A Bride's PORTRAIT

OF DODGE CITY, KANSAS

ERICA
VETSCH

BARBOUR
PUBLISHING

ISBN 978-1-61626-506-9

This book is a work of fiction. Names, characters, places, and incidents are either products of the author's imagination or used fictitiously.

For more information about Erica Vetsch, please access the author's website at the following Internet address:
http://webpages.charter.net/ericavetsch/home.html

Cover design: Faceout Studio; www.faceoutstudio.com

Published by Barbour Publishing, Inc., P.O. Box 719, Uhrichsville, OH 44683, www.barbourbooks.com

Our mission is to publish and distribute inspirational products offering exceptional value and biblical encouragement to the masses.

Printed in the United States of America.

K

Praise for *A Bride's Portrait of Dodge City, Kansas*

In this book, Ms. Vetsch gives Dodge City a reputation of civilized gentility not often found in romances about the "Queen of the Cattle Towns." History in the hands of a master storyteller is displayed. With many deep emotions the author weaves a powerful tale of conflict, suspense, and romance. Kudos to Ms. Vetsch for capturing this historical era and giving readers a novel filled with wonderful characters, several unique subplots, and a surprising twist on the last page!
—Irene Brand, bestselling author of *Love Finds You under the Mistletoe*

Erica Vetsch captures all the excitement of the old West with her compelling tale of love, greed, and intrigue. Strong, endearing characters, vivid writing, and a fast-paced plot make this a delightful read. You won't want to miss this one.
—Margaret Brownley, author of the Rocky Creek Romance series

I've read several shorter romances by Erica Vetsch. At the end of each I've wanted more, a longer story, a chance to stay with her charming characters a little longer. I got my wish with *Bride's Portrait of Dodge City, Kansas*. Erica's first full-length romance novel is charming; action packed with a hero to sigh over and a heroine to cheer for. And even in this longer book I wasn't ready to let go of Dodge City or Addie's and Miles' love story. As always, Vetsch brings a setting, her characters, and their love story blazing to life.
—Mary Connealy, author of *Doctor in Petticoats*

When I was a little girl, I loved spaghetti westerns and television shows like *The Big Valley* and *The Virginian.* Not only was my love for story satisfied but my interest in history as well, especially when true-to-life characters made "guest appearances." In *A Bride's Portrait of Dodge City, Kansas,* Erica Vetsch has done what the movies and television series of the '60s did. She has brought adventure, romance, relationship, and true-to-life characters to a western setting. This is the perfect "lose yourself" book.
—Eva Marie Everson, author of *Chasing Sunsets*

This story has mystery, suspense, and not just one, but two romances all set in a lush landscape of historical detail. The surprise ending leads to a satisfying conclusion. This book is bound to please readers who like to be transported back in time to enjoy a solidly constructed tale.
—Linda Ford, author of *Prairie Cowboy*

As rowdy as cowboys fresh off a cattle drive, yet as subtle as trail dust over faded tracks, *A Bride's Portrait of Dodge City, Kansas*, offers the reader a powerful story of long-guarded secrets tucked behind photography props and deputy badges—desperate measures to hide the truth capable of destroying lives. Erica Vetsch indulges the excitement of the old West using charm and sensitivity with every click of the camera shutter, making the reader sigh and smile well beyond the last page.
—Audra Harders, author of *Rocky Mountain Hero*

Erica Vetsch delivers a rollicking adventure, where greed blurs the line between good and evil, and secrets lurk in Dodge City alleys. Only forever-love can salvage the mess brewing in the wild, wild West. You'll love this one!
—Patti Lacy, author of *The Rhythm of Secrets*

Vivid descriptions, captivating characters, and a compelling plot woven with mystery is brought to life in Erica Vetsch's historical romance set in the old West. *A Bride's Portrait of Dodge City, Kansas*, is a delightful page-turner.
—Gail Gaymer Martin, novelist and speaker

With books like *A Bride's Portrait in Dodge City, Kansas*, Erica will soon be hitting the bestseller lists. Romance, history, suspense, comedy, and engaging characters come together in a rip-roaring tale set in one of the West's wildest towns. Be sure to take your own picture of this one. . .you'll want it to last longer.
—Aaron McCarver, co-author of the bestselling Spirit of Appalachia series

Erica Vetsch captures rough and wild Dodge City with such clarity, my nose practically tickled from the dust. Addie is a warm, admirable heroine who charmed me with her determination. *A Bride's Portrait of Dodge City, Kansas*, is a wonderful story about the illusion of fresh starts and the peace that comes with forgiveness.
—Stephanie Morrill, author of the Reinvention of Skylar Hoyt series

A Bride's Portrait of Dodge City, Kansas, blends all the flavors of the old West in a delicious recipe of love, determination, and forgiveness that delivers to the last morsel. With this story, Ms. Vetsch has whetted our appetite for more. Encore!
—Lois Richer, author of *A Family for Summer*

Dedication

To my husband, Peter,
a man of courage, character, and compassion

Author's Note

While most of the characters in this story are fictitious, the characters of Charlie Basset, Luke Short, and Bat Masterson are taken from the annals of Dodge City history. I have tried to stay true to the historical record, with one noted exception: Bat Masterson's proclivity for keeping printed material stacked in his office is fictional and entirely of my own creation.

Chapter 1

June 1, 1878

Uncle Carl had taught her that the customer should be accommodated no matter what, but surely there were limitations. Addie Reid pressed her fingertips against her temple. "You want to do what?"

"I want my picture made with my horse."

"Sir, this isn't a livery stable. I do serious portraiture."

The cowboy—so prototypical of the breed as to be comical with his wide hat, sunburned face, and bat-wing chaps—waved a scrap of newsprint in her face. "Read this here ad. It says 'Come to Reid's Photography to get your portrait taken with your trail pards and best friends.' This is your ad, ain't it? You are Reid's Photography?"

A small pang twisted Addie's heart. She was now. *What if I can't do this alone?*

"Well?"

"Yes, that's my advertisement, and this is Reid's Photography."

"Good. Then I want my picture made with my trail pard

and best friend. I've got good cash money. Trail boss paid us off an hour ago. I got spiffed up down at the barbershop and headed right here."

"But sir, a horse? The advertisement is intended for humans."

"That horse"—he pointed through the open door to a dusty animal dozing in the sun on Front Street—"is the best friend and trail pard I've ever had. He's smart and gentle and has forgotten more about cow work than I'll ever know."

Which was either an accolade for the horse or an insult to the cowboy. She blew out a breath. "I can't haul the camera out into the street." Though she wouldn't risk moving the Chevalier for a simple portrait, perhaps she could use her smaller Scovill. Though the print would be smaller, too.

"I don't want no outside picture. I want it taken in the studio with one of those fancy backdrops. And I want the picture to be about this big"—he held up his hands about a foot apart—"so it will look good in a frame on the wall."

That ruled out the Scovill. A print that size would need the bigger camera. Her mind trotted back to what he'd said, and her jaw dropped. "You intend to bring a horse inside?" Jamming her hands on her hips, she shook her head. "No. Impossible. I'll take your picture, and it will be a good one, but the animal stays outside."

He tugged the corner of his enormous moustache. "I reckoned as much. No gumption. Should've known better than to come to a woman photographer. A man would understand. Guess I'll go over to Donaldson's. He offered to do it for me, but I wanted to give you a try at it first, since you're new in town and all. He said you'd be too timid."

Stung, Addie straightened. "Wait. Don't go." Donaldson's Photography three blocks down would be her biggest competitor, and Heber Donaldson had been the most vocal about the new photography shop on Front Street stealing his customers. "We can work something out." But it would have to be worth her while. She hesitated then quoted him a price.

The cowboy grinned. "That sounds fine to me. Donaldson was almost twice that. Don't you worry. My old Mudslinger's gentle as a spring breeze, and he'll stand quiet." He removed his hat and smoothed his hair. "You got a back door or something? I can lead him in that way."

"No, he can't come in through the back. That door's blocked off." She eyed the paisley-scattered rug in her reception room. "I suppose you'll have to lead him through here." This was ridiculous. Why was she even contemplating such a crazy idea?

Money. Pure and simple. She needed customers and couldn't afford to turn one away.

The cowpoke jammed his hat back on. "I'll fetch him in." He hustled outside as if afraid she might change her mind.

Which she should do. A horse in the studio?

Old Mudslinger's hooves clomped on the boardwalk and through the doorway, muffled on the carpet. She winced to think of horseshoe-shaped marks on the pretty red and blue rug but shrugged. *Worry about the bank manager. Worry about convincing him to let you assume the mortgage. And while you're at it, maybe you should worry about how you're going to get this beast to hold still long enough for the exposure.*

"This way." She hurried into the studio ahead of the horse and cowboy. The animal brought with him a whiff of sweaty hair and barnyard, hay and leather. Lovely. "Don't let him near the camera." In the center of the long room, her pride and joy, a glossy new Chevalier, stood on a tripod, the black drape hanging nearly to the floor. She crossed to a bench along one wall and pulled her order book toward her. Snagging a pencil from a jar, she held it poised above the page. "Can I have your name, please?"

"Call me Cracker. Everybody does."

"Very well, Mr. Cracker." She wrote the name and the date.

He guffawed. "Not mister. Just Cracker. It's a nickname I picked up because I love those little oyster crackers like they serve over at the Dakota House. Can't get enough of those tiny things. I been called Cracker for about as long as I can remember."

Cracker and Mudslinger. Fran was not going to believe this.

"Cracker, I've three backgrounds you can choose from, but I would suggest the landscape." She crossed the studio and tugged on the rope that raised the canvas curtain painted to look like a drawing room and lowered the heavy drape painted to look like rolling hills.

"Say, that's dandy." Cracker rested his arm across his saddle.

Mudslinger stood still, one hind leg tucked up a bit, his ears drooping. Perhaps getting him to stand still wouldn't be a problem. Might be more challenging to make him look alive.

Addie wrestled a plaster pedestal and a wicker chair out of

the way and quickly folded a fringed piano scarf and tucked it away on a shelf. "Just what did you have in mind for a pose?"

Cracker rubbed his chin. "I want you to get all of us in the picture. Head to tail and hat to hooves. And could you make sure you get my rifle in the picture, too?" He patted the gunstock sticking out of a scabbard on his saddle. "This picture's for my mama back in Uvalde."

Why a picture intended for his mother would need to be bristling with guns, Addie didn't know, but once again Uncle Carl's voice in her ear reminded that above all else, she must try to accommodate the customer.

"Lead him around here then, so the rifle is on the side facing the camera. Are you going to be astride?" She stepped back as Mudslinger's haunches came around. If the man wanted to be in the saddle, she'd have to move the camera back, which would reduce some of the detail. . . Her mind slipped into working mode, and she began to consider the lighting and the exposure time, the focal point, and how to achieve depth of field.

"Naw, I'll just stand beside him." Cracker looped the reins over the saddle horn and placed his hand on the pommel. He lifted his chin, shoved his hat back so it wouldn't shade his face, and stared off into the distance. "Like this. Like we're standing on a hill looking over a herd and dreaming of home."

Addie hid a smile. Cowboys might like to be thought of as firebrands and fearsome, but most were just boys with romantic notions and fierce pride. "That will be fine. You wait here while I prepare a plate. It won't take me a minute."

She ducked into the darkroom at the back of the building,

struck a match to light the lantern, and lowered the red glass covering. Rosy light bathed the room, the workbench, the trays, and the rows of bottles and chemicals necessary to her job. She closed the door, shutting out all sunlight, and reached for a large glass slide to begin the process. Uncorking bottles and preparing the wet-plate washes, she shook her head again. A horse in her studio. If word got out, she might have a stampede of equine customers. Would that make the bank manager more amenable to her taking over the mortgage?

Just thinking of the meeting with the bank manager this afternoon made her hands shake. In her haste, she splashed a bit of silver nitrate on her cuff and wrist. *Grrr.* Grabbing the ammonia bottle and a rag, she dabbed at her skin. If she didn't get it off now, it would turn blackish-blue and take ages to wear off. Twisting her lips, she scowled at the once-white cuff now blotched.

She took precious moments to roll up her sleeves like she should've done right away and donned her work apron to cover her straight, blue skirt. She wouldn't have time to go back to her boardinghouse to change before meeting the bank manager, so now, in spite of the warm day, she'd have to don the matching jacket to cover the stain on her sleeve.

Finally, she had a prepared plate in the lightproof box. Entering the studio once more, she noted that neither cowboy nor horse had stirred. "I'll just get this into the camera. You'll both have to stand completely still until the plate has been exposed for the proper length of time. If you move even a little, the picture will come out blurred." She removed the lens cover and ducked under the drape to peer through the camera. She emerged, backed the camera up about a foot, and sighted again. Perfect. After replacing the lens cap, the black drape stifled all light. Operating by feel, she slipped the glass plate into the back of the camera and closed everything up.

When she emerged from beneath the cloth, she took a moment to tighten the combs keeping her upswept hair from teasing her face and studied Cracker. She approached him for some final adjustments. "Put one foot a bit in front of the other and let your left arm hang loose. You'll look more natural that way." She smoothed his collar and tilted his hat a bit more. The sunshine from the skylight overhead should provide enough illumination that she wouldn't need any flash powder. Just as well. The pop and glare of a flash might startle even the dozy Mudslinger into bolting.

"Make sure you get my pistol and knife in the shot." Cracker patted his gun belt.

"Of course." This was for his mother, after all. "Now relax, but hold completely still until I give you the word." She stepped back, surveyed the tableau, trying to see things through the camera lens in her mind, to see the finished product and predict if it would please the customer.

Gently, she unscrewed the lens cap. "Hold it." She counted off the seconds, added two more because the horse and saddle were so dark, then replaced the cap. "There. You're done."

Cracker relaxed a fraction then grinned. "Great. When will it be ready?"

"You can pick it up tomorrow, but you'll have to pay for

it today." Uncle Carl always required payment from a cowboy before developing the picture, and she intended to follow his example. If she waited until Cracker came to pick up the photo tomorrow, chances were his money would've disappeared, siphoned off in one of the saloons or gambling halls. What took the average cowboy three months to earn on the trail up from Texas could be gone in a matter of hours in a cow town like Abilene or Dodge City, Kansas.

Cracker dug into his pocket and produced a wad of bills. He peeled off a couple, grinned at her, and added a third. "There you go, lady. A little something extra for you. And I'm going to tell everybody I know to come here to get their picture made."

He grabbed Mudslinger's reins and tugged. The animal roused, shuffled his feet, and ambled toward the door. When he came abreast of her camera, he paused.

Addie let out a shriek.

Cracker yanked on the reins, but it was too late. "Whoops. I sure am sorry about that. He ain't exactly housebroke, you know."

An hour later, Addie had scrubbed the studio floor and her hands several times. Praying none of the stable odor lingered on her clothes, she stepped into the Dodge City Bank. The sturdy, brick building faced Front Street, as her own shop did, the main artery into and out of town bisected by the Santa Fe Railroad tracks. North of the tracks only about half the businesses were saloons. South of the Santa Fe rails, saloons, gambling dens, dance halls, and houses of ill repute abounded.

The smells of ink and beeswax furniture polish drifted over her. Everything in this bank bespoke prosperity, from the shiny woodwork to the burgundy velvet wallpaper to the gleaming brass hardware. A row of teller windows took up the left-hand wall. Patrons stood patiently in line waiting for their turns, and Addie took her place at the tail end.

Lord, please let the bank manager understand, let him give me a chance to prove I can do this. Because, truthfully, I have no idea what I'll do if he says no.

"Miss Reid?"

Someone touched her arm, and she realized she was standing in the middle of the bank with her eyes closed. Warmth spread across her cheeks, and she looked up into the bank manager's stern visage. "Mr. Poulter." She forced his name past her constricted throat.

"Please come this way. I'm glad to see you believe in being prompt. I despise being kept waiting." He sounded like he had a lemon rind stuck in his throat. Sour and raspy.

She followed, her pulse beating loudly in her ears. He led her to the half-wall that separated the civilians from the cash and held open the gate. Not a squeak from the hinges. Darting a glance at his intense expression, she doubted the gate would have the nerve to sound off.

"Please be seated." He waved her to a straight-backed and uncompromising chair set square before his immense desk. Behind the nameplate and blotter, Mr. T. Archibald Poulter settled into leather luxury.

"I'm afraid I'm not sure why you wished to meet with me, Miss Reid. I am sorry for your loss, but I've looked over the agreement between this establishment and your deceased uncle." He spoke slowly, as if she might have trouble keeping up with his words. "The terms are very clear. As I told you at the funeral, in the event of your uncle's death, the mortgage is due in full. If you cannot pay the loan, the collateral will be forfeit."

She hadn't forgotten how he had approached her as she walked away from her last relative's burial service and given her the news. He couldn't even wait until the next business day. Word had it that Archie Poulter had a heart of pyrite. Cold, yellow, and pretty much worthless.

Try nice first. The reminder, floating through her mind from a long-ago schoolteacher, surprised her. Trouble was, Miss Ambrose had never met this bank manager.

"I, too, have read the documents, Mr. Poulter." Though it irked her to be treated as if she had no more sense than a prairie chicken, she kept her voice reasonable and professional. "I understand the terms of that agreement. I am not here to dispute them. I'm here to negotiate a new agreement with myself as proprietor of the business. I wish to assume the loan at the current terms."

His thin brows shot down over his hawk-like nose. "Yourself as proprietor?" He shook his head. "I'm afraid that would be impossible. The bank has never loaned money to an unmarried woman to finance a business. Unless. . ." He leaned back in his chair and studied her. "Unless you have a male relative or business partner who would be a cosignatory on the loan?"

Addie moistened her lips and stifled the urge to roll her eyes. "No, there's no one else. But if you call in the mortgage now, all you'll get is photographic equipment and an empty building. The studio itself is collateral for the loan. Surely it would be in your best interest to let me continue running the business and paying on the mortgage."

He steepled his fingers under his chin. "Ordinarily, I would agree with you. It would be better to have another merchant assume the note. However, Heber Donaldson was in here just this morning, and he indicated he would be interested in purchasing the repossessed equipment from the bank. And a building on Front Street is never difficult to sell or rent. The bank wouldn't lose any money by calling in the loan."

Heber Donaldson. A thorn in their flesh from the moment she and Uncle Carl had stepped off the train three months ago. She throttled her handbag in her lap, clenching her fingers to stop them from shaking. "Mr. Poulter, please. The studio is my livelihood. It's all I know how to do. Without the studio, I have no way to support myself. I assure you, I'm a very good photographer. I know the business from the ground up. Photography, developing, bookkeeping. I've helped my uncle for years. If you won't give me a new loan, will you please give me time to pay off the debt? I'm only asking for six months." She'd have to live sparingly, and the summer season would have to be better than good, but she'd scrimp and save and scratch and claw to keep the studio. Six months would be pushing it, but she could do it if he'd only give her a chance.

"Six months?"

"Just until the end of this year. By January 1, I'd be loan-free, and the bank would have the entire mortgage repaid with interest."

He squared up some papers on his immaculate desk and appeared to consider her request.

Hope sprang up when he didn't automatically shoot her down, but as the minutes crawled by, worry began to blot out that feeble hope.

Finally, he looked up. "I tell you what. I'm prepared to give you an additional three months to get your affairs in order. Ninety days. The mortgage will be due in full at that time, no excuses. The regular, monthly payments will be due on the first of the month as usual, with a balloon payment on. . ." He opened a drawer and withdrew a small calendar. "August 29. That's ninety days from today, June 1."

"Ninety days?" She swallowed. "That's not fair. There's no way I can raise that kind of money in just three months."

"Miss Reid, it's more than generous when you consider it would be within the bank's legal rights to call in the loan today. When you view it in that light, I think ninety days is fair."

So, he was prepared to let her slave away all summer, making the monthly payments, then call in the loan and selling the studio to Donaldson. And she was helpless to stop it.

"I'd advise you, Miss Reid, to forget about trying to run a business and find yourself a husband. I realize you've barely had time to get settled in this town, and to be faced with bereavement so soon after arriving makes the situation more difficult." He toyed with the pin piercing his necktie just below his chin. "In fact. . ." He studied her face and let his eyes wander over what he could see of her from behind his desk.

She immediately wanted to scrub her skin with ammonia all over again.

"In fact, I wouldn't be averse to discussing an arrangement with you. You're a comely woman, and I have recently decided that it was past time I thought about getting married."

His audacity sucked her breath away. Threatening to yank her business, her livelihood, away from her one second and hinting at marriage the next? Addie rose and skewered him to his chair with her glare. "Mr. Poulter, I accept only the extension of the loan. In ninety days, I will pay the entire mortgage. Until then, I would prefer to keep our dealings entirely professional." She dug in her purse and produced a small roll of bills. "This is the payment that is due today. I will see you in one month with another installment."

Chapter 2

"I had a hard time convincing him to lean against that pedestal, but I think it turned out perfectly, don't you?" Addie studied the photograph before slipping it into the cardboard frame. She ran her finger over the silver lettering in the corner of the frame and smiled.

REID'S PHOTOGRAPHY STUDIO, DODGE CITY, KANSAS.

Fran Seaton looked over Addie's shoulder. "Bat Masterson has the most piercing eyes I've ever seen. They can turn my insides cold even on a day as hot as today."

Addie studied the portrait of the newly elected sheriff of Ford County. Though he wore a fine suit and natty bowler, and she'd posed him casually with his forearm resting on the plaster pillar, it was his eyes that drew attention. A hint of humor, a lot of grit, and absolutely no fear. Exactly what she'd been trying to capture with her lens. She doubted she'd even be able to tint a photograph to accurately capture the vivid blue of his eyes. Too bad there was no way to take color photographs. But it was one of the best portraits she'd ever done, color or not.

"Stop looking so smug." Fran poked her shoulder. "I know it's a good picture. I'm sure he will appreciate your skill. Let me see what else you've got." She scooped up a stack of newly developed portraits from the corner of the desk and plopped onto a red velvet settee Addie used for posing families. "Bat's handsome, but not what I'm looking for. Can you imagine looking across the breakfast table at those eyes every morning?" Fran shuddered. "I have a feeling any girl who tries to catch Bat Masterson will find herself trying to tame a tiger."

Addie put the sheriff's photograph into an envelope and fastened the clip. "Maybe you can go with me to deliver this after work. You might run into Jonas." A teasing smile tugged at her lips. It hadn't taken Addie long to find out Fran's views on nearly every male in town, especially Deputy Spooner.

"Ugh. No thank you. Bat might be a tiger, but Jonas is as scary as a bowl of oatmeal. Though you might be interested to know that Bat hired Miles Carr as a deputy. Jonas says he's getting his badge today."

"Is he? That's nice." Addie feigned nonchalance, but her ears pricked. The gunsmith had always been quietly polite when they'd passed on the street, but she'd never spoken to him.

"I think you two would make a lovely couple. He's so tall and—I don't know—watchful? I always get the impression he's kind of sweet on you."

"You're a romantic goose." Addie smiled fondly at Fran. "You see hearts and rainbows where none exist. Concentrate on your own affairs of the heart and leave me to my solitary existence. If you want to talk about how someone gets watched by someone else, let's talk about the way Jonas can never take his eyes off you."

Fran flipped through the photographs. "I've got my heart set on someone tall, dark, and handsome. Jonas is none of those things. Hey, this one has possibilities. What about him?"

Addie joined her on the settee and peered at the photo. "If you aren't careful, all your daydreaming about a romantic encounter is going to get you into trouble. Tall, dark, and handsome doesn't mean a man has a good character or is even nice. You can't judge a man by his portrait." And didn't she have reason to know the truth of that statement?

"I can tell plenty from the portraits you take. Look at Bat's. That picture tells you a lot about the man. You captured him perfectly."

Addie couldn't deny the pleasure Fran's compliment gave her, but she shook her head. "That's because we know Bat—at least a little. The papers are full of him, and we see him around town. You're reading into his photograph what you know of the man. These"—she tapped the stack in Fran's hand—"are total strangers. You should be careful. Not everything is as it seems in this life, and that goes double for men."

"Well"—Fran shrugged—"a girl has to start somewhere." She held up a photograph. "Tell me about him."

With a sigh, Addie took the picture. A young, sunburned, intense man looked back at her. "He's like half a dozen others in that stack. A Texan. Maybe twenty years old? Like all of them, he wanted to make sure I posed him so his gun and holster showed, and I couldn't talk him out of wearing those wooly chaps. They looked ridiculous and smelled worse."

She wrinkled her nose, remembering the pungent cow odor that had filled the portrait studio every time he moved. Cowboys made up the bulk of her business, and without exception, every man wanted his likeness struck in full regalia with his rifle or his handgun. Alone in the photograph or posing with his trail mates, every puncher wanted to look as fierce as possible. He wanted the world to know he was a cowboy and proud of it.

"What is this?" Fran held up another picture. "Are you serious?" She shoved a red-gold curl off her cheek and tucked it behind her ear, leaning over the picture. Her emerald eyes turned to Addie, wide and questioning.

"I knew you'd like that one." Addie laughed.

"A horse? You let someone bring a horse into the studio?"

Addie shrugged. "He said his horse was his best friend, and he fully intended to get his picture taken with his best friend. He even brought in the advertisement. Thank you for writing that up for me, by the way."

Fran held the picture up to the light streaming through the front windows. "Was he drunk?"

"Not at that time, though I have a feeling he hit the saloons pretty soon afterward. Most of them do." Addie shook her head. "I thought it might be a problem getting the horse to stand still for the length of time it would take to expose the slide, but he was so placid, I think he fell asleep. Though he did leave me something to remember him by." She pinched her nose and screwed up her eyelids.

"No!" Fran made a face. "He didn't!"

Addie sighed. "I do suffer for my art." She pantomimed agony, putting the back of her hand against her brow and fluttering her lashes until they both dissolved into giggles.

The photograph of the horse and cowboy had come out even better than Addie had hoped. Almost as good as the one of Bat Masterson. She'd love to put the horse portrait in the window as an advertisement, but she was afraid it would give potential customers too many ideas. One horse in the studio was enough.

"With the way cowboys are pouring in here to get their portraits taken, you'll have everything paid for and enough money to last through the winter by the Fourth of July." Fran quickly made her way through the rest of the photographs. "What did Poulter over at the bank say yesterday? I meant to come by last night and get all the news, but I had to stay late at the store." She shrugged, shaking her head. "Will they let you assume the loan?"

Addie's middle clenched at the thought of Mr. Poulter and the loan. Eighty-nine days left. "Well, after I disabused his mind about marrying him—" She stopped to enjoy Fran's gaping and blinking. "He agreed to give me ninety days to pay off the loan."

"Wait, wait, wait. Marriage? Mr. Poulter asked you to marry him?" She grabbed Addie's arms and gave her a shake. "Tell me everything."

Addie laughed, though the bank manager's leering assessment still lingered in her memory, making her flesh crawl. "He didn't come right out and say it. Rather, he told me to give up ideas of running a business and find myself a husband. Then he said he'd given some thought to getting married, and I was, in his words, a 'comely woman.' "

Fran's eyebrows rose. "I hope you spit in his eye. Of all the nerve. He's old enough to be your father."

"I didn't spit in his eye, but I did agree to his terms on the loan. Somehow I've got to raise the money. I thought he might give me six months, and if I worked hard, I'd just about be able to do it, but he's already had an offer on the place. Heber Donaldson." Addie grimaced.

Fran sank onto the settee and let her head fall back to stare at the ceiling. She blew a puff of air that lifted her bangs. "What is this town coming to? Heber's been jealous of you since you arrived. He had most all the photography business sewed up before you came. A couple of photographers drifted into town last year, but he dropped his prices and they couldn't match him. But you've got him worried. And he and Poulter are friends." She shot Addie a concerned glance. "Be careful. There are politics and power and prideful men in this town, and they wouldn't hesitate to force you out if you had something they wanted."

Loneliness swept over Addie, a longing for Uncle Carl and for Abilene and the life she once knew. For the security of a home and someone to belong to, someone of her own to stand beside her to fight life's battles. Instead, she was alone.

Seeing Fran's troubled face, Addie put on a false bravado. "Don't you worry. I'm tough enough to take all comers. You wait. I'll find a way to pay that loan off, and Heber can go jump in the Arkansas River. He won't get his hands on this studio or the equipment."

"Then a lot is riding on you having a good season. I hope you can do it. I don't want you to have to close the shop. I've been waiting for two years to find a best friend in this town. I'm not giving you up." Fran shook her finger at Addie. "I wish I could help you, but we're just making ends meet at our place. The expansion of the feed business took all the money my brothers had saved up. Everything I make at the store goes to help pay the bills. Linc mentioned possibly looking for an investor or two to help out with the cash flow. Say. . ." She brightened. "Maybe that's what you need. An investor. If you had some backing, it would ease the burden. Maybe even pay off the loan entirely. Wouldn't that feel good, to go plunk the cash down right in front of that smug Mr. Poulter?"

Addie allowed herself a moment to imagine the satisfaction paying off the note early would have. But she shook her head. "I don't want an investor. I want to make it on my own. An investor would want to have a say in how I ran the business, and after the loan was paid off, I'd lose a percentage of the profits to a partner. If I'm going to be a success as a photographer, I have to do it myself."

The weight of the bank mortgage hung over her. All the equipment, most of the props, the backdrops, the glass slides, the development chemicals, even the frames and stationery, nearly everything had been purchased by Uncle Carl new when they came to Dodge City after losing his photography studio in Abilene. And then his heart had given out before they could open the shop.

Fran picked up the stack of portraits she'd tossed onto the settee and held them against her middle. "You want to be careful, Addie. Dodge City isn't exactly the best place for a woman on her own. I'm lucky my brothers let me out of their sight long enough to go to work, and they wouldn't if we didn't need the money. I wish you'd come live with me at our house. I'd feel better if you left the boardinghouse. My room isn't big, but it's got to be safer than Mrs. Blanchard's rooming house."

Addie shrugged. "My room is right next to Mrs. Blanchard's, and I haven't had any problems. Half the men who live at the boardinghouse are cattle buyers only here for the season, and they spend all their time downtown doing business. No one has given me any trouble."

"You haven't had much trouble because it's early yet. The trickle of cows and cowboys we've seen is nothing compared to the flood that's coming." Fran handed Addie the pictures and got to her feet. She smoothed her lace collar and straightened the pleats on her jade-colored dress. "When the herds start coming in every day, this town will bust wide open. That's why Bat's hiring new deputies, and I imagine the town marshal will as well."

"Then there's sure to be a deputy around when I need one. I'm not going to complain about the cowboys being in town. Nobody loves having his picture taken as much as a cowboy fresh off the trail. They're my bread and butter and some of the jam."

Addie stretched and brushed at her skirt. Uncle Carl

hadn't approved of mourning clothes, said it flew in the face of everything the Bible said about eternal life for those who knew God. Consequently, Addie wore her customary plain, ivory blouse and straight, blue-gray skirt.

Though Fran fussed at her to wear more feminine gear and encouraged her often to come into the mercantile to see the latest inventory, Addie refused. Fran might be trying to catch a man, but Addie wasn't—not ever again. She was a businesswoman.

Besides, she didn't have the money for fancy clothes. Everything must go toward reducing the mortgage. If it wasn't for her, Uncle Carl wouldn't have lost the Abilene studio and had to start over. She owed it to him, and to herself, to make a success of this business.

Fran plucked a parasol from the prop box and opened it, twirling the lacy umbrella and tilting her head. "If you kept regular hours, one of my brothers could stop by to see you home safely when he came for me, but you're locked in your darkroom until all hours some nights."

Addie tapped the stack of photos into a neat pile and squared it up with the corner of her desk. She picked up a paper clip that had somehow found its way out of the box and returned it to the proper place so everything was neat and tidy. "Long hours are part of the job. When you're the only employee, you get to do everything. Photographs, developing, retouching, advertising, cleaning, bookkeeping, and sales."

"Speaking of sales, have you heard back about the Arden Palace?"

Grimacing, Addie propped her hip on the desk and began rolling down her sleeves. She frowned at the creases, but wrinkles were better than stains and acid pinholes. "Mr. LeBlanc said he'd let me know by tomorrow. I'm trying not to get my hopes up, but I can't help thinking what this would mean for the studio. The photos would appear on posters all over the state and maybe even in *Harper's* if you can believe what LeBlanc says. Heber put a bid in, and he let me know he expected to win the job."

"Wouldn't it be wonderful to see one of your photographs in *Harper's*?" Fran checked her reflection in the mirror, fussing with her hair and smoothing her eyebrows with her little finger, her heart-shaped face framed by the parasol. She wrinkled her nose. "You'd do a much better job than Heber Donaldson. He's too homely for words and an old crank besides." With an airy wave, she took in the studio. "You're so creative, and you've got that fabulous camera. Heber doesn't have anything that can touch it."

Addie smiled and walked over to trail her fingers down the heavy, black drape hanging from the back of her Chevalier wet-plate monorail view camera. "I wanted Uncle Carl to start out a bit more cautious, but he was determined to make this studio as nice as the one he had in Abilene. He ran into some. . .difficulty in Abilene and lost his business. I think it was a matter of pride to him not to scale back when we got here." She sighed and caressed the gleaming wooden case. "It might be the best one in town, but it isn't paid for yet. With Poulter clamoring for the mortgage money, I really have to get the Arden commission."

The regulator clock on the wall chimed the hour. "Uh-oh." Fran snapped the parasol shut and tossed it in the prop box. "The mercantile calls. I'd better scoot." She headed for the door. Opening it, she turned back as the bell jangled. "Let me know how Bat likes his picture."

Addie's eyes returned to the portrait of the new sheriff. It was good work. Maybe if she showed it to Henri LeBlanc, it would provide the encouragement he needed to give her the commission to photograph the Arden Palace Theater.

Miles Carr lowered his right hand and shook Bat Masterson's. The weight of responsibility tugged at the brand-new badge pinned to his vest, even as a grin tugged at his lips. He glanced down at it and read: DEPUTY SHERIFF, FORD COUNTY, KANSAS.

Bat's eyes pierced him. "Deputy Carr."

"Congratulations." His friend Jonas stepped forward and shook Miles's hand, too. "I know you've wanted this for a while."

Jonas was right. Miles had wanted this for a long time. As long as he could remember. Now, to have the chance to serve alongside the likes of Bat Masterson, Charlie Bassett, Wyatt Earp, Bill Tilghman. . . His heart beat faster. Living legends all. Could he prove himself worthy to be counted among them? Could he live down his heritage and prove to himself and everyone else that he was good enough to be a lawman in Dodge City? The toughest, bravest young men in the West? Though at twenty-six Miles had a year on his new boss, Bat had such presence and reputation, he seemed much older.

Bat riffled through a set of keys and selected one. "I know you have your own sidearm, but a pistol and a rifle come with the badge. I find it handiest to keep the rifle here at the jail." He unlocked the gun cabinet behind his desk and withdrew a Colt and a holster so new the belt stood out stiffly and creaked as he folded it over before handing it to Miles. "You might prefer your own, but this gun has some stopping power. And it's intimidating to unruly cowboys." Bat slid the gun from the holster, cocked it, and sighted down the long barrel. Lowering the hammer, he flipped it in his hand and offered it, butt-first, to Miles.

Miles took the walnut-handled firearm, testing the weight. Guns were as familiar to him as a skillet to a bunkhouse cook. He'd been around them all his life, and until recently, he'd worked at the gunsmith's on Front Street. Whether shooting or repairing, there wasn't much about a gun he didn't know. "Can't go wrong with a Colt. You know the saying. 'God made men, and Colonel Colt made them all equal.'" He checked the cylinder, pointed the pistol at the far wall, and pulled the trigger. The click of the hammer coming down on an empty chamber snapped through the room. "The action is a little stiff. Do you mind if I file it?"

"It's your gun. If you want an easy pull, file away." Bat picked up his silver-topped cane. "You and Spooner will be working the same shifts, since you know each other well. The biggest chore is keeping the cowboys from ripping up the town every night." Light came into his pale eyes, and his moustache twitched. "They've been known to paint the town a very vivid shade of red. As county deputies, your jurisdiction is wider than the city police, but with the number of herds expected to come in, I've put you and Spooner at the disposal of the town marshal's office. Charlie Bassett will treat you right. County and city share the jail and the jailer responsibilities. I'll be around whenever I'm not out chasing horse thieves."

Bat handed him a box of cartridges, and Miles shoved bullets into the loops on the belt. Then he loaded five bullets into the gun, leaving the one under the hammer empty. Slinging the belt around his hips, he buckled it and holstered the gun.

"We give the cowboys quite a bit of leeway," Bat said. "That's the way the merchants and the mayor want it. Drovers roll into town, and the minute the herd is sold, they get paid off. Not long after, they're spending that money in the stores and saloons around town. We don't want to discourage this behavior." Bat tapped his cane on the floor. "Some of the townsfolk will bend your ear, telling you to come down harder on the cowboys, but don't let them sway you. Without those wild Texans and their cash, Dodge City would just be a former buffalo-hide camp."

Miles flicked a glance at Jonas. "So, go easy on the cowboys, but keep them from tearing up the town."

"It's a pretty tight line sometimes." Jonas shrugged. "For the most part, the men you'll go up against will be drunk, which works for you and against you. A drunk is usually easy to corral, but he's also unpredictable. You just have to use your judgment."

The door opened, and Addie Reid stepped inside. Miles drew a slow breath. Miss Reid had captured his attention the first time he'd passed her on the street, and he had found his mind straying to her more often than he wanted to admit. Foolish thoughts, since everything about her spoke of quality and class. If she knew who he really was, about his past, she'd run fast in the other direction. He couldn't seem to stop noticing the smallest details about her, though.

A few brown curls had escaped the coiled braid on the back of her head and brushed her cheeks. Gray-blue eyes widened, blinking to accustom themselves to the dark interior of the jail after the sunshine outside. A long strap slung crossways over one shoulder held a case at her hip.

"Excuse me, Sheriff. I was just on my way home and wanted to drop this by for you." She opened the case and withdrew an envelope. "I'm really pleased with how it turned out, and I hope you will be, too." She handed the sheriff the packet and turned to the deputies. Smiling first at Jonas, her eyes moved to Miles.

He had the odd sensation that she could see into his thoughts. He'd never been so scrutinized before, and he wanted to squirm.

Bat slid a silvery cardboard folder out of the envelope. "Miss Reid." He swept a glance at Miles and Jonas.

Miles realized his hands were fisted at his sides. He forced himself to relax.

"Have you met my deputies? Jonas Spooner"—he pointed with his cane—"and Miles Carr. I just swore Miles in a few minutes ago."

"Congratulations, Mr. Carr. I believe I've seen you in the gunsmith's shop next to my studio." Thick lashes fringed her eyes, and her lips were full and curved.

Before he could formulate an answer, Bat cut in. "An excellent likeness, don't you think?" He held the photograph up for them to see. "I had my doubts about the pose, but you've proven me wrong, Miss Reid."

"I'm glad you trusted me. It came out even better than I expected." She fastened the closure on her case.

Miles studied the tan leather box, an unwieldy accessory for a woman to carry, and realized it was a camera case. That made sense.

Jonas lifted a sheaf of papers from the corner of the desk. "I finished going through these Wanted posters and culled the ones we know are dead or in jail. Do you want me to burn them?"

"No, tear them in half. I'll use them as scratch paper." Bat continued to study his picture. "The city council was talking about having all the deputies' photographs taken soon. I'll recommend they consider giving the job to you, Miss Reid. If anyone can make silk purses out of a bunch of sows' ears, you can."

She didn't respond to his jest. Her cheeks paled, and her eyes bored into the paper Jonas held up. The Wanted poster of Cliff Walker. Train robber. Murderer.

Jonas caught her stare and flipped the paper over to study it. "Whew, he was a bad one, wasn't he?"

A cold finger of guilt stirred Miles's guts. He masked his

features, turning to stare out the front window at the street. Of all the Wanted posters to turn up here on this day.

With a ripping sound, Jonas tore the paper across. "We don't have to worry about him anymore. Arrested, tried, found guilty, and hanged. One of that no-account nest of Walkers from up by Abilene. I sure would've liked to have been in on the posse that finally tracked him and his gang down."

Bat shoved at another stack of papers on his untidy desk. "No, you wouldn't have, son. I was leading that posse, and it was the hardest ride and the closest shave I've ever had on a chase. Cliff Walker came within a gnat's eyebrow of shooting my head right off my shoulders before we cornered him, and he ran out of ammunition." He turned to Miss Reid. "One of the boys will see you to your boardinghouse, ma'am. Be a good idea if from now through the end of cattle season, you don't walk by yourself downtown."

"I'll see her home." Miles couldn't wait to get out of the sheriff's office. Bat and Jonas exchanged grins at his eagerness. Heat prickled across his chest. He didn't want Miss Reid to get the wrong idea, but she was a good excuse to leave. He didn't need any reminders about how lawless the Walker gang had been. Not when he'd been considered one of them just a few short years ago.

Chapter 3

Fran chewed the end of her pencil and frowned at the ledger. Hap had been at it again, scrawling in her neat receipt book with his spidery, hurried penmanship. And it was up to her to make sense of the scribbles. Now, if it had been Wally, the numbers would be neat as a shiny new pin right out of the package.

Hap Greeley and Wally Price, cousins, business partners, and as different as chalk and cheese. And once more squabbling.

"Why did you order pickled beets?" Wally's fussy voice whined down the store. "You know we can get those locally."

"They were a bargain. Don't worry. We'll be able to sell them. I already got an order for a case from the Dodge House Hotel." Hap's voice, full of nonchalance and bonhomie, boomed. "You worry too much, Wally. We're primed to have the best season of our lives. The store's chock-full of inventory, and cowboys are stampeding up the trail right to our doors."

Fran stood on tiptoe and leaned her elbows on the counter to see past the notions case to where her bosses stood by the cold stove.

Hap, big and loose-limbed, with baggy gray trousers and

a striped shirt, leaned against the counter. His sleeves were shoved up to reveal hairy, meaty forearms, and his boots had earflaps that slapped when he sauntered through the store. He took off his spectacles and rubbed them with his big, red handkerchief. "It will be a good year."

Wally, immaculate in a starched white apron and black sleeve covers, held his clipboard against his snowy shirtfront. "If we don't have a good season, I'll know just where to lay the blame." Wally consulted the clipboard. His rosy face always looked freshly scrubbed, and Fran speculated that he used a ruler to part his greased hair. The white line bisecting his scalp was razor straight.

"Don't worry about it." Hap returned his glasses to his bulbous nose, dug his fist into one of the candy jars lining the counter, and popped a sourball into his mouth, rolling it until it made his cheek jut like a gopher's. "I told you, we're going to have a great season." He caught Fran leaning over the counter and winked at her. "With you and Frannie here seeing to things, there's not much chance of anything going wrong. Best thing we ever did, hiring Fran. The cowboys fall all over themselves to buy whatever she suggests to them."

Fran smiled. Hap had to be the most easygoing man in Dodge. He never scolded her if she was late for work, and when it was his turn to pay her, he usually managed to slip a couple of extra dollars into her pay envelope. The only person who ever got under his skin was Wally, and Wally had to work at it.

Wally squatted and began checking things off the list on

his clipboard. "If you'd help out more around here, instead of hanging out over at Shanahan's or the Alhambra all the time, Miss Seaton and I wouldn't have to see to everything ourselves. You'd think, with a half-interest in this mercantile, the store would garner more of your attention than a gambling hall."

Fran sighed and closed her ledger. Hap and Wally fought like an old married couple. And always about the same things. Hap's gambling and Wally's worrying. If they hadn't been left the store jointly by their grandfather, they never would've gone into business together, she was sure. But in the year since she started, Wally's harping rarely made a dent in Hap's good nature—or his gambling, and Hap's slipshod bookkeeping and fortune's favorite outlook hadn't rubbed off a bit on the straitlaced Wally.

"Miss Seaton, if you could clear some shelf space behind the flour bins, I'll put away some of these beets, though what we're going to do with more than two hundred cans of pickled beets, I'll never know." Wally's fussy, pencil-thin moustache twitched, and his nearly black eyes rolled.

"You'll think of something, Wally-me-lad." Hap smacked him on the shoulder, making Wally stagger and drop his pencil. "I believe I'll go out and drum us up some business. Fran, you hold the fort, right?"

The bell over the door jangled, and three cowboys strolled in. Wide-brimmed hats, easy rolling gait, tinkling spurs, and brash manners. Fran picked up her feather duster. Ignoring them, she went to the front windows and stretched to flick the duster along the top casing, being sure to raise her arms high enough to show just a hint of petticoat and ankle.

"Whooeee." One of the cowboys whistled low. "If I'd have known there was a new clerk in this store this season, we'da made it our first stop."

Fran glanced over her shoulder and returned to her dusting. She stifled a sigh. Run-of-the-mill drovers. Again. When was someone exciting going to come through the door? Still, they looked ready to spend, so she should do her best by Wally and Hap and wait on them. She walked behind the counter and laid aside the duster. "What can I do for you boys?"

The tallest one grinned and leaned on the counter. "Well now, just a smile from your pretty lips would do for a start. We've been on the trail a powerful stretch of time. I haven't seen a pretty face in way too long." He jerked his thumb at his *compadres*. "Just these two ugly mugs and a dozen more just as homely, all the way from Uvalde."

One of his friends scowled and elbowed him over, jostling for room. "I ain't as ugly as you." He stuck out his hand, checked it, and then wiped it on his trousers before offering it to Fran again. "They call me Brazos Bill. And what would your name be, darlin'?"

She let him shake her hand and almost laughed when his pals demanded their own handshakes. Simple, uncomplicated cowboys. "You boys are just in off the trail? You must be in need of a lot of things then. New clothes? Candy? A gift to take back to your mothers or your sweethearts?" Fran always tried to steer the conversation toward mothers, wives, and sweethearts, just to keep the cowboys in line. Though they were high-spirited and full of fun—as long as they hadn't been drinking—cowboys were fairly predictable.

She directed them toward the table in the center of the mercantile. Piles of shirts and pants in all sizes and colors lay in stacks on the long narrow top, and others hung from hooks and hangers on a rail overhead. "Everything you could want in the way of clothing, you'll find there. Boots and hats are on the wall here." Fran waved to the bank of shelves piled with boxes and the hat stand on the counter. She tilted her head and tapped her chin with her finger. "I think you'd look very handsome in brown. It would match your eyes." She held up a dark brown shirt with mother-of-pearl buttons.

As Hap had pointed out, cowboys had a tendency to buy most everything she suggested, and this group was no exception. She had to be careful not to abuse the power she wielded, though Hap encouraged her to use it. She didn't want to bilk the cowboys out of their hard-earned cash. It was a fine line, and she wasn't always sure she walked it correctly.

Wally beamed from behind the counter, totting up their purchases and taking their money. He wrapped the packages in brown paper and tied them with twine before disappearing into the back room.

When the Texans had their arms laden with purchases, two of them strolled out, but Brazos Bill stayed behind.

Fran returned to her dusting, but she was aware of Bill watching her every move.

"Say, when do you get off work here? I'd be pleased to buy you dinner at the hotel and maybe take in a show? I hear they put on a real good show over at the Comique." He pronounced it Com–ee–cue like most of the cowboys.

A tinge of excitement tugged at her, but at the same time disappointment encroached. She wasn't in the slightest bit interested in Brazos Bill or any of the Texas drovers. And while she'd love an opportunity to have dinner at the hotel and see a show at one of the theaters, she knew her brothers would never approve of her going out with a stranger. There was really only one man they would approve of her seeing. Her fingers curled around the handle of the feather duster.

The door chime rang out again. She glanced at the doorway and pressed her lips together. Speak of the devil.

She was at it again. Chatting with some cowboy.

Jonas used his heel to close the door and opened his coat so his badge and gun were on full display. "Afternoon, Fran." He nodded and sauntered up to stand beside the cowboy.

Fran shot him a "leave me alone" kind of glare and composed herself to looking all feminine and sweet again.

The cowboy straightened from lounging on the counter. "Fran, is it? Mighty pretty name for a mighty pretty girl." His grin had more than a whiff of wolf about it, and Jonas took a firm grip on himself so as not to shove the Texan's teeth down his throat. It wasn't this poor kid's fault he'd wandered into Fran's store and fallen for her looks. Fran was a mighty powerful draw.

Jonas tilted his head and raised his eyebrows at her. When

she stared back at him with wide green eyes, he jerked his chin in the cowboy's direction, silently asking for an introduction.

She crossed her arms and huffed, blowing her red-gold bangs off her forehead. "Jonas, this is Brazos Bill. Bill, this is Deputy Jonas Spooner of the Ford County sheriff's office."

Bill nodded but didn't offer to shake hands, which was fine by Jonas.

"You just off the trail?" Jonas asked to be polite, though everything about the cowboy, from his work-stained clothes to his rank odor, shouted trail herd.

"That's right. Ramrod paid us off about an hour ago." Bill turned to face Jonas square, his muscles rigid. "I ain't doin' nothing wrong."

"I didn't say you were. Cowboys are welcome in Dodge City. We have a few rules, but most drovers don't find them too hard to live with."

"Rules? What rules? I don't remember too many rules last season." Bill scratched his hair over his right ear and squinted.

"Things change. The most important rule is: no firearms inside city limits. You can check your guns at the jail or one of the hotels." Jonas stared hard at the pistol tucked into the cowboy's belt. "Everything else is pretty much routine. Don't ride your horse into the saloons, don't cheat at cards, don't harass the womenfolk." Jonas tilted his head toward Fran, who gripped her feather duster as if she wished it was his neck.

"Since when is it harassing the womenfolk to talk to a store clerk?" Bill held his open hand out to Fran. "Have I said one harass-ful thing to you?"

"No, you've been most gallant. Deputy Spooner tends to be overly cautious."

"Then you'll come out with me tonight?" The cowboy's face split in a wide grin once more.

Jonas pressed his lips together and folded his arms across his chest. "You talked to Linc this afternoon, Fran?"

Fran glared back for a moment and shook her head. "I'm afraid I won't be able to have dinner with you. My brothers expect me home right after work."

"Brothers? How many brothers?"

"Four," Jonas supplied. "They run the feed store over by the depot. You might've seen them. Seaton's Feed and Seed? Closest thing to grizzly bears we have around here, those Seaton boys."

Brazos Bill gulped.

Fran's brothers had as much of a name for themselves in Dodge City as Bat Masterson himself. Burly, surly, and without exception willing and able to take on a bull buffalo bare-handed. They, more than any other, were the main reason why Fran hadn't gotten herself into more trouble with her flirting ways.

"The Seaton brothers." Bill rolled the idea around in his head for a minute. "You're their sister? Well, if they expect you home tonight, I'll just have to find other company, though it won't be as delightful as yours, I'm sure, Miss Seaton." He doffed his big hat. "You'll be certain to tell them I wasn't harassing you in any way, right? Good day." Snatching up his purchases, he all but bolted for the door.

Jonas laughed. "Works every time." He jerked when Fran

whacked him with the duster. The cloud this produced made him sneeze. "What?"

"Why do you always have to ruin everything? You're worse than my brothers, even Stuart, and he's the worst of the lot." She plonked her elbows onto the counter and rested her chin in her hands. "It's not flirting to be nice to customers, and Wally and Hap won't appreciate you running off every man who comes in here and pays me some attention. You're not my keeper, you know."

"I do know." Jonas leaned down so his eyes were on the same level as hers. "Though I'd be happy to take on the role. Your brothers worry about some cowpoke getting the wrong idea. You're too pretty for your own good and their peace of mind."

She stuck her lower lip out. "They might as well be prison wardens, the way they order me around. And you are, too. Beats me why they don't mind you hanging around all the time."

"Your brothers and I have an understanding. I promised I'd look after you while you're in town, and that's what I'm going to do. You about ready to head home?"

Her mouth opened. "You have an understanding with my brothers? They've hired you to babysit me?" She sure looked cute when she was outraged, which was a good thing, since she seemed to be spitting mad more often than not when he was around.

"They aren't paying me to look out for you. It's part of my job as a deputy. I'd do it for anybody, so don't get all het up."

Wally Price came out of the back room. "This day has gotten

away from me entirely. I didn't do half the things I wanted to. I suppose it's near to closing time. Miss Seaton, you did an excellent job with those cowboys. They bought far more than if I'd have been the one to wait on them." He seemed to notice Jonas for the first time. "Deputy Spooner."

"I've come to see Miss Seaton home. Her brothers just got a big delivery of feed at the store, and they asked me to come fetch her."

"Very good." The fussy little shopkeeper checked his clipboard then his watch. "You may go, Miss Seaton. I'll see you bright and early tomorrow morning, and we'll deal with these beets." His narrow moustache twitched like a rat's whiskers.

Fran grabbed her purse and hat from under the counter, stopping to check her reflection and pin the hat to her upswept curls.

Jonas noticed the curve of her neck and the way a few wisps of hair played at her nape, and his heart bumped faster. Smothering his tender feelings for her, he took her elbow. "Quit primping. You look just fine. Every cowboy within eyesight of you will be gawking. You won't even have to flirt."

"You don't have to grab me up like a flapjack. I can take care of myself, you know."

He gentled his hold on her arm. "One of these days you're going to tangle with the wrong man and find yourself in a heap of danger."

"At least it would be an adventure. Better than the boring same-old, same-old I see every day."

Chapter 4

"The best thing about being a lawman is that no two days are ever the same." Bat leaned back in his chair and propped his feet up on the corner of his desk. His hat sat at a rakish angle, and he tapped the round, silver head of his cane in his palm. "There's always something popping up to keep things lively."

Miles dabbed his rag into the saddle soap and rubbed at the holster in his hands. "So, tell me more about what the merchants and saloon keepers have to say about enforcing the law on Front Street." He wanted to know exactly where he stood, so as not to run afoul of his new boss.

"There is a war going on in Dodge City. It's fought in the newspapers and at the polls. The mayor and myself and several others think we should—within reason—give the cowboys a free hand. Some of the local bigwigs want us to come down hard on the cowboys, keep them corralled, maybe even instill a curfew, if you can believe such a thing."

"A curfew, in Dodge? I don't know how you could enforce it without bloodshed." Miles held the leather belt up to the candlelight. Even this early in the season, hours after sundown, people still strolled the sidewalk outside, piano music rolled from the doorways of the saloons and theaters, and shouts and laughter ricocheted down the street. The theaters wouldn't close until about three in the morning, and the saloons wouldn't close at all.

"That's what I told him. The cowboys come to town expecting to let their hair down and play the curly wolf. They're looking to buck the tiger and get drunk and carouse with women of ill repute. All we ask is that they let us take their guns while they do it."

Miles's chest squeezed. Just because something was legal didn't make it right. The gambling, drinking, and immorality of Dodge City flew in the face of everything his newfound faith and God's Word told him. He didn't condone the behavior, but Bat was asking him to go light on the men who were doing the sinning. "What about the townsfolk? Don't they have a right to be safe?" He asked the question as innocently as possible. He didn't know his new boss well, and he didn't want to get him riled.

"Sure they do. But they live in Dodge City, the Queen of the Cattle Towns. If they want to be safe, they should go live in Topeka or somewhere. This is the West. The men work hard, and they play hard, too. Those same townsfolk like the money that rolls in every year, but they can't have it both ways. They have to take the cowboys as they are and the hijinks that go along with them. Dodge City is the last place in Kansas where Texans can bring their cattle. The legislature has pushed them out of Abilene, Ellsworth, Newton, and Wichita. They say it was the tick-fever and the sodbusters who swayed them, but I have a feeling it was the preachers and the schoolmarms." Bat had warmed to his subject, and his eyes glowed.

"Most all the deputies and policemen in town side with the merchants and saloon keepers. In fact, most of the law enforcement in this county has investments in businesses on Front Street." Bat smoothed his moustache and ran his fingers down his lapel. "I've invested from time to time myself. I even owned a part of the Lone Star Dance Hall. You'd be wise to put your money into something like that. This town is a cornucopia of opportunity for a young fellow like you. Sink some money into one of the gambling houses or theaters and rake in the cash."

Miles bent to rub the leather harder, working the oil deep into the holster to make it supple and waterproof. "I'll have to have a look around." Investing wasn't a sin, though he'd steer clear of the saloons and brothels and such. Maybe the gunsmith's where he'd worked until recently. Or the saddle shop. Or even the livery. The buying and selling of horses was big business in Dodge City. A man could make a profit there. "Though I'll have to wait until I get paid." He grinned.

"Dodge City and Ford County pay their lawmen better than anywhere else in the West. You'll have a stake together in no time."

Jonas strolled in through the open doorway. He carried his rifle over his shoulder. "Things are livening up out there."

Bat swung his feet to the floor. "You can watch the jail, Spooner, though that won't be hard. Just the one prisoner, and he's asleep. Carr and I will take a stroll around, poke our heads in a few places, see what we turn up."

Miles's breath quickened, and his muscles tensed. His first patrol as a lawman. He made short work of slinging his gun belt on and holstering his weapon then checked that his badge was in plain sight. Forcing himself to relax, to steady his breathing, he took his hat from the rack by the door and settled it on his head.

The sheriff's boots rang on the boardwalk, and Miles matched his strides. Though Bat carried a cane, he showed no sign of a limp or any pain from the bullet he'd taken in the hip a couple of years ago. His eyes scanned the road and seemed to miss nothing.

Miles copied the action, sweeping the wide street and every window and doorway.

Cowboys clustered on the porch of the Long Branch Saloon. Rollicking piano music rolled through the open doors of the Saratoga, and down the street, the Alamo appeared to be doing a brisk business.

"There are more than a dozen saloons in town at the moment, and about twelve hundred residents. That number will more than double by midsummer. Both the residents and the saloons." Bat nodded to the cowboys as they passed through the crowd. "Evening, boys."

Miles searched every man with his eyes, looking for a weapon or signs of any mischief. Most of the young men had flushed cheeks and lurching movements, the beginnings of being knockdown drunk. They crowded into the saloon, laughing and jostling.

"They'll be sorry specimens by morning." Bat spoke mildly, as if he didn't care much one way or another.

"And broke, most likely. Nobody wins bucking the tiger except the dealer. I've never seen a faro game that wasn't crooked." Miles rested his hand on the butt of his pistol. "The saloons are fleecing the cowboys, and they're mostly too green and too drunk to know it."

"Gambling houses aren't running a charity. Nobody's making those boys go in there and gamble or drink. They could keep their money in their pockets and head home like good little lambs. All we're doing is providing a little entertainment. It's not like we're robbing them at gunpoint. They put up their money and take their chances." Bat frowned at him. "You sound more like a preacher than a deputy. You aren't against gambling and drinking, are you?" The smile that tugged at Bat's lips told Miles he thought the very idea a joke.

Miles's mouth went dry, and he scrambled for something to say that would be the truth and yet still keep Bat's respect. Nothing came to mind. "I think it's a shame that they risk their lives and break their backs getting longhorns up that trail, then, in the space of a couple of days or a week, everything they earned is gone."

His belly flipped. What a watered-down, tepid answer. *Where's your courage, Miles Carr?* But he had to keep his boss's respect, didn't he? How could they work together, count on each other in a pinch, if Bat thought he was some kind of weak-willed Bible-pounder? Spouting off about how things were run in this town was his quickest ticket to losing his badge. He could do the job and keep his faith to himself.

"Might be a shame for them, but it's good for the merchants here." They passed the saddlery shop and paused before the windows of the photography studio. Though the blinds were drawn, slits of light appeared around the edges of the glass. Bat nodded toward the door. "She's working late again. I've warned her of the dangers of being downtown after dark, but she doesn't listen."

Addie Reid. Miles let a picture of her float through his mind. A pretty little thing and game, too. Trying to make a go of the photography studio in spite of her uncle's death. Though he admired her grit, he didn't see how a girl could run a successful business in this town. She didn't have anyone to protect her, and she seemed to have no fear letting cowboys traipse through the studio all day. Now that he was a deputy, he would make it a point to keep a closer eye on her place.

The gunsmith's shop next door was dark. Bat let the head of his cane trail along the siding until they got to the display window. "Shanky has some fine weapons. Does all the gunsmithing for the county. But you know that, I guess." Bat eyed a brace of derringers behind the glass. They lay in a velvet-lined box on a display shelf. Miles had worked on the pair himself just a few weeks ago.

They resumed their walk in the direction of the cattle yards. Far out on the prairie, the glow of sparks and steam announced the imminent arrival of the late-evening train. The long, mournful whistle rolled toward the town.

Miles touched the badge on his chest. A rush of pride

washed over him, just as it had when he'd taken the oath and first pinned on the star. On the heels of that good feeling came a twinge of guilt. He had ducked voicing his views on the vice in this town. He should come clean. About that, and about his family connection to the Walker Gang. Then let Bat decide if he wanted to keep him on. He cleared his throat. "Bat."

The lawman stopped. He smoothed his moustache, his eyes piercing Miles.

At the last minute, Miles's courage failed him, as he envisioned Bat demanding the badge and gun back and, worse yet, hauling him to the jail and throwing him in a cell for being part of the Walker Gang. The law in Kansas had no love for the Walkers, and it wouldn't matter a plugged nickel that he hadn't done anything wrong. Being related to that nest of thieves would be enough to get his neck stretched in these parts.

Bat's eyebrows rose as he waited.

Miles voiced the first dumb thing that came into his head. "Anything else I should know about being a lawman in Dodge?"

The sheriff shrugged. "Mostly it's a case of being in the right place at the right time. Learn to smell trouble before it starts, and keep your gun handy."

Turning to retrace their steps, Miles's badge became even heavier. Being handy with a gun was second nature, and he'd long been able to smell trouble. But was he in the right place at the right time? He was new at this whole Christian thing. Could he be both a lawman and a believer? Would he have to give up one to be the other? If Bat ever found out who he was, being both wouldn't matter. He could find himself on the other side of a cell door faster than he could say, "Arkansas River."

Addie straightened and pressed her fists into the small of her back. She tended to lose all track of time when she was working, particularly when she was sequestered in the darkroom, but her rumbling stomach told her it must be past the supper hour.

Lifting the last print out of the warm acid fixing bath, she rinsed it and laid it on a sheet of glass. With her roller, she squeezed the excess water from the photograph and held it up to examine it in the rosy light of the red-glassed lantern on the wall.

Two more touch-up jobs awaited her attention, but that was fine, close work that needed a steady hand and sharp eyes. Better to leave it until tomorrow.

She lifted the red globe from the lantern, and golden, bright light filled the room. Clipping the last portrait onto the wire overhead to dry, she rolled her shoulders to ease the tension in her neck.

Working alone meant much longer hours than when she and Uncle Carl had split the developing duties. Tomorrow she would mount the dry photographs into cardboard frames for the customers to pick up. She inventoried the portraits she'd taken that day, judging the effects she'd tried to produce with each one.

By far, the best had been the Easton family. The butcher, his wife, and their three adorable sons. She'd posed them all together then persuaded Mr. Easton to allow her to photograph just the boys. At six, four, and two, they were stair steps in short pants. Golden halos of curls, rounded cheeks, sturdy legs, and engaging smiles. She'd set the middle boy on a brocade chair and placed the youngest beside him. The oldest boy she'd leaned against the plaster pedestal, much as she had Bat Masterson a few days ago. He'd been against the pose until she'd mentioned he'd look just like the sheriff. The picture had come out beautifully, and she had a feeling the Eastons would be very pleased. Maybe they'd even consent to letting her display a copy of the picture in the front window to entice other families to come in for a sitting.

Her final task was to store the chemicals and tidy everything up for the next day. This took her almost as much time as the developing, as some of the compounds used were volatile and, if treated casually, could injure or even kill. Uncle Carl's cautions and directions ran through her head as she closed up bottles of acid, lye powder, nitrates, and more.

Emerging from the dark room, she breathed deeply, trying to dispel the chemical smell from her nose. Working in such close quarters with so many strong emulsions and acids left her brain foggy. If only she could find a way to get clean air into the little room without letting in even the smallest bit of light.

Laughter and footfalls rang out from the boardwalk in front of the studio. A glance outside told her not only had she missed supper at the boardinghouse but darkness had fallen. She checked the clock. Eleven o'clock? She groaned and caught sight of her reflection in the mirror on the wall. "You've done it now, girl. Didn't Sheriff Masterson warn you about being downtown alone after dark?"

Four blocks to her boardinghouse. Between here and there, six saloons, two dance halls, the mercantile, and the jail.

And a gauntlet of cowboys.

They loitered on every porch, sauntered from saloon to saloon, and though most would treat a woman with deference, a few were truly dangerous—especially if they were under the influence of liquor. Life had taught Addie that coyotes often hid behind a mask of chivalry.

Still, she couldn't stay here all night. Taking one last look around the studio, Addie picked up her hat and bag and blew out the lantern. Things would only get worse if she waited. Last thing, she strapped on her camera bag. Though the Chevalier was her pride and joy, she would never leave her smaller Scovill behind. One never knew when a photographic opportunity might arise.

Locking the door behind her, she returned the key to her handbag and gripped the cloth sack close to her body. Petty thieves had been known to slice the cords of a lady's reticule to steal it off her wrist, and they weren't always careful with their knife. The camera case bumped familiarly against her hip. She wore the strap diagonally across her chest, which she knew wasn't ladylike, but carrying the camera that way ensured it wouldn't slip off her shoulder and also left her hands free.

Music rolled and light spilled from the windows and doorways of the saloons and dance halls. Her studio, tucked between a leather goods shop that boasted the "best fitting boots in the West" and a gun shop, was a good location for garnering foot traffic and drop-in business but not so good from a security standpoint. Still, it wasn't right next door to a saloon, which would've been much worse.

Squaring her shoulders, she stepped out of the recessed doorway and headed west. Clumps of men dotted the boardwalk between her and her destination. She took a deep breath, kept her chin up, and walked with purpose. If she acted scared, it marked her as easy prey.

When she reached the first group of cowboys, the odors of the stockyards, hard work, tobacco, and horses assailed her. They jostled, elbowed, and laughed. A match scratched off a boot sole, and one of them lit a huge cigar, puffing clouds of smoke into the night air.

Though they stood aside to let her pass, she could feel their eyes on her. Refusing to cower, she looked straight ahead, praying no one would stop her. She really needed an alarm clock in the darkroom. Something to help her remember the time and never get caught out like this again. Though once she'd started the developing process, she couldn't stop halfway through.

Her breath came a bit easier as she passed by the group. Perhaps she would make it just fine after all. Then she came abreast of the Long Branch.

A rowdy crew of firebrands lounged and joked on the porch. "Whooeee, lookit here." One cowboy elbowed his companion. "They sure do grow 'em pretty here." He stepped directly into her path, and she was forced to edge around him. "Hey there, little lady. Can I buy you a drink?" He had flushed cheeks and looked to be about eighteen. She kept walking, and he sidled along with her. His chaps flopped, and his spurs clanked with each stride.

"No, thank you."

He frowned and breathed beer fumes across her face. She kept walking, but he crab-stepped to get around in front of her. "There's no call to be uppity. Just one drink. No harm in that."

Addie started to inhale, but the alcohol on his breath hit like a blow. A cough exploded from her throat. She gasped. "Really, sir, I have to go. I don't want a drink. I just want to get home." Though she trembled, she tried to hide it. These men were like wolves. If she showed the least bit of fear or weakness, they would pounce on it. Her hands gripped the strap on her camera case.

"I'll go with you, then. Can't be too careful here in old Dodge." He shoved his hat back and tucked his thumbs into his belt. "My name's Brazos Bill. What's yours?"

His eyes were glazed, and his exaggerated gestures told her he was past halfway to drunk. Not only was he in no condition to protect her from anything, he might get the wrong idea the minute they were out of sight of the others.

"I'll be fine on my own, thank you. Why don't you go back to your friends?"

He scrubbed the side of his head and kicked his toe against the end of a bench under the window. "I think I'd rather make friends with you." His hand snaked out and grabbed her wrist.

"I asked you polite to come in and have one little drink."

She tugged against his grip, but his fingers didn't budge. "Sir, please. You're hurting me." Her breath came fast, and her heart bumped. His friends had gone into the saloon. She didn't know whether to yell or not. Would screaming make him let go or would it bring more cowboys? Why hadn't she realized how late it was getting?

"You gonna have that drink with me?"

"Let her go." The icy command came from the darkness of the alley behind her.

She swiveled her head to look, but she couldn't see anything in the deep shadows.

Brazos Bill stiffened, and his grip tightened, making her fingers tingle. "This ain't none of your affair."

"I said, let her go."

Boots scuffed on the dirt, and she discerned a darker space in the blackness of the alley. Her throat tightened. Something sinister and powerful came from that shape.

"Mister"—Bill scowled—"I'm talking to the lady. You should move along and go find your own gal."

Addie wrenched her arm but couldn't break free. Her skin burned and the bones of her wrist ground together. She'd have bruises for sure.

The man in the shadows emerged. Light from a window gleamed off the star on his chest.

A breath whooshed out of her at the same time Brazos Bill sucked in air.

Miles Carr.

The cowboy's grip loosened a fraction, but he didn't let go. "What is it with you deputies? Can't a fellow talk to a girl in this town? First it was that clerk at Greeley's, batting her lashes and playing all flirty. Now it's this one"—he lifted her hand—"waltzing through town, offering herself as fair game, then crying when someone takes her up on it."

Addie gasped. "I did no such thing. I have a right to walk to my own home unmolested by drunken cowboys. Now unhand me, you. . .you Texan!"

Deputy Carr closed the distance between himself and the cowboy. "I've asked you twice to unhand the lady. If I have to ask again, I'll arrest you for assault."

Bill quivered.

The deputy stood his ground, and the look in his eyes chilled Addie and fired her blood at the same time. Gratitude, that was all it was. For his rescuing her. It had nothing to do with how handsome and courageous he was. Nothing at all.

Flinging her hand away, Bill backed up a step and raised his hands shoulder-high. Disgust lined his suntanned face. "Fine. Take her. She ain't worth a night in a cell. This town sure has changed. Everywhere I look there's a deputy telling me what I can and can't do."

To Addie's amazement, Miles relaxed a fraction and slapped the cowboy on the shoulder. "I'm sure you'll find something else to do tonight."

Brazos Bill strode off toward the Long Branch, and Miles turned to her, a fierce expression in his eyes. "What do you think you're playing at, strolling through town after dark?

You're lucky I came along."

She pressed her hand to her chest and gulped. "Thank you. I thought he was going to drag me right into that saloon."

The scowl painting the lawman's face eased. "C'mon. I'll see you home."

He took her elbow, and she could feel each of his fingers through her sleeve. She needed to remind herself of what had happened to her the last time a man made her heart flutter and her breath hitch. And she was of no mind to go down that road again.

Miles had wanted nothing more than to push his fist through that cowboy's face. The fire burning in his belly at the sight of Miss Reid trying to get out of that drover's grip didn't abate as they walked away from the scene. The only thing that had kept him from littering the street with the man's body had been Bat's caution to use a light touch where the cowboys were concerned. At least he hadn't had to draw his gun.

They walked in silence the remaining blocks to Mrs. Blanchard's Boardinghouse. Miss Reid didn't ask how he knew where she lived, and he didn't offer to enlighten her. The only rooming house on this end of town was Mrs. Blanchard's, and she was also the only landlord who had women residents—reputable women, anyway—so it didn't take much detective work to figure out.

They reached the porch of the boardinghouse, and Miss Reid turned on the step to face him. Their eyes were on the same level, and the starlight picked out the blue glint in hers. He backed up half a step.

She pressed her lips together, swallowed, and gave him a polite smile. "Thank you for coming to my rescue. That man really frightened me."

"You had reason to be scared. You shouldn't be out this late without an escort." The gruffness in his voice surprised him, but it was better than the shouting he wanted to do. "Bat said he'd warned you about that."

She nodded, and he noticed the slight upturn to her nose. Some aroma clung to her clothes, like medicine or soap or something. Probably the stuff she used to make her pictures.

"I have orders to fill, and once I get into the darkroom, I tend to lose all track of time." She shrugged, spreading her hands like a little girl.

Her appeal made him even gruffer. "Next time you work late like this, raise the blinds in one of your front windows when you're ready to go home and me or one of the other deputies will walk you home. Good night, ma'am." He tipped his hat and strode away from her to resume his patrol, leaving her standing on the steps.

A block away, the lights and sounds of Front Street pulled him along, reminding him that he was a lawman and he couldn't afford any distractions, no matter how pretty they might be.

Chapter 5

"I have chosen you, *mademoiselle*, because I believe you have a gift." Henri LeBlanc waved his hands with all the fervor of his Gallic nature. "It is you who will capture the essence of my beloved theater, as you have captured my heart." He imprisoned Addie's hand, bent from the waist, and kissed the air just over the backs of her fingers. "The talent you displayed with your portrait of our esteemed sheriff convinced me you were the one I have been looking for."

They stood in the opulent foyer of the Arden Palace Theater, scheduled to open in just three more days. Addie withdrew her fingers and crossed her arms at her waist. "Mr. LeBlanc, what would your wife say?" She tilted her head and raised her eyebrows. Fran, standing just behind her, snickered. Knowing better than to take the Frenchman's words seriously, Addie waited for his response.

He laughed, flicked a handkerchief from his pocket, and dusted the gleaming handrail leading to the second floor. "You think she would lead me to the guillotine, no? Not my Gisette. She would agree with me, that you"—he nodded to Addie and included Fran in the gesture—"are like two beautiful roses. You compliment my beautiful theater with your very presence."

Fran giggled again. Addie cast a glance over her shoulder at her friend. Eyes wide, lips parted, Fran appeared to be trying to see everything at once. Not that Addie could blame her. Every surface in the Arden Palace shone with sparkling newness—plush carpeting, velvet drapes, textured wallpapers, gilt frames. The smell of new paint lingered.

The front door swung open, and Addie stifled a groan. Heber Donaldson, red-faced and glaring, stomped in. "LeBlanc, what is the meaning of this? You can't possibly choose *her* over me. I'm the most respected and experienced photographer in the county." He jabbed his finger toward Addie but didn't look at her. Instead, his eyes bored into the little Frenchman. "This is an outrage."

LeBlanc shrank back and patted his forehead with his handkerchief. He darted a look behind him to the safety of the office doorway and swallowed. "*Monsieur*—"

Donaldson ignored his protest, turning on Addie. "What did you do? Offer to take the photographs for free? That's the only way you could've undercut my bid. You're getting too big for yourself, girlie. Why don't you go back to the kitchen where you belong?"

"Monsieur, please, this is most inappropriate—" The proprietor tried to step in, but Donaldson rounded on him again.

"I'd like to know what you think you're playing at, LeBlanc. I thought we had a deal." Donaldson shook his finger in LeBlanc's face. "You're supposed to give the job to me."

"No, no, nothing was certain." He raised his hands, his brow scrunching. "I discussed it with my wife, and she preferred the mademoiselle's portraiture."

"Ha! That explains it. Skirts usually stick together. I might've known you'd be under your wife's thumb."

Addie shot a look at Fran, whose eyebrows rose and jaw dropped in a "do you believe this guy" expression.

The little Frenchman's dark eyes snapped fire. "That is enough, monsieur. You will not come to my establishment and insult me this way. Your bid was submitted and considered, but we have elected to give the job to someone else. I would prefer it if you would leave now. The mademoiselle has work to do." He pointed to the door, stuffing his handkerchief back into his pocket and smoothing his lapels.

Donaldson scowled, his face getting even redder. "You'll be sorry about this, girl. You'll be sorry you didn't quit and turn everything over to the bank. This job won't matter. You'll never make the payments, and by the end of the summer, you'll be washed up." He slammed the door hard enough on his way out to rattle the chandelier.

Addie took a shaky breath. "Where would you like us to start, and is there anything in particular you'd like photographed?" Her knees trembled, but she strove for a professional demeanor, as if getting bawled out by a competitor hadn't bothered her in the least.

She rested her hand on the cart she'd used to haul her equipment to the theater. A cart had been necessary, because for a job this big she'd packed up the Chevalier and brought it over from the studio. Anything less would be inadequate. This tableau called for a large print. But she had her smaller Scovill along as well. Best to be prepared.

LeBlanc's smile, though not as broad as before Donaldson's interruption, returned. "I should think you would know what is best. What I had envisioned, it is for the photograph to make the viewer want to see my beautiful Palace." LeBlanc ran his hand down a lovely fluted column. "I should like to see some of the detail but also the grand openness of the theater. Yes?"

Addie nodded. "I would like to take a portrait of you as well. Perhaps here in the foyer, under one of the paintings? Or beside the ticket window. The scrollwork here would photograph beautifully."

"What about by these potted palms?" Fran touched the tip of one of the fanned-out leaves.

LeBlanc couldn't decide, posing himself in one place and then another before changing his mind altogether. "No, no, not a picture of me. It will be best to take only my beautiful Palace."

Addie, conscious of time ticking away, began lifting boxes of equipment. Fran followed suit. They entered the opulent auditorium and stood still for a moment. The grandness of the décor and the sheer size of the room sent a covey of quail darting around her insides. "Thanks for coming with me. With no natural light in the theater, I'm going to need someone to help me with the magnesium powder flash."

Addie unfolded the legs of her tripod in the center aisle. As she'd requested when LeBlanc had delivered the excellent news that he'd given her the commission, every chandelier had been lit and every wall sconce glowed brightly. Even the boxes on the second floor had lamplight streaming from them. "I'll take a few with the curtains drawn across the stage then a couple with them open."

"How many all together?"

Addie grimaced. "I brought enough plates for twenty exposures. I know that's a lot, but I've never photographed something on this scale, so I want to try a lot of combinations. I wish Uncle Carl were here." Though she'd been confident enough when she put in her bid for the job, now that she was faced with it all her uncertainty and self-doubts came roaring back.

"I never thought Donaldson would show up here." Fran shook out the camera drape and handed it to Addie. "Bad enough that he stood in the middle of the mercantile yesterday and announced that LeBlanc was out of his mind to hire an amateur for such a job. He even hinted that you had used your 'feminine wiles' to get the bid. Though he did assure everyone that after you ruined the job, LeBlanc would be only too glad to come crawling to him, Heber Donaldson, a *real* photographer."

Addie grimaced and pressed her hand against her stomach. "I don't understand why he's so upset. There's plenty of work to go around."

"He's just jealous. Before you opened your studio, his was the only studio on Front Street, and he got most of the cowboy business. He knows he can't compete with you, not your photography and not with the cowboys. They would much rather have a pretty girl take their pictures."

"I just hope he's not right about this job being too much for me." She hated to admit the extent to which his tirade had rocked her.

"You can do this. And I'll stay, even if it takes all day." Fran set the box with the wet-plate slides on one of the plush, velvet chairs. She put her hands on her hips. "What should I do first?"

The preparations for the first picture took much longer than Addie had hoped, but thankfully, Mr. LeBlanc left them alone. She sighted through the camera and framed the shot to include the entire stage and the first two boxes on either side of the second floor. *Depth of field. Focus, exposure, angle, lighting.* Addie rehearsed everything her Uncle Carl and her own practice had taught her and tried to forget how important this commission was. If she fell flat on her face, the bank would call in her loan, and her dreams and vision would disappear into the prairie air.

"Be careful with those two boxes. Keep them separated." She pointed to the two containers of flash powder ingredients. For safety's sake, she didn't carry them in the same box. Photographers had been known to burn down their own studios when flash powder ingredients got out of hand.

Fran helped where she could, and she put her own artistic talents to work straightening the folds of the stage curtains and even running upstairs to fuss with the drapes framing each private box. "What this place needs is some flowers." She leaned over one of the boxes. "Especially the foyer, but even in here. Imagine a couple of big vases of roses or carnations on either side of the stage. Wouldn't that look spectacular?"

"Where are we going to get those kinds of flowers in the middle of Kansas? How about a few Indian paintbrush stalks or sunflowers or yucca stems?" Addie set up her scales for measuring out the combustible elements she would need for the flash and paced off the distance between the camera lens and the curtain. She did a few quick calculations in her head.

"You're right." Fran's voice echoed in the vast room. "Too bad. They would look great." She disappeared from the box and soon emerged though a side door.

Addie finally had the magnesium powder and potassium chlorate measured out and in the holder. Her hands shook as she lit a long taper candle and handed it to Fran. "I'll be under the drape. When I point to you, touch the flame to the edge of the pan." She demonstrated with her finger. "Don't look at the pan when you do, or you'll be seeing black spots and stars. The flash powder will ignite and make a very bright light."

A tight band of tension wrapped itself around Addie's middle, and a sinking feeling of having bitten off more than she could chew started in her chest. With chilly fingers she loaded the first plate into the camera by feel, careful to keep it concealed from all light. She ducked under the drape, the familiar, closed-in, airless feeling of the heavy cloth isolating her from everything but the view through the lens. Allowing her eyes to accustom themselves to the darkness, she reached around to the front of the camera to remove the lens cover. She had to stretch, because she'd extended the accordion-pleated bellows on the Chevalier to full-length, using every inch of the monorail mounting. With a dry mouth, she raised her right hand and pointed toward Fran, remembering to close her eyes.

Pop! Foof!

The familiar minor explosion of flash powder blasted the room with a light so bright she could see it even with closed eyelids. Her eyes popped open, and she reached around to cap the lens. When everything was dark and covered, she emerged from under the drape. Triumph trickled through her and loosened her stomach muscles.

"Wow!" Fran lowered her arm and peeked over her elbow. "Did it work?"

"I think so, but the proof will be in the developing." Addie tucked her thumbnail between her teeth and clamped down, surveying the room for an interesting angle. "I'm thinking we'll do another shot from here with a longer exposure and no flash powder. I'd like to capture the feel of an opening night with all the soft lights."

She set up and took picture after picture, from the balcony, from the foyer, from the stage looking outward to the seats and boxes. She even took one from well back in one of the boxes with only the stage in view, perfectly framed by the box curtains. Every photograph with the Chevalier took an age to set up as she had to prepare a new wet-plate and flash powder for each new location. As she held the watch in her palm timing the exposure, she knew in her heart the pictures would be good. She recapped the lens. Time for a little fun.

"Fran, go raise the curtain again and stand on stage. Pretend you're the actress you always wanted to be." Addie repacked all her equipment and lifted her Scovill. The dry-plate technique was so much quicker, though it didn't provide quite as sharp a detail nor could she print large photographs with it.

Fran grinned and vanished behind the drapes. A few thumps and bumps and the massive curtain parted to reveal a large stage. A painted landscape on canvas provided the backdrop. At least it wasn't advertisements as some theaters used. Fran struck a pose, lifting one hand, palm up as if beckoning to someone in the first box. She clutched the lace at her throat with the other hand and filled her expression with pleading.

"Hold that." Addie rested the Scovill on the back of one of the chairs and uncapped the lens. "Don't move or you'll just be a blur." She counted off the seconds in her head. "Okay, you can relax."

They took several more portraits, each one sillier than the last, before Addie announced she was out of plates. "That will have to be it. I think I used a whole month's allotment."

"Allotment?" Fran straightened from where she was almost hanging out of one of the balcony boxes and began braiding her hair. The Rapunzel pose Fran had suggested had sent them both into a fit of giggles that made taking the picture hard.

Addie removed the plate from the camera. "Yes. I'm on a strict budget, and photographs just for fun can be expensive. I've given myself an allotment of dry-plate money, and I think I've used it all up for this month." And she'd better cut that allotment back from now on if she was going to have any hope at all of paying off the mortgage. Only about ten weeks to go and she hadn't made much of a dent, though this commission would be a big step in the right direction.

Fran came down and sat on the edge of the stage between two footlights. She crossed her ankles and let her legs swing. "You haven't mentioned the little scrape you got into last week on the way home." Her green eyes held a slight accusation. "I've been waiting for you to tell me about it."

Addie repacked the Scovill, nestling it into the case and clipping it into place so it didn't slide around. The clips had been a good idea, even if the man who had thought them up and fashioned them for her hadn't been such a good idea for Addie.

"How did you hear about it?" She kept her voice neutral, though her heart did a little flip-flop. How many times since that night had her thoughts turned for no good reason to the newest deputy in Ford County?

"Jonas told me. I guess Miles must've told him." Fran hopped off the stage. "Did he really save you from a wild cowboy and walk you home in the moonlight?"

Addie turned away and wrinkled her nose at her friend's romantic notions. "It wasn't like that."

Fran hurried up the aisle until she stood in front of Addie. Placing her hands on Addie's shoulders, she gave her a little shake. "Then tell me how it was. Who was the cowboy?"

She shrugged off Fran's hands and sat in one of the plush seats. Fran plopped into the row behind her. Addie turned and stacked her hands on the back of the chair. She had been trying to forget about that night, and she'd been scrupulous about watching the time so as to be home before dark, but she could see Fran wasn't going to let her off without hearing the entire story. "He said his name was Brazos Bill, and he wanted me to go to the saloon with him for a drink."

"Brazos Bill?" Fran's voice shot high. "Are you joshing me? He came into the store and asked me out to dinner. I'd have gone, too, but Jonas shoved his big nose into my business and ran him off."

"You should be thankful. I wouldn't like to think about what might happen to a girl in the company of Brazos Bill when he's been drinking. Jonas did the right thing."

"Oh pooh on Jonas Spooner. The man's worse than all my brothers combined. A mother hen has nothing on Jonas."

Addie shook her head and wondered what it would be like to have someone that protective of her. Though, come to think of it, Miles had done a very good job of protecting her that night. "When are you going to see that all Jonas's blustering is because he loves you?"

"But I don't want him to love me. I want him to leave me alone."

Addie looked up from stowing equipment. "Do you? Do you really?"

"Tell me what happened the other night." Fran evaded her question and got busy gathering things up.

"Brazos Bill grabbed hold of my arm and wouldn't let go. I thought he might drag me right into the saloon. But Miles happened on the scene and changed Bill's mind for him."

Fran sighed. "Romantic. And exciting. Like a knight

rescuing a fair maiden. What did he say to you when he walked you home?"

"He told me I was foolish to be out alone after dark, and he was right."

"That's all? Surely he did something or said something that could be considered romantic."

He had arranged for her to signal one of the deputies if she had to be in the shop late and needed an escort to the boardinghouse, but did that qualify as romantic? And if it did, was she willing to share that, even with Fran? "No, he just did his job, told me to be more careful in the future, and left me on the steps."

Fran frowned in disgust. "Men are so dense."

"You're dense if you don't get in on this." Deputy Ty Pearson counted a roll of bills.

Miles and Jonas stood on the front porch of the sheriff's office and watched the activity on the street. Ty had been going on for quite a while, and Miles was heartily sick of it. Jonas nudged him and jerked his chin. Miles followed his gaze and found Addie and Fran crossing Front Street, pulling a cart laden with boxes.

"Think we should go help them?" Miles whispered out of the side of his mouth.

Jonas shook his head. "I offered to help them when they headed out, but Fran set me back right quick. They were on their way to photograph that new theater of LeBlanc's."

At least Addie was doing business in the daylight when the streets were pretty safe. Miles didn't take his eyes off the pair until they disappeared into the photography studio.

"I'm telling you, it's the easiest money I ever made. You two won't ever get rich on a deputy's salary." Ty licked his finger and riffled through his cash once more. "Invest in one of the businesses. I started out south of the deadline because that's all I could afford, but now I've got enough to buy into one of the places on Front Street."

"There's nothing south of the deadline but brothels and booze joints."

Ty looked up, the gleam of greed in his eyes. "So? That's where most of the cowpokes spend their money. A little companionship and rotgut. No reason why I can't make a buck or two off it. They ain't hurting nobody."

Miles's gut clenched. "They're hurting each other. How many knife fights have we broken up down there? How many times does one of those girls get knocked around? I've only been a deputy for a couple of weeks, and I've already had to fetch the doctor for three of those girls."

Jonas nodded. "What they're doing is morally wrong and goes against everything God tells us is right in the Bible. It might not be against the laws of this county to visit the brothels or to get blind, stinkin' drunk, but it sure is contrary to the laws of God."

Miles wanted to squirm at the slack-jawed look Ty gave Jonas, and at the same time, he wanted to applaud Jonas's fearlessness in speaking up. Where Miles hid behind logic and reasoning as his motivation for standing against the avarice in Dodge City, Jonas came right out and said God didn't approve of the sinning. Though Miles was fairly new to his Christian faith, he wondered if he would ever be as bold as Jonas, as matter-of-fact and open. He hoped it would be a long time before he was asked point-blank to defend his faith.

Ty shoved his bankroll into his pocket and rested his hands on his narrow hips. "I think you missed your calling, Spooner. You should've been a preacher. You should carry a Bible instead of a gun. Though I don't know as the Good Book would be much help down across the deadline when the bullets start flying." He threw back his head and laughed. "That the way you feel, too, Carr?"

Prickly sweat broke out on Miles's chest and his mouth went dry. He flashed a look at Jonas, but his friend's face was expressionless. He was saved from having to answer when Bat strolled out of the office and stretched. "Evening."

Ty wasn't ready to be done with the conversation. "Hey, Sheriff, I was just telling these boys they should get in on some of the action and buy into one of the businesses like you and me done. Tell 'em how dumb it would be to miss out on this opportunity."

Bat reached into his vest pocket and pulled out his watch. "I've mentioned it to both these gentlemen before. They're grown men. They can decide on their own."

"They're fools if they don't." Ty leaned against the hitching post, his expression clearly saying he already thought Jonas was a fool and that he wasn't so sure about Miles.

Bat snapped his watch shut. "I want you boys to stay close to Springer's place tonight. Dora Hand's performing down there, and it looks like it's going to be another packed house. Ty, I want you and Miles at the front door checking weapons, and Jonas, I want you in at the bar."

"Boss, why can't I be at the bar?" Ty took off his hat and ran his hand through his hair. "I'd sure like to see Dora perform. I hear she's good."

"She is very good. I want Jonas inside because I can trust him not to drink while he's in there." Bat bent his gaze on Ty, who squirmed.

Must be a story there. If Bat knew Miles well enough, he'd know Miles never touched the stuff either. But Bat *didn't* know Miles well enough, and Miles hadn't done or said anything to make Bat think he might be as devout as Jonas. Again he felt a thrust of guilt.

"As to the investing," Bat said, "I can understand Jonas's reluctance to buy into one of the more. . .salubrious endeavors here in town. Are you interested in something else? I've heard the livery is looking to expand, as well as the hotel."

Jonas shook his head. "No sir, I think I'll hang on to my money. I've got my eye on a little spread just south of here, and I've just about got enough money saved up to buy it. When I've got the money all put together, I'm planning on getting married and settling down to ranching." Jonas squared his shoulders as if he expected another ribbing from Ty.

Ty straightened and took a deep breath, but before he could say whatever he was bursting to say, Bat cut across the conversation. "I always admire a man who sets a goal and goes after it, regardless of what others might think." He clapped Jonas on the shoulder.

Miles knocked a dirt clod off the boardwalk with the toe of his boot. Not only had he missed a chance to stand up for his faith, but he'd also missed a chance to impress Bat. If he jumped in now, he'd just sound stupid. Why couldn't he be more like Jonas, who had no fear in just being himself?

But Miles didn't want to be himself. He wanted to be so much better than anything he'd been in the past.

Chapter 6

What do you mean I can't go?" Fran set the coffeepot down on the stove hard enough to make the stove lids rattle.

Her eldest brother, Linc, tipped his chair back to lean against the wall and hooked his thumbs under his suspenders. "You can't go out at night by yourself, and none of us can take you. We've got to deliver four loads of feed to the fort, and we'll probably stay over."

"You could leave early. Nothing says you have to stay." She glared at each of her brothers. When Nathan grinned and ducked his head, she narrowed her eyes. "Just why are you staying over?"

Jack and Stuart, the twins, stood as one, mumbled their thanks for the meal, and scooted out the door like raccoons with their tails on fire. Nathan, pinned in the corner by Linc, looked like an animal in a trap. He studied his tin plate and dabbed his finger on a couple of cornbread crumbs.

Linc dug a toothpick from the pot in the center of the table and stuck it in the corner of his mouth. "We've been invited to a little shindig the quartermaster is giving."

Fran sucked in a breath. "A party at the fort?" She was immediately torn. A party at the fort with all those officers in uniform or tickets to opening night at the Arden, a gift from Mr. LeBlanc after they'd finished the photographs? "If you won't let me go to the Arden, then take me to the party."

Nathan snickered but subsided when Linc raised an eyebrow in his direction. Though Nathan was older than Fran by more than a year, sometimes he acted like a kid. Not so with Linc, who acted more like a father to them all than an older brother.

He turned his bland stare toward Fran. "You haven't been invited to the fort. It isn't that kind of party."

Frustration bloomed in her chest. "So I'm supposed to sit at home waiting for you while you get to go visit friends? I have an invitation." She dug the card from her pocket. "Mr. LeBlanc had them specially printed just for opening night. Addie's going. It's not like I would be alone."

"You might as well be. Two helpless lambs in a town full of wolves. You're not going out at night without a proper escort, and since we won't be here to do it, home you'll stay. If Addie goes, that's her business, though she should know better than to go alone."

"If you'd let me go with her, she wouldn't be alone."

"I've said all I'm going to say on this matter." Linc pushed his plate back and picked up his coffee cup to drain it.

Nathan shot Fran a sympathetic look, but he obviously wasn't so sympathetic he'd give up an overnight at the fort just to see her safely to and from the Arden.

She was going to have to do it. They left her no choice. And she'd have to hurry before Linc left for the day. Her lower lip trembled, and she turned her back to her brothers. After a second or two, she sniffed and let her shoulders shake just a bit. With little effort she squeezed two tears from her eyes and let them roll down her cheeks. She made a show of digging for a handkerchief. When she couldn't find one, she lifted the hem of her apron to dab at her eyes, though she was careful not to disturb the tear tracks. A sob escaped her throat. The more she thought about missing opening night, the easier the tears came.

She waited for it, almost smiling when Linc's chair scraped on the floor. "Now, Frannie, don't cry." His big hands engulfed her shoulders. "You know I don't like to see you cry."

She shrugged, but his hands didn't move. "I don't think it's so much to ask. After all I do around here. The cooking, cleaning, washing, not to mention working at the store." Though she kept the apron hem pressed to her lips, she made sure he could hear every anguish-infused word.

"You do work hard." Linc patted her shoulder with awkward tenderness, his voice so sad guilt poked her with pitchfork prongs.

"And I don't ask for much in return. One evening. I was looking forward to it so much. It isn't every day a girl gets an invitation to an opening night. Can't we reach some kind of compromise so I can go?" She lifted her face to him at the precise moment two more tears fell.

He all but crumpled.

At his pained expression, she did feel bad. But she was so close to getting what she wanted. . .

"We've already told the quartermaster when to expect us with the feed. I can't back out now." He looked tortured.

Her chin quivered, and she blinked her wet lashes. "Please, Linc? For me?"

Nathan edged around the table. "Say, Linc, I have an idea. Why don't we get someone else to walk Fran to the theater? It doesn't have to be one of us."

Fran's tears stopped. The idea took hold in Linc's eyes, and the lines disappeared from his face. "That's a fine idea, Nate. We can ask Jonas to see her safely there and back."

Her jaw dropped. "Jonas?"

"Deputy Spooner would be just the man to ask." Linc folded his arms across his chest and looked down at her. "In fact, I wouldn't trust anyone else with the job."

Her mind scrambled to salvage the situation. "What about one of the other deputies? Jonas might be on duty or not available." She shot a glare at Nathan for coming up with the idea and putting it into Linc's head. The way Linc had grabbed onto it said not even a full-blown crying jag would dislodge it.

Nathan scratched the hair over his ear. "Jonas is free. I ran into him yesterday, and he said he was going to the opening night at the Arden anyway. He won't mind stopping by here to pick you up and bring you home." He grabbed his hat from the peg by the door. "We'd best scoot, Linc, if we're going to meet the train and unload that wheat."

"I don't want Jonas Spooner to accompany me." Fran

jammed her hands onto her hips, all pretense gone.

Linc flipped his wide-brimmed hat onto his short, red-gold hair. "You'll go with Jonas or you won't go at all." Nathan and Linc shared a conspiratorial look on the way out the door, and their laughter drifted through the open kitchen window.

Fran picked up a dishcloth and whipped it at the door. They'd planned this from the outset, and she'd fallen right into their trap.

Jonas Spooner. Fran sighed. It wasn't that she didn't like him, but he was so very. . .ordinary. She couldn't remember a time when she didn't know him. As kids growing up in Missouri, he'd always been around, frogging with her brothers or fishing or playing ball. And even then he'd carried her books and given her small gifts, never shy about showing his affection for her. When her brothers proposed moving west and opening a feed store and bringing Fran along to housekeep for them, it had seemed perfectly natural for Jonas to come along. That was the trouble. Jonas was more like a brother than a suitor. She just couldn't see him in those terms.

Aware of the clock ticking, she hustled through the kitchen chores. She had ten minutes before she needed to be at the mercantile, which was plenty of time. But only three days to decide what to wear to opening night, which wasn't much time at all.

Opening night. Anticipation feathered across Addie's skin as she checked her reflection in the mirror over the washstand.

For such a special occasion, she'd piled her brown curls high, letting them fall in a cascade down her neck. A few tendrils lay on her cheeks—her much-too-pink cheeks.

"Stop it," she told her mirror-self. "You're merely following orders and using common sense. Miles Carr is only doing his duty as a peace officer."

Her mirror-self didn't appear to be listening, because her eyes glowed with anticipation and her mouth wouldn't quit smiling at the thought of seeing him again, and of having him see her dressed up for once.

Stepping back, she tried to get a full-length view of her gown, though the small mirror was a challenge. She smoothed her hand down the burgundy polonaise, her fingers bumping over the twenty cloth-covered buttons from her throat to her waist, feeling hollow and excited at the same time.

She'd bought this dress more than a year ago for the Cattlemen's Ball in Abilene, for *him*, for the night when she had been sure he would propose. A week before the ball, her world had fallen apart. And she'd never worn the beautiful dress, packing it away with her hopes and dreams and not taking it out of her trunk until today.

Determined to shake off the past and only look forward, she made sure the folds of her bustle and train lay just so and that the cuffs of the long, tight sleeves were straight. Fan, gloves, bag. Her Scovill lay on the end of the bed, snug in its case. Though she didn't feel wholly dressed without it, she knew she couldn't lug it with her tonight.

Picking up the invitation, she couldn't help the self-satisfied smile that tugged at her lips. Mr. LeBlanc had gone into raptures at the photographs she'd delivered to him. A fountain of French accolades poured from him, and he proudly presented her with the invitations to opening night.

Fran had been thrilled when Addie gave her one. Though she'd been less than thrilled yesterday afternoon when she'd announced that her brothers had maneuvered her into accepting Jonas's escort to and from the theater. Addie had almost gone to the sheriff's office to cancel her need for a deputy escort, figuring that Jonas could take her as well, but she'd decided against it. Jonas had her support in courting Fran, and she wouldn't do anything to derail his efforts.

The fact that Miles Carr would be seeing Addie to the theater had nothing to do with it.

Addie flicked the fan open and covered the lower half of her face, checking her reflection one last time. Too eager by far. She grimaced and headed downstairs.

Mrs. Blanchard sat in her rocking chair, her fingers flying, knitting needles clicking, creating yards and yards of lace. Addie had often speculated that if her landlady's knitting needles had been made of wood, she'd have long since started a fire. What she did with all that lace was a mystery. Nobody had that many petticoats.

Mrs. Blanchard looked over the top of her glasses and appraised Addie. "My, don't you look lovely, my dear."

"Thank you."

"Your gentleman is just coming up the walk." She craned her neck just slightly to peer out the window.

Addie flushed. "He's not my gentleman. I called in at the sheriff's office for a deputy to escort me to the theater, and Sheriff Masterson assigned Deputy Carr to the task." And that was all. Really.

Mrs. Blanchard's almost-nonexistent eyebrows rose, and her needles moved faster. The doorbell click-buzzed instead of ringing. "I should get that fixed someday."

Since she made this remark every time someone used the bell, Addie didn't put much stock in the comment. She gathered her skirts, told her heart to stop bumping so crazily, and opened the door.

Air crowded into her throat. From his brushed cowboy hat to the tips of his shiny boots, Miles Carr was immaculate. Even his badge gleamed. The only incongruous note to his attire was the gun belt slung low on his hips. "Evening, Miss Reid. You ready?" He offered his arm, a smile playing about his lips.

Though a warm evening breeze blew across her temples, her fingers tingled as if chilled. "Thank you for seeing me to the theater. I'm taking your warning not to walk through town alone to heart."

"I'm glad. You sure look pretty. Looking like that, I might have to draw my gun to fight off the cowboys tonight."

Pleasure shot through her. He thought she looked pretty. *Watch yourself, girl. You've had your head turned before. He doesn't mean anything by it, and you're not looking for a beau.*

She looped the handles of her fan and purse over her wrist and put her hand into the crook of his elbow. His formal dress set up a small panic in her chest. Did he think he was her date for the evening? She only had the one invitation, having given Fran the other. When she'd requested an escort to the theater, had someone misunderstood? But how did one ask without sounding ridiculous?

He matched his stride to hers, his eyes scanning the street ahead. Most of the windows along Front Street were lit, and cowboys strolled the boardwalks. The persistent lowing of cattle from the yards drifted on the breeze, as familiar to Addie by now as the all-night band music from the Long Branch.

She snuck glances up at Miles, hoping he wouldn't notice but unable to stop herself. Strength and integrity. Those words drifted through her mind, and she realized that had been her first impression of Miles, and that impression had strengthened each time she met him. But she didn't trust her own judgment. She'd been fooled before. Why didn't her heart seem to be listening to her head?

A steady stream of people headed toward the brightly lit Arden Palace, and Addie and Miles joined it. Women in fancy dress, men in suits, all with an expectant air. Cowboys wore their best clothes, some so new they still bore the creases from being folded in shirt boxes. The jingling of spurs mingled with the fluttering of fans.

LeBlanc had plastered the town with posters and flyers announcing opening night, each one bearing at least one of her photographs. The expense he'd gone to using such a new printing technique—he'd had to go all the way to Kansas City and back to find a printer with the necessary skills and equipment—must've been enormous, but it seemed to have paid dividends, judging by the size of the crowd.

"Looks to be a full house." Miles's eyes never stopped moving over the people on the porch. "Hope everyone behaves himself tonight."

The last person she wanted to see was Heber Donaldson, so of course they ran into him first. He glared, snorted down his long, hooked nose, and stomped away.

Mayor Kelley strode by, resplendent in evening dress, and Henri LeBlanc seemed to be everywhere in the crowd, greeting people, accepting congratulations, gesturing with large movements and a wide smile. "Ah, *cheri*, you came. I have reserved seats in a fine box for you. Number four." He took Addie's hands and kissed her cheeks. "It is going to be a wonderful night. Your photographs were *le magnifique*." He waved to a poster beside the front doors. Her name figured prominently, just as LeBlanc had promised it would.

Before she could thank him, someone clouted Miles on the shoulder. "You made it."

Jonas with Fran on his arm.

A pretty flush decorated Fran's cheeks, and she was exquisite in green, but she had a battle-glint in her eyes. "You've seen me to the theater, Jonas. I can take it from here." She tried to free her hand from his arm, but his shot up to cover hers.

"I wouldn't dream of leaving you here alone, Fran. I told your brothers I would see you to your seat." He smiled blandly, and Fran's protests bounced off him.

Addie darted a look at Miles. "Jonas can accompany me to my seat, too, if you'd prefer."

"It's no trouble." To her relief, he dug in his coat pocket and produced a ticket. "I had a hankering to see this particular play, and Bat expects us to make our presence known in the theater to keep the cowboys from breaking herd." He handed the ticket and her invitation to one of the deputies at the door. "Evening, Ty."

"Well, don't you look the curly wolf tonight?" The deputy named Ty glanced at Miles's sidearm at the same time he tipped his hat to Addie. "Evening, miss." He jerked his thumb to the table beside him where three revolvers lay. "Already collected some firepower off some civilians."

Miles nodded and put his hand on the small of Addie's back to guide her to the stairway leading to the balcony boxes. She could feel each of his fingers as though he touched bare skin, and icy-hot chills raced along her arms and affected her breathing. The air grew close around her, and she flicked open her fan.

Fran and Jonas followed close. An attendant swept aside the heavy curtains to the box where Fran had pretended to be Rapunzel, and Addie almost giggled, not daring to look at Fran. Four chairs sat around a small table, and music from a string quartet drifted up from the orchestra pit in front of the stage.

Addie took the chair Miles held for her. Fran did the same, but with less grace for Jonas. The shorter deputy wore a dark suit that stretched across his broad shoulders, and everything about him exuded steadfastness and stability—the exact opposite of the ideal Fran dreamed about and often rhapsodized over.

Addie shook her head, settled her belongings, and looked up to thank Miles for his consideration before he left to find his own seat. But instead of leaving, Miles and Jonas hung their hats on the rack in the corner of the box, and each took a chair at the table.

"What are you doing?" Fran's voice carried, and people from the lower level looked up at them. She flushed and glared at Jonas.

He scooted his chair just a bit closer to hers. "I'm going to watch a play. I bought a ticket." He waved the stub of pasteboard at her before tucking it into his vest pocket.

Addie turned to Miles. "You, too?"

He nodded. "LeBlanc said we could sit up here. I hope you don't mind."

She should, but she didn't in the least. Amazing how she'd gone from anxiety to relief to anticipation, all in a short amount of time. She hardly knew what to think or feel. All she knew was that she wasn't in the least disappointed that Miles was staying.

Scanning the crowd to give herself time to gather her thoughts, she took a few deep breaths. Her eyes lit on a face turned up and staring right at her. Her breathing stopped, and her heart started knocking against her ribs.

Vin Rutter's pale, almost colorless eyes bored into hers.

How had he found her?

Miles found himself staring at Addie. When she'd answered the door at the boardinghouse, it had been all he could do not to blink and stand there like a slack-jawed idiot. Whatever she'd done to her hair, it looked great. He wanted to bury his hands in those curls and let the silky strands twine around his fingers.

Rubbing his palms on his thighs, he turned his attention to the crowd below. Conversation hummed and people filed into the seats. Their box attendant appeared with a tray of fancy bits of food and offered them their choice of beverages. Jonas ordered lemonade for everyone.

Fran looked like she wanted to wring Jonas's neck. She was sure pretty enough, but why Jonas continued to pursue her in the face of her obvious dislike of him was a mystery to Miles. Though when Jonas set his mind to something, he was awfully hard to deflect, and to hear him tell it, he'd had his mind and heart set on Fran for a long time.

He glanced at Addie again, taking in her profile. Her nose tilted up a little at the end, and her lips were parted. That dress she wore fired his blood. Not in the least revealing, it covered her from neck to toes and all the way to her wrists, but the cut of the reddish fabric showed off her womanly charms. She was the prettiest girl in the room, and she was with him. Sort of.

Something seemed different about her getup, though he couldn't pick it out right away. He almost snapped his fingers when he struck on what was missing. Her camera case. A laugh made it as far as his teeth before he choked it off. She went everywhere with that case, even to church.

A small commotion downstairs drew his attention. Two cowboys shoved at each other, but before Miles could even stand, LeBlanc was on the scene and the combatants sat down.

That's when he saw him.

Vin Rutter. He'd know those dead eyes anywhere.

Miles's mouth went dry.

Vin's eyes bored into his, and a smirk decorated his face. He sketched a wave and tilted his head in a mocking salute, and Miles's hands fisted on his thighs.

Addie sucked in a breath, and Miles broke eye contact with Vin. Her face had gone pale, and her hand pressed to her stomach. Her other hand gripped her folded fan until it shook. Was she unwell? He touched her shoulder, and she turned wide eyes to his face.

The houselights began to go out, and to his surprise, she scooted her chair closer to his. She beamed a smile his way brighter than the footlights, and his stomach muscles tightened. When she reached out and patted his hand where it rested on his leg, tingles shot up his arm, and he found himself clasping her fingers in his. They were chilly in spite of the warm room.

"I'm so glad you are here with me. It's going to be a wonderful night."

Fran's eyebrows rose from across the table. "Addie?"

Addie shrugged and kept her hand in Miles's. Jonas grinned.

Miles's mind reeled. Caught between apprehension at Vin's being in Dodge and the sensation of holding Addie's hand and sitting so near her, he couldn't think straight. He was grateful when the curtain went up and the performance began.

Addie clung to his hand through the entire first act and kept her attention on the stage. Miles couldn't have told anyone even the most rudimentary bits of the plot. His mind batted thoughts, tossing between Vin and Addie.

When intermission was announced, Fran bounced up without waiting for Jonas to pull out her chair. "I'm going to get some ice cream. Don't you want to come with me?" She sent a direct look at Addie, bombarding her with the message that she wanted Addie to come.

"No, thank you. I'd rather stay here." She turned to Miles. "You don't mind, do you?"

Far from minding, he had to quell his relief. The last thing he wanted was to run into Vin Rutter in a crowd. "We'll stay. You go on."

Fran and Jonas disappeared and returned in plenty of time for the second act. Fran's eyes shone, and it seemed she had forgotten her peeve at having to endure Jonas's company in favor of enjoying the evening. Addie remained quiet, only answering direct questions and those briefly. Fran finally gave up trying to draw her into the conversation and concentrated on her ice cream.

Miles watched the house seats below, keeping his eye on Vin. Rutter appeared to be alone, but in the crush, it was hard to tell. It was surely no coincidence that he'd landed in Dodge City, but what could he be after? Vin never acted without careful deliberation. It was the reason he was a free man at the moment and not languishing in Leavenworth. Wily and smooth, Vin Rutter knew how to wriggle out of trouble better than a greased snake.

By the time the play ended, Miles was a bundle of nerves. Addie had stayed so close to him he could smell her perfume—

like flowers, though he couldn't have identified the particular bloom. Heady, and he would've loved to savor it if he wasn't so distracted.

When the last curtain call ended, the houselights came up again, and conversation replaced applause. The crowd stirred, gathering belongings, talking, and laughing, clearly in high spirits.

Fran sighed and sat back in her chair. "What a wonderful evening. Wouldn't it be something to have two buccaneers fighting over you like what happened in the play? How would you ever choose? Sebastian was so wickedly interesting and Barnabas was so brave and good." She sighed and fingered the string of beads at her neck. "Though I suppose Fiona made the right choice eventually. Oh, I never want this night to end."

Miles tried to gauge Addie's feelings. She'd been so quiet. Though this wasn't a by-the-book date with his asking her out and her accepting, he was still her partner for the evening, and he couldn't help but feel he'd somehow failed her, that she hadn't enjoyed herself. Yet, she'd held his hand for most of the play, staying with him in the box rather than escaping during intermissions, and still held his hand as if she never wanted to let go. That had to mean something, didn't it?

He gave up trying to navigate the maze of the female mind and stood. "I'm afraid we'll have to be leaving soon. I'm on patrol tonight." He pulled Addie's chair out as she rose.

Fran's face crumpled for a moment before brightening. She glanced down at their entwined hands and back at Addie's face.

Addie smiled, though her lips were tight. "See you, Fran."

Jonas and Fran left ahead of them, and Miles shepherded Addie toward the steps. She stopped at the head of the stairs and threaded her arm through his as if they'd been courting for months. His hand came up to cover hers in the crook of his elbow. He was at a loss to explain her behavior, but he was equally at a loss to stop himself from responding to it.

Threading their way through the thinning crowds, he led her through the lobby and out onto the porch. An evening breeze scudded up the street, whipping a bit of dust into the air and teasing the tendrils of hair on her cheeks.

Out of newly established habit, he scanned the area.

Vin stood across the street, his features clear in the light streaming from the the Lady Gray Comique Theater. Miles gritted his teeth. When Vin stepped into the street and began sauntering his way, Miles, almost without meaning to, slid his coat aside to free his gun hand.

Then Addie laid her head against his shoulder, totally distracting him. "I'm tired. I think we should head to the boardinghouse, don't you?"

Her pale face so close to his threw all thoughts of Vin out of his head. He nodded and started up the street. For a whole block she kept her temple against his shoulder, and her closeness was all he could think about. When they turned the corner off Front Street, darkness surrounded them, and she straightened and took a deep breath. Her hand relaxed on his arm, and she gave him a trembling smile.

They stopped at the foot of the steps to Mrs. Blanchard's, and she turned her face upward. Moonlight bathed her features, making her eyes seem bigger and more lustrous than ever. "Thank you for seeing me safely home."

"You're welcome." His voice sounded gruff. Then, because he couldn't seem to stop himself, he did what he'd been wanting to do all evening—since he'd first laid eyes on her a few months ago, in fact. He slid his arms around her waist and drew her toward him. She fit perfectly into his embrace, and slowly, giving her time to run if she wanted to, he lowered his lips to hers.

Sweet. So sweet.

She sighed against his lips and returned the pressure, entwining her arms around his neck. He wondered if his head or his heart would explode first, and without breaking the kiss, his hands came up and buried themselves in her curls.

Soft.

His fingers tangled in the brown strands, and he cupped the back of her head, deepening the kiss. He never wanted it to end, and when he realized that, he knew he had to stop. He eased back and, before he could stop himself, snatched one more kiss from her pretty lips.

Her eyes fluttered open, dazed and dreamy. Manly pride that his kiss had so thrown her off balance made him grin. One of her hands lay against the flat of his chest, her fingers just covering the edge of his badge. Could she feel the thundering of his heart? They stood, locked together as if in a spell.

The curtains twitched, and the knob on the front door rattled.

Addie sprang back, and she touched her lips, her eyes still bemused and bewildered.

"Good night, Miles."

She disappeared up the stairs and into the house, leaving him standing in the moonlight, looking after her like a lovesick bull calf.

Chapter 7

Addie brushed past Mrs. Blanchard with her gaping face and blinking eyes and sought the refuge of her room. When she closed the door on the outside world, she leaned against it and pressed her hand against her chest to still the wild throbbing of her heart.

"Oh Addie girl, what have you done?" Fingers trembling, she struck a match and lit the lamp on her bureau. Immediately her reflection in the oval mirror caught her eye, and she gasped.

Her hair tumbled about her shoulders in wild disarray, and she remembered the feel of Miles's hands plundering her carefully arranged curls. Several hairpins dangled from the mass, and if she didn't miss her guess, she'd find more decorating the sidewalk. Her lips were pink and just a hint puffy, and she couldn't resist touching them again.

Closing her eyes, she was instantly back in his arms, his lips pressed to hers, the feel and smell and very essence of Miles Carr fusing to her. And she'd kissed him back with a passion that had both exhilarated and frightened her.

"Stop it!" Her eyes flew open, and she stared at her reflection. None of this was supposed to happen. She was playing with fire, and well she knew it. What had possessed her throwing herself at Miles that way?

The cause of her trouble seemed to superimpose his image over hers in the mirror. Vin Rutter, with his pale, dead eyes and narrow slash of a mouth. Here. In Dodge. Watching her. The minute she'd spotted him, cold, thorny terror had crawled up her windpipe and lodged in her throat.

Without really being conscious of it until now, she'd sought the protection Miles and his badge offered. Heat curled through her chest and flooded her cheeks when she thought of how she'd held his hand all through the play, trying to draw strength and courage from him, trying to tell herself that Vin and all he represented was in her imagination, or at the very least in her past and couldn't hurt her.

But that had been a fool's paradise.

Guilt followed hard. She'd shamelessly used Miles, leading him on, flirting outrageously—enough that even Fran had noticed and promised a reckoning in the morning. Addie swallowed. Vin had been waiting outside the theater. The terror had returned, and instead of telling Miles the truth, what had she done? Cuddled up to him and steered him away like some brazen hussy from one of the brothels south of the deadline.

Mortified, she clutched her hands at her waist and pressed her stomach to still the raging guilt. Shame licked at her skin, and she poured some water from the pitcher into the basin to bathe her hot face.

Dabbing at her damp cheeks with a linen towel, she went to stand by the open window, hoping the night breeze would blow some clarity into her head. Though her thoughts bounced around like tumbleweeds in a tornado, one remained paramount in her mind.

The kiss.

She couldn't get it out of her thoughts, but somehow she would have to. Somehow she would have to find a graceful way to retreat and pretend it never happened. It had been wrong to use Miles the way she had, and if Vin started any trouble, she might've just sucked Miles into it. "Addie," she groaned, "how could you be so stupid? You had no business getting involved with Miles."

Seeking to ground herself, to remember why she had to walk warily where all men were concerned, she reached for her Scovill case. The familiar scarred leather box brought her back to reality. Unbuckling the latch, she lifted the camera from its nest and set it on the coverlet. Though the room was dark and the interior of the camera case darker, she needed no light to find the small, velvet tab along one side. She pinched the fabric and tugged, opening the false bottom of the case and tipping the fat, square photo album out into her hand.

She brought the lamp to the bedside table and turned up the wick. Her fingers traced the Moroccan leather cover and the gilt edges with their silver corner protectors. Sixteen photographs, her own work. Her first foray into portraiture. The first inkling that she might have a talent for capturing life through a lens.

The spine creaked as she opened the book. His face greeted her.

Cliff Walker. Not that she'd known it at the time.

No, when she'd taken this photo, he'd called himself Clem Wilson. A traveling salesman for a sewing notions company.

Black hair, intelligent brown eyes, a smile that could turn a woman's insides to warm mush. And a tongue that ran with honeyed words to turn a girl's head.

She turned the page, and in spite of everything, a chuckle escaped her lips. Clem—no, Cliff, she reminded herself—leaned against the plaster pedestal he'd so proudly constructed for her. The same pillar she'd convinced Bat Masterson to rest his elbow on for his portrait. And what would Bat say if he knew the notorious Cliff Walker had posed in the same manner for her camera just over a year ago?

She studied the photograph again. His hat sat at a rakish angle, and his eyes burned with laughter—and what she'd mistakenly thought was love. All humor fled, and a lump clogged her throat. Flipping through the pages, she studied each well-known picture briefly before moving on. Rational thought began to trickle into her mind to replace the wild feelings Miles's kiss had engendered.

Cliff Walker, an accomplished liar, suckering her with his flattery, pretending interest in her work as a photographer, professing his love. And all the while, he'd been hiding his identity, hiding the fact that he was the leader of the bloodiest gang of thieves and killers Kansas had ever produced. He had courted her and promised her the moon, even while he and his gang robbed trains, plundered banks, and murdered innocents who got in their way.

She'd known nothing about his other life until the U.S. marshals arrived on her doorstep looking for him. Even now their disdainful looks and accusing comments made her squirm. They'd tried so hard to pull her into the investigation, sure she had known all along of his true identity, sure that she was an integral part of the gang. In the end, she'd been cleared, but it had been a harrowing time. The townsfolk in Abilene had withdrawn, those she thought were her friends separating themselves, leaving her alone to face the accusations with only Uncle Carl for support.

Addie pursed her lips and traced the edge of one of the pages. Cliff lounged under a tree beside a sluggish creek near Abilene, his long legs stretched out in the prairie grass and his hat tipped over his nose so that only the lower half of his face was visible. He hadn't even known she'd taken this picture until she showed him the developed print. A picnic blanket lay beside him. Such lighthearted fun, but under it all, a sinister secret that had ruined not just her life but Uncle Carl's as well.

How had she been so naive? She'd asked herself that question a thousand times. Cliff's arrest and trial had shocked her and killed any love she felt for him. Day after day she'd sat in that courtroom listening to the evidence and the testimonies of those Cliff had harmed. The prosecutor peeled away the layers of lies and deceit and revealed the killer behind the charming face. Justice had been swift, and Cliff had been hanged two days later.

Shattered, Addie had set about putting back together the broken pieces of her life. But healing wouldn't be possible in the hostile atmosphere of Abilene. Cliff had hurt too many people there for her ever to be free of the stain of her involvement with him. She couldn't even walk down the street without someone hurling harsh words or worse at her.

A week after the trial, someone threw a lit torch through the front window of the photography studio. The reception room and the workroom beyond had gone up in flames before the volunteer fire brigade got the blaze under control. The hostility toward the Reids had been so great, that if the neighboring buildings hadn't been in danger, Addie was sure they would've just let the studio burn. As it was, she and Uncle Carl only managed to salvage the props from the prop room and his boxes of glass slides. When the flames reached the darkroom, the developing chemicals ignited, destroying the rest of the building entirely.

The local police hadn't pursued the culprit too hard. Addie had the feeling they thought she and her uncle had only gotten what they'd deserved.

A black fist of remorse pressed under her rib cage. Everything destroyed, and the blame lay squarely with her. If she'd never taken up with Cliff, they'd still have the shop in Abilene, her Uncle Carl might still be alive, and she wouldn't be so alone and scared.

And now Vin Rutter was here. She'd met him once when Cliff had brought him to town, though of course he'd introduced him as a business associate. She'd tried to like him for Cliff's sake, but his fishy eyes and lack of visible emotion had chilled her. If only Cliff had radiated that same dangerous essence, she'd never have fallen for his lies.

She had no illusions as to Vin's reasons for being in Dodge City. After Cliff's trial, at which he refused to name any of his accomplices, the gang had scattered, fleeing into Indian Territory rather than be caught in Kansas.

But Vin had returned, and only one thing would've brought him back.

Her. And what he thought she knew.

She was all he could think about.

Miles leaned against the clapboards of Greeley and Price Mercantile, careful to stay to the shadows of the alley while he watched the street. He'd shed his suit coat at the jail but still wore his best trousers and vest. The starch in his shirt chafed his skin, but the discomfort had been worth it. At least he hadn't looked out of place at the theater.

Horses galloped by, their riders anxious to get to the dance halls, saloons, and gambling dens before every last drop of revelry had been wrung out of the night. Music, laughter, shouts, voices. In the occasional lull, he could hear coyotes yapping out on the prairie, and the metallic clinks and pings as the steam engine sitting at the depot cooled.

He'd kissed her. And not just a brotherly peck either. He'd snatched her up like the last biscuit on the plate and crushed the breath right out of her. His blood raced at the memory, and he had to force himself to relax his tense muscles.

What had he been thinking?

He'd been thinking that he was with a beautiful woman who had intrigued him from the minute he first laid eyes on her. A woman who had changed from remote to receptive in the blink of an eye.

He frowned. The female of the species baffled him, but no more than he baffled himself. He had a list as long as his arm why he shouldn't get involved with a woman right now, and what had he done? Jumped in boots, badge, and all.

A door slammed across the street and footsteps rang out on the wooden outside staircase running up to the second story of the saloon. A woman entwined her bare arms around a cowboy's neck for a lingering good-bye in the moonlight, the tail end of a shameful transaction that had nothing to do with love. Disgust sloshed in his belly.

A snippet of scripture floated through his head. Something about the beam in his own eye.

Miles's face flushed, and he rubbed his palm against the back of his neck. An hour ago he'd stood not three blocks from this spot right here and kissed the daylights out of a woman he barely knew. A sigh forced its way past the guilty knot in his throat. He'd enjoyed every second of that kiss.

He wasn't good enough to court someone like Addie. With his more-than-checkered past, he'd only manage to drag her down if the truth ever came out. He needed to prove himself first, put some more distance on his unlovely youth, and ground himself as a lawman and a man of faith.

Though he'd done precious little on the faith front. He seemed to duck every chance he got to speak boldly about God and what God thought was right.

Lord, I'm asking for You to give me boldness to stand up for what's right, to speak up when the chance comes to identify myself with You. I've ducked it too much lately. I really want to be used by You, to be bold for my faith, but I need Your help. I need Your wisdom.

His plea for wisdom had his thoughts straying again to Addie. Surely there was some way to work this out, because he found himself wanting to court Addie, to make her his for always, thoughts that had never entered his head about a woman before. Maybe, after he'd shown her and the rest of the town that he was a man of good character—law-abiding and upstanding—he could ask permission to call.

"You're looking good, Miles."

He whirled, his hand going for his gun, shocked that someone had snuck up on him so easily and even more shocked that it was the man he'd been on the lookout for.

Vin raised his hands. "Easy there, my dear boy. I'm not armed." The fake Southern accent Vin employed grated across Miles's skin. Though Vin found it useful for charming his way into and out of trouble, it made Miles's blood simmer.

Letting his gun drop back into his holster, Miles straightened. His unprofessional lack of attention galled him. Anyone could've walked up, stuck a knife between his ribs, and he wouldn't even have known. Of all the green, amateur, stupid mistakes.

"What do you want, Vin?"

Even in the dark of the alley, Vin's eyes glittered, reminding

Miles of two pebbles surrounded by hoarfrost. "Is that any way to greet an old friend?"

"There's no friendship between us."

Vin's mirthless laugh pricked him. "And whose fault was that?" He stroked slender, pale fingers down one of his lapels. "You and your uppity mother, acting like you were too good for us. Old Man Walker said he'd never let either of you go, but I guess you both got out eventually. Such a tragedy, her taking that way out. How long's it been? Ten years?"

Miles shifted his weight, never taking his eyes off Vin's face. "He killed her. As surely as if he'd pulled the trigger himself. Poetic justice that he dropped dead a few days later. Doc said it was a heart seizure, but you'd have to have a heart first." Though he'd struggled to forgive his stepfather for the years of abuse and anger, he hadn't quite managed it. . .at least not for long. Forgiving the old man for driving his mother to take her own life—that was going to take a lot more prayer and effort.

"You disappeared before they threw the first shovelful of dirt into his face."

Miles shrugged. "Seemed the thing to do, with Cliff taking over for his father. Worst mistake my mother ever made, marrying into the Walkers. I'm glad I got out when I did, what with Cliff branching out into train robberies. Turned a bunch of mean dogs into a pack of killer wolves. He was vicious before I left, and he got worse after."

"Well, rest assured, the antipathy you had for your stepbrother was mutual. Cliff used to spit on the ground whenever your name came up."

Enough about the past. "What are you doing here, Vin? I thought you and the rest of the boys were hiding out in Indian Territory since the trial."

"I could ask you what you're doing here as well, though after tonight, I have a fair idea. You're such a dark horse, Miles. I never would've suspected it of you. All that talk about finding God and being forgiven." Vin sneered. "Clever of you to follow her here and insinuate yourself into her life. Tell me, does she know?"

He frowned. "Who are you talking about? Does who know what?"

"The delightful Miss Reid, of course. I saw you with her tonight, and very cozy you were, too. What did she say when she found out you were related to Cliff?"

Miles sucked in a breath. Vin knew Addie?

Vin feathered his fingers through his hair, his light movements reminding Miles of his dexterity, both with cards and with a gun. "Ah, I see from your expression that Miss Adeline Reid is once more clueless as to the true identity of her suitor." He tipped his head back and let out a derisive *ha*. "This is too rich. So smooth, too, coming from you. I always thought you were a tell-the-truth-and-shame-the-devil type, and here I find you insinuating yourself into Cliff's former paramour's life."

Miles's mind reeled. "What are you talking about?"

Vin's eyebrows climbed. "Stop playing games. I admit I'm chagrined that you should've arrived here first. I only learned of her whereabouts last week." He reached into his inner pocket.

Miles tensed, his gun filling his hand and training on Vin in a blur.

Vin stiffened and stilled. "My, my, you are a suspicious fellow these days. Allow me?" He inclined his head toward his hand still stuck in his jacket.

"Nice and slow."

A folded paper emerged. With excruciating patience, Vin opened the page and smoothed it out before turning it so Miles could see. A flyer for the Arden Palace. Miles had seen a hundred of them plastered about town. Vin pointed to the bottom right corner, and Miles didn't need to read it to know what it said. PICTURES BY ADELINE REID, REID'S PHOTOGRAPHY, DODGE CITY, KANSAS.

"What do you want with Addie?" He lowered his gun a fraction but kept it trained on Vin. Vin never wanted anything good for anyone but himself, and his interest in Addie made Miles's skin itch.

"If you must continue this charade, I'll play along." Folding the paper, Vin sighed. "Adeline Reid is the one-time fiancée of our dear, departed Cliff. The woman he claimed was his soul mate, the one person on earth who really understood him, who would make his life complete. Of course, their courtship met a rather abrupt end when the State of Kansas stretched your dear stepbrother's neck, but there it is."

Cold realization sluiced over Miles. "Addie?" Cliff's fiancée? His soul mate? Bile churned in Miles's stomach, burning hot.

Vin arched one eyebrow, a strangely black curve on his milky-white face given his pale hair. "Stop pretending you didn't know. Why else would you be here?"

"Addie and Cliff." Miles whispered the words, testing out the idea. It made him sick.

"That's right. The same little honey you were billing and cooing with tonight." Vin's narrow shoulders shook. Vin flicked the badge on Miles's chest, making him jerk back and raise the gun again. "I'd venture to say you didn't inform your boss either. I doubt the people of Dodge City would take too kindly to having a member of the Walker Gang—however much on the outskirts he might've been—on the county payroll."

Miles clenched his jaw, hating the knowing look coming from Vin's reptilian eyes. Vin thrived on wielding power over others. And everything he knew about Miles and about Addie gave him a great deal too much power.

Chapter 8

Fran tucked a stray curl up and clasped her hands against her chin, pressing her thumbnails against her front teeth, and feigned interest in the window display she'd been working on all morning, pretending she hadn't noticed the strikingly handsome man at the end of the counter who had been watching her since the moment he came in. She tilted the bonnet on the display stand to show the cluster of silk flowers better.

Curiosity wriggled up her spine. He perused the timepieces behind glass and moved on to the fobs, cuff links, and cigar cases before coming back to the pocket watches.

When he'd first entered, Wally had approached him with an offer of assistance, but the customer had declined. Lean and pale, he wandered the aisle and ran his hands over the merchandise. He dressed too fine for a cowboy but not flashy enough for a professional gambler. His skin was too pale for him to be a farmer or any kind of an outdoorsman, and yet he had an aura of capability to him that roused her curiosity. Indefinably not a drummer, a salesman, a banker, nor any of half a dozen other occupations that came to her mind.

Fran prided herself on being able to size up every customer—both their purchasing needs and their probable income—quickly, but this man had her baffled. Time to get some answers.

"Are you sure there's nothing I can help you with?" Fran approached him, fingering her lace collar and the two buttons she'd left open for coolness at her throat.

"I'm actually killing a little time before an appointment." His Southern accent flowed over her like melted butter. "Didn't I see you at the Arden Palace last night? In one of the private boxes?"

Pleasure feathered through her. "You might have." She studied his chiseled features up close, the straight nose, high forehead, intelligent eyes, finely cut lips. Handsome was hardly the word for it. His hair was as pale as the December moon, but his eyebrows were two dark slashes, and his eyelashes were equally dark, making his eyes seem even paler. Fascinated, she couldn't look away. "I attended opening night with friends."

"I knew it." He snapped his fingers. "One does not forget such a beautiful woman. A lady such as yourself, refined and genteel, stands out in one's memory." A slow smile stretched his thin lips. His eyes drew her, almost as intense as Bat Masterson's himself. "My name is Vincent Rutter. My friends call me Vin, and I do hope you will count yourself among that number. And you are?"

My, my, my. Very smooth, much more polished than a cowboy. "Fran Seaton, Vin." She caressed his name with just enough intimacy to draw another smile. A little thrill shot up her spine. Was this, at last, the mysterious stranger she'd dreamed about? The one who would sweep into town and carry her away for a life of romance and adventure? Though lately she'd become more and more aware that her adolescent fancies were silly, a part of her still longed for them to be true.

His eyes roamed over her face and form, and she swallowed. He had a knowing, practiced way about him, not awkward and overblown like most of the men who came into the store. This man was different, and that difference intrigued her like none had before.

"You've got a fine store here." He waved to the laden shelves and items hanging from rows of hooks overhead. "You must do a land office business."

Fran picked up her feather duster. Dusting was a constant need in this windy, dirty town, but she also preferred to be doing something while she chatted up customers. "We do, though not usually until afternoon. The townsfolk drift through in the mornings, and the cowboys come in the afternoons, after they've slept off the night before." She tilted her chin and raised her eyebrows, inviting him to understand her meaning.

Though her brothers might try to hedge her around and keep her protected, she was no babe in the woods. No one could live in Dodge City for long without having at least an inkling of what went on. Some of her most frequent customers were the working girls from the saloons, dance halls, and "houses of negotiable affection" as she'd heard one of the girls put it. . .accompanied by a broad wink.

"A man could do quite well for himself in this town, I

imagine. A businessman, that is."

She smiled and swiped the duster over a stack of Hap's pickled beets on the counter. "That would depend on the business. Some do very well. Are you a businessman?"

His thin lips twitched. "You could say that. I'm in acquisitions, most recently with the railroad." Though he smiled, the humor didn't affect his eyes, which remained trained on her as if he had her in his crosshairs. Aha, why hadn't she considered he might work for the railroad? That explained his rather cosmopolitan air and the quality of his clothing.

Something thudded in the back of the store, and voices drifted toward them. "I'm telling you, Hap Greeley, if you don't stop, this partnership is through, cousins or not." Wally shouldered his way through the storeroom doorway, bent under the weight of the bag of flour on his shoulder. "I'm killing myself keeping this place open, keeping the shelves stocked, keeping up with the ordering. And what are you doing? You're sitting on your backside in some rat hole of a saloon playing poker. When was the last time you waited on a customer or checked a packing slip?" The bag of flour hit the floor with a powdery thump. Wally dusted his hands and wiped the perspiration from his forehead. "I'm working myself into an early grave to keep you in poker chips." He aimed his voice toward the storeroom doorway.

Hap, untidy and amiable as always, clomped out of the stockroom carrying an open can of peaches. He stuck his pocketknife into the can and fished out a slice of fruit. It plopped off the tip of the knife back into the syrup, and a glob of liquid splashed up on his glasses. "Confound it." He set the can and his knife on the counter, and out came the giant, red handkerchief.

Fran made a mental note to wipe down the counter after they'd gone, since she was sure it now bore more than a trace of peach syrup.

"Wally, you worry too much. I told you I'd put the money back, and I did."

"But you didn't ask me before you took it. If you'd have lost that game last night, we'd be staring up from the bottom of a pretty dark hole."

"Well, I didn't lose. I'm on a hot streak right now, and I was lucky to get a seat at that table at all. It's a thousand-dollar buy-in, and you have to wait for a place to open. I'd still be there now if you hadn't come in screeching like a scalded cat. Made us look bad, Wally." He frowned and stabbed another peach. "Not exactly the best image to be leaving the businessmen of this town with, is it?"

Wally's face went from red to purple. He scanned the store, saw Fran with a customer, and grabbed Hap by the arm, dragging him to the storeroom and slamming the door behind them.

Fran sighed and set aside the duster in favor of opening her order book and ledger and making what she hoped were intelligent-looking marks in one of the columns.

Vin's dark eyebrows rose. "I take it those are the proprietors? You don't seem surprised by their bickering."

"Happens every day." His eyes had an almost reptilian

quality that mesmerized her, especially this close. She tucked in her lower lip, and those eyes narrowed. "Nobody fights like family. They're cousins who inherited the store from their grandfather. Wally works, and Hap plays poker, and somehow they keep it all going, though Hap's getting worse. Last night, instead of depositing the day's receipts in the bank, he took them to a high-stakes poker game. Wally found out this morning and hit the roof."

"A thousand dollars to buy in for a poker game? This store must really be doing well." He rubbed his thumb across his fingertips, and for the first time, his eyes sparked to life. "I might have to see if I can get into that game."

She couldn't decide if she was disappointed or further intrigued. On the one hand, he had just admitted to being a gambler, but on the other, the thought of plunking down a cool thousand didn't seem to faze him. She came down on the side of intrigued. "The store does very well. Some days we take in so much money we need a deputy escort to take the cash to the bank in the evening."

He leaned in close, inviting her to do the same. With a slight huskiness to his voice, he whispered, "You know, it wasn't fair of you to go to that play last night."

"It wasn't?" She whispered, too, a delicious tremor playing across her skin.

"You completely distracted me from the actors on stage, and I imagine I wasn't the only one."

She fervently hoped the blush she could feel in her cheeks was the becoming kind and not the you've-been-out-too-long-in-the-sun kind. Though she scrambled for something coy and witty to say, she couldn't think of a thing.

"I noticed you had companions in your box with you. A couple and another young man? Perhaps the young man is your beau?"

"Oh no, Jonas is just a friend." She could've bitten her tongue off. Rushing to assure him she was unattached? Ugh.

"I see. Well, that relieves my mind. What about the others with you last night? Friends? They seemed most devoted to one another."

Fran frowned and toyed with her pencil. She hadn't had a chance yet to talk to Addie, but it was high on her to-do list. "Addie Reid and Miles Carr. Addie's my best friend."

"Oh? She seemed familiar to me. Is she new in town?"

"She's been here a few months. She and her uncle came here from Abilene, though her uncle passed away recently. She's running the photography studio up the street, Reid's Photography."

"She works alone?"

"She does, and I'm so proud of her. If it had been me, with that whopping big mortgage and all alone, I think I would've just folded up and died. But she's making a go of things. And she'll get that note paid off before it's due. She told me she would, and I believe her. Come the end of August, she'll own her business free and clear."

He leaned his elbows on the counter. "I think you're made of sterner stuff. I imagine you would've come up with a plan to survive." Again his slash of a mouth lifted at the corners.

"Perhaps your friend has a nest egg put away or she knows she's going to come into money soon, and that's why she's so certain she can repay the loan."

It wasn't quite a question, and Fran shrugged. "Addie doesn't have any extra money that I know of, but we're coming into the busiest part of the season. She's got lots of customers every day, and she's getting some attention because she took some fabulous photos of the new theater. That was her work on the posters. Did you see it?"

Wally emerged from the back room, his face still dusky red, and opened the flour sack to empty it into a bin. Hap shuffled out, looking sheepish, his hands in his pockets and his glasses sliding down his nose. He hitched them up and sidled out of the store, keeping his head down as he passed Wally and giving Fran a quick wink before stepping out into the sunshine. Wally watched him go and folded the flour sack into precise squares. He frowned in Fran's direction.

She grimaced and closed the ledger. Though her bosses wanted her to chat up the customers, particularly the male customers, dawdling with someone who didn't look like he was going to make a purchase at all was another matter. "Vin, as much as I am enjoying talking to you, I do have to get some work done. This window display is driving me crazy. Something's not right about it, but I do have to get it finished before the afternoon rush."

Footsteps sounded on the boardwalk out front, and Jonas walked through the doorway. Though with the light behind him she couldn't see his face, she knew his silhouette as well as she knew her own name. Her lips pressed together. Couldn't she go a day without his coming in to check on her? Bad enough that she'd been finagled into letting him escort her to the theater last night.

Several of the ladies who had come in this morning had asked if she and Jonas were now keeping company. As if she would! And now Vin might think she wasn't telling the truth about Jonas not being her beau.

Jonas put on his most pleasant expression, hoping for once Fran wouldn't bite his head off. They'd parted amiably enough last night to give him a glimmer of hope that she was coming around to her old self, the girl he'd fallen in love with. When his eyes lit on her chatting with yet another strange man, his resolve to be pleasant slipped a notch.

"Morning, Fran." Jonas sauntered toward her, smitten as always with her fresh, golden beauty. Would it ever pall on him? Would he ever get used to it? Would she ever outgrow her flirtatious ways and see that they were perfect for each other?

He eased back his jacket lapel and hooked his thumb in his vest pocket. "Howdy." He nodded to the stranger. "Don't believe I've had the pleasure." This man definitely wasn't a cowboy, but what he was remained to be seen.

Fran braced her palms on the counter and leaned forward. "Jonas, this is Mr. Vin Rutter. He works for the railroad."

Jonas sized him up. Lean, well-dressed, pale as a catfish belly, and with a pair of eyes that reminded him of ice-cold nickels. Rutter. He'd heard or read that name before, but where? It teased his gray matter, but he couldn't quite lay hold of the thought he sought for. Jonas filed it away to think about later. A railroad man. Hmm.

"Vin, this is Deputy Jonas Spooner." She said his name with just a hint of exasperation. "Was there something you wanted, Jonas?"

Rutter stepped back from the counter. "Miss Seaton, it's been a pleasure. I hope you're able to solve the dilemma of the front window display, and I look forward to seeing you again. . ." He paused, and his eyes roved over everything he could see of her behind the counter. "Soon."

Jonas fisted his hands and straightened. Jealousy writhed in his gut, and he had a fierce desire to send a right hook through Vin Rutter's leer. Warning bells went off in Jonas's head, an instinctive reaction that this man could be dangerous. Where had he heard that name? He kept his eyes on the man all the way out the store before he turned to Fran. "You're playing with fire. Again."

Her wide green eyes got wider. "I have no idea what you mean." Her heels tapped on the floor as she headed toward the front of the store.

He strode after her. Catching her elbow, he stopped her and spun her around. "That wasn't some cowboy you were flirting with. When are you going to realize you can't play with a wolf and expect it not to bite you?"

"Vin's no wolf." She shrugged off his grip. "He's a perfectly nice gentleman who works for the railroad. And I wasn't flirting." Her conscience twinged. "And even if I was, there's no law against being nice to customers. You coming in here to harass me is getting to be a tired old habit. I can take care of myself, regardless of what you or my brothers think."

"That's just it, Fran. You can't. You're too beautiful for your own good. The cowboys are bad enough, but you can't play your little games with a man like Vin Rutter. There's something about him that gives me the creeps."

"Do you know something specific that makes you say that, or is it just your jealousy?" Her pointed chin went up as it so often did around him lately.

He sighed and lifted his hat to thrust his fingers through his short hair. "I don't know anything specific, no, but I plan to find out everything I can about him. Until I do, you stay away from that man."

She gasped and turned her back on him, shoving things around in the front window, toppling bonnets off hat stands, and knocking a beaded purse to the floor. Her shoulders quivered, and her back was so straight he thought it might snap. "Jonas Spooner. . ." His name came out sharp as a sewing needle. She turned, and if glares could start a fire, his face would be smoldering right now. "You have no right to say who I will and will not see. You don't know anything about Vin, and yet you're willing to malign his character. You're jealous, and that's that." She pointed to the door. "Get out of here. I don't want to see you right now."

He backed off, shaking his head. He'd come in determined to be pleasant, and now she was chasing him out like a stray mongrel. Shoving his hands into his pockets, he nodded. "I'll go, but mind what I said. You try to pet a wolf, and he'll bite you."

When he walked out into the sunshine and past the window, something inside the store smacked into the glass at his eye level. Little spitfire. Prickly as a box of straight pins. If he ever did manage to win her heart, he had a feeling he'd never be bored again.

Chapter 9

Miles wiped his palms on his trousers and gripped the door handle. For days, he'd rehearsed what he would say to Addie when he saw her, but everything he came up with made him sound like a donkey.

He'd meant to see her sooner—the day after their kiss, in fact—but Bat had rousted him before dawn to ride with a posse chasing a pair of horse thieves. Riding for hours in the blazing early summer heat had given him plenty of time to think and prepare what he would say, but he wound up chasing his thoughts and running in mental circles. The memory of their kiss would distract him, followed hard by the knowledge that she had been Cliff's girl. . .and round and round he went.

Twisting the handle, he let himself into the studio. Armchairs flanked the door, with some potted ferns and small tables. Photographs hung on every wall of the front room, mostly portraits but a few landscapes and buildings and such. Centered on the right-hand wall, a large picture of the interior of the Arden Palace held pride of place.

But it was the portraits that drew his eyes. Dozens of cowboys, singly and in groups. Lots of hats and chaps and spurs and guns. There were some businessmen—he recognized a couple of local lawyers, one of the town's doctors, and the preacher at the Methodist church. Children stared solemnly back at him, in their best clothes. Then he turned to study the pictures on the left-hand wall.

Miles sucked in a breath. These were completely different. Like moments caught in time. A cowboy down near the stockyard stroking his horse's mane, his eyes keen on the horizon. A black woman bent over a washboard with a hundred lines and wrinkles bearing testimony to the long journey her life had been. Deeply seated in her dark eyes, he saw wisdom and long-suffering.

Another picture made him smile. A baby sat in a washtub in someone's yard. Sunlight gleamed off the halo of blond curls, and a perfect little hand, like a star-shaped rowel, reached for a sunflower bobbing near the tub. Soap bubbles surrounded the tot, and he could just make out the edge of a calico apron fluttering on a clothesline. The picture was so natural, and the baby looked so real and happy, Miles thought if he touched it he could almost feel the soft skin and the slick of bubbles.

A dozen other photographs hung on the wall, each one a sliver of life caught unaware. Unlike most photographs where the subject faced the camera in awkward stiffness, Addie seemed to capture her customers in a relaxed moment, as if they had no notion a camera was pointed their way at all. Her skill impressed him.

"Miles?"

His chest squeezed. Turning, he tried for nonchalance. "Afternoon."

She stood, framed by the doorway that led to the back of the studio. One graceful hand held the doorjamb, and the other propped a heavy book against her waist. Those blue-gray eyes made his stomach do flip-flops. "Good afternoon."

He rubbed his hands on his trousers again. "I'm sorry I didn't come to see you before now."

"Jonas told me you were out of town." She looked him in the eye, and the only indication that she might be thinking of their last meeting was a bit of color in her cheeks. Of course, that might be caused by the warm day, too.

"Horse thieves." Why did his tongue feel like a wooden shovel?

"I understand you apprehended the offenders?" She shifted the book on her hip, and he read the words FAMILY ALBUM on the velvet cover.

"They're in the jail, or the 'Hotel de Spooner' as Bat's calling it." Jonas was currently splitting jailer duties with one of the town policemen while several of the county deputies followed up on leads. The horse-thieving ring was proving bigger and broader than they had imagined.

Miles remembered with a jolt why he was standing in her parlor and dug in his pocket. "This here's my chit for getting my portrait taken. From the sheriff's office." He swallowed against his tight shirt collar. "Bat thinks it's asking for trouble posting the names and pictures of all the peace officers, but he's been outvoted by the county board."

She looked up from scanning the paper he'd given her. "Why is that asking for trouble?"

He shrugged. "Why give out the names and faces of the lawmen to a bunch of cowboys full to the skin with ruckus juice? They might look at it more as a shopping list of who to shoot than any deterrent to crime." Miles realized he still had his hat on and snatched it off. *The manners of a prairie dog.* He smoothed his hair, conscious that in his haste he'd dragged it all askew. "So, can you take my picture now, or should I come back later?"

Neither one of them mentioned the big bull buffalo in the room—the kiss. And crowding to the front of his mind was everything Vin had told him about her. Her innocent air might be a hoax. Was the fact that she hadn't mentioned the kiss they had shared a sign that she was a cool customer when it came to men? How could he find out without revealing his own connection to Cliff?

Had she loved his stepbrother?

He shoved that thought away as unworthy. It didn't matter in any case. Everything Vin had told him meant she could never be his.

She folded the paper and tucked it into her skirt pocket. "Now is a good time. I don't have another appointment until after three."

Miles followed her into the back room, his innards warring over what he wanted to believe and what might actually be the truth. He stepped through the doorway into her studio, and his eyebrows rose.

A large room with a skylight surprised him with its open, airy feeling. Various pieces of furniture sat around the perimeter—a settee, several chairs, and an assortment of stools like the ones the piano players used in the saloons with seats that screwed up and down. Blankets, tapestries, and drapes hung from a row of hooks along one wall, and at the rear of the studio, several canvases hung from the ceiling, ready to be pulled down or rolled up for backdrops. A huge, boxy camera on a tripod dominated the center of the room with a black cloth hanging from the back almost to the floor.

He breathed in the smell of fresh pine and paint mingled with a faint chemical odor.

"This is quite a place." He rotated his hat brim in his hands. "Really nice."

"You sound surprised. What did you expect?"

"I don't know. I heard you had a mortgage you were trying to pay off. I figured"—he raised one shoulder—"you'd be scraping by without so much equipment or something. . ." His voice trailed off, because he hadn't really given it much thought, just assumed from the bits and pieces he'd heard from Fran and Jonas that money was tight for her. And here was all this stuff, everything shiny new and fully stocked.

"You can't sell anything out of an empty cupboard." She dragged a stool to the area before the camera. "Without the proper equipment, a photographer can't take the kinds of pictures that will please the customers and have them coming back for more. I also cater to a wide clientele. I have to have the right props and furnishings to suit everyone from cowboys to city commissioners and everyone in between."

He sat where she indicated, still holding his hat. "Do you take a lot of pictures of commissioners?"

"I take photographs of whoever wants one. Family portraits, cowhands who want to commemorate their trip up the trail. This morning, I took pictures for the girls from the Lone Star Dance Hall." She lifted the drape on the back of the camera and flipped it to the side.

"The Lone Star?" His voice shot up. "What kind of pictures would those girls be wanting?" Surely she hadn't taken any of those risqué ones some of the women in that part of town liked to pass out as advertising. His face got hot at the thought.

Her eyes appeared over the back of the camera. "They were perfectly respectable photographs. Did you know that several of those ladies have families back East? Families who have no idea what those girls do for a living? Every single one who came in here today was dressed like she was ready to go to a church supper and she stayed that way." Addie stepped around the legs of the tripod, her hands resting on her hips. "I do good work in this studio, respectable work. They wanted pictures of themselves to send home. To let their families know that they were all right. I don't condone lying, and I have no control over what those girls tell their families, but those were good, decent pictures I took."

Miles held his hands up, palms facing her. "All right." He wanted to laugh at her spitfire answer, but the fighting light in her eyes told him he'd be safer not to. "I understand. I didn't mean anything by the question." Her vehemence both reassured him and discomfited him. She didn't condone lying. Was it lying not to tell someone something? Not to mention that he knew her former fiancé? More than knew him, in fact?

She relaxed and let her hands drop. "I'm sorry. It's just that every photographer is approached at one time or another about taking pictures that should never be made. I don't hold with provocative poses or pictures taken to advertise what they're selling, and I don't want my name associated with such a sordid practice as taking pictures intended to lure and inflame. It makes me a little. . .defensive."

He could understand that. Just like he didn't want his name associated with the doings of the Walker Gang. Just thinking of what Addie might say if the truth came out made his guts squirm.

"If you'll wait here, I'll get a plate started in the darkroom." She whisked away, disappearing behind a door to his left.

He studied the capped camera lens, like some great, black, lidless eye, and let his gaze wander the room again. So much new equipment. Had Addie been in collusion with Cliff and his nefarious activities? Or was she an innocent casualty in the war the Walker Gang had waged on decent people for the past few years?

She reemerged, wiping her hands on a cloth and checking a clock on the wall beside the darkroom door. "That will hold for a few minutes while we get everything situated out here."

"How'd you get involved with photography?"

"My Uncle Carl was a photographer. He worked for Matthew Brady as a photographer during the War and struck out on his own afterward. My father was a Union soldier. He died at Chickamauga, and my mother died not long after the War ended. Uncle Carl came for the funeral, and afterward, he packed up my valise and took me with him in his caravan wagon. We lived out of that wagon—a converted ambulance from the War—for a couple of years, traveling from town to town where he'd take portraits and I'd help him develop them. We finally settled in Abilene when the first herds came up the trail. He opened a studio, and we lived there until recently." She fussed with something on the back of the camera, not looking at him. "Then we moved to Dodge City. Uncle Carl thought the prospects would be good here."

They'd left Abilene not long after Cliff's trial and execution. Did that mean Cliff had meant so much to her she couldn't stay in the town where he'd died? Or had the citizens of Abilene made it too difficult for her to stay? His thoughts milled like a herd bedding down for the night.

She stepped close and took his hat from him. "We don't want this in the picture." Tilting her head, she studied his face until he grew uncomfortable.

"Do I have dirt on my face?"

"No." She smiled, but it seemed detached. "I'm framing the portrait in my mind to get just the right angles and lighting."

"Are all those pictures in the front room yours?" He tried to ignore the warm feeling of her fingers as she placed them under his chin to raise it just a fraction and turned his head to the right.

"Yes." Addie stepped back then approached again to push

his shoulders down a hair. "I'm thinking a three-quarters shot."

"How do you make them look so. . ." He sought the word. "Relaxed?" That wasn't quite it, but he couldn't think of how to put it.

"The trick is in not telling the subject to relax." A real smile teased her lips this time, and something warm sprang into his chest. "Portraits aren't about how the person looks in real life. A good portrait shows the subject as they think they look or even more as they wish they looked. A skilled photographer uses every weapon in her arsenal to produce a portrait that diminishes a customer's faults and showcases their strengths."

"Weapons? Like what?" Did she think he had a lot of faults that needed diminishing?

She rummaged in a box on a table and pulled out a square of cardboard with an oval cut into it. "Like this. I put this over the lens to diffuse the edges and give me an oval exposure. A photographer uses light, angle, exposure, props, filters, diffusers, and especially her knowledge of the subject to take a portrait. It also helps greatly to know what the portrait is to be used for. Commercial photography like the Arden Palace shots or the posters of Dodge City lawmen won't be staged the same way a portrait of a deceased baby or a woman who wants a picture to send to her sweetheart." She ducked behind the camera and peered through the lens. "A portrait can hide or reveal, and both can be a result of a photographer's skill."

What did she see when she looked through her camera at him? And what did she know about him that would be revealed by her obvious skill? He shifted and grimaced, then tried to get back to the way she'd positioned him.

"You can move for now, but once I get you into your final pose, you'll have to be still for the exposure or you'll come out all blurry." She emerged from the drape, smoothing her hair into the twist on the back of her head.

"You take pictures of dead babies?"

She sighed, crossed her forearms on top of the camera, and rested her chin there. "I do. It may seem gruesome, but for the families who commission the picture, it's often the only reminder they have of a loved child who passes away. I often prefer, if possible, to take a picture of the mother holding the child, so she will always have that link to her baby. I can't imagine the pain of losing a child, and if I can mitigate it in any way, then I try." She went back to work adjusting, focusing, posing his shoulders again, and tilting his chin. A few cranks pulled a shade partway across the skylight to shield him from some of the glare.

There was a lot more to photography than he'd ever imagined. And a lot more to Addie Reid than he'd imagined, too.

Addie looked through her lens at Deputy Miles Carr and tried to maintain her professional air. It was the only way she could think of to get through this first awkward meeting since the night he'd walked her home from the Arden. The night when she'd practically thrown herself at him out of fear of Vin Rutter. The night Miles had kissed her senseless.

She needed to stop babbling about photography and think,

or his portrait would come out all wrong and everything she'd said about being a skilled photographer would blow up in her face. If he sensed her unease, he would tense up. Instead of talking about herself, she should talk about him. "How are you adjusting to being a deputy sheriff? Do you like the work?"

For the first time, his eyes lost their wary look and took on a shine. "It's the best job I've ever had. I can't believe I get to work with men like Bat and Jonas. Most everyone likes them, and those that don't at least respect them."

Ah, her first inkling of what he would want in a portrait. "I read the article in the paper about the posse and capturing those horse thieves. It sounds like you acquitted yourself well."

He shrugged. "We worked as a team. Bat knows his onions. Though they had a head start, he had a feeling they were headed to Trinidad, since one of them had family there. We went across country and got around ahead of them near the state line. Then it was just a matter of waiting until they showed up."

"You make it sound so simple."

"I'm learning that being a lawman can be simple if you do it right and everything falls the way you hope it does. I read once where someone said that chance favored the prepared mind. That's a big part of being a lawman in Ford County. Being prepared for just about anything. It isn't enough to have a reputation. You have to be able to back it up with a quick hand, a steady nerve, and determination to succeed." Passion for his job glowed in his expression. His hand fisted on his leg, and he leaned toward her a bit.

This was just what she wanted to capture. "Wait right here while I get a plate." She hurried to the darkroom, closing the door behind her before parting the heavy, woolen curtains. By feel, she reached the pan holding the plate she had just washed with collodion. Lifting it, dripping from the solution, she slid it into the box that would protect it from light until she could get it into the camera.

Slipping from the darkroom, she hurried to the Chevalier and ducked under the smothering drape. With instinct born of much practice, she inserted the plate into the back of the camera. Silver nitrate dripped from her fingers, and she wiped them on the edge of the drape.

"All right. We're ready." She approached Miles once more and readjusted his pose. "Tuck your thumb just under your jacket at the waist to hold it back, because I want your badge to show up well in the picture."

The gleam of pride leapt into his eye once more, and his jaw lifted just a hitch. Exactly as she wanted. Stepping back, she removed the lens cap, counted to five, and replaced it. "Perfect."

He smiled at her, the same smile he'd given her the night of the play, and her heart bumped harder. "Thank you. I've never had my picture taken before, but you've made the whole process a pleasure."

"You've never had a portrait taken?" She blinked. "Not ever?"

Miles retrieved his hat from the chair where she'd placed it earlier and held it before him. "There wasn't much money for that kind of thing when I was a youngster, and what with one thing and another, I guess I never got around to having one taken since I left home. Nobody to send it to anyway." He shrugged. "When will the picture be ready?"

"I promised the county board I'd have them done by this weekend if they could get all the officers to come in. You're the last one, actually."

"Do you think I could get a copy of my picture? I'd pay you for it of course."

"Sure. You can drop by for it on Monday, or I can bring it by the jail."

"I'll stop in for it."

She tried not to let herself feel glad that he'd be coming by again. Neither of them had mentioned the kiss or that night at all. And what did that mean?

Miles stared at his likeness. It was him, and it wasn't.

When he'd stopped by for it on Monday morning, unable to hide his eagerness, Addie had been setting up for a family portrait and couldn't spend time with him. He'd handed her his coins and taken the little cardboard folder, tipping his hat and escaping the rowdy kids and harried parents. How she would ever corral them into sitting still for a picture was a mystery, but he didn't doubt she could do it.

He traced the silvery scrolling letters on the bottom of the frame while staring at the photograph. Addie's skill made him take a deep breath and shake his head. Everything she'd said about capturing people the way they wanted to be, how they wanted to see themselves, was present in this picture. For the first time in his life he saw more than a dirt-poor kid with no prospects or a weedy offshoot of a larcenous family tree. Looking back at him was a lawman. Someone who stood for something good and decent. Someone who could command respect. Someone with a future.

For the first time he really believed he could overcome his past and be the man he wanted to be.

Chapter 10

Firecrackers went off in the street for the hundredth time that day. July Fourth, cowboy-style.

Fran held the lengths of dress goods high to allow her passage through the throng in the mercantile and stepped into the comparative calm behind the counter. She ripped a length of brown paper from the roll and reached above her head for the string holder. It hung just out of her reach down the track, and Fran grabbed the metal cage and dragged it toward her before snipping off a length of twine. The paper crackled as she wrapped the fabric into a neat bundle and tied it up. "Here you go, Mrs. Blanchard. Three lengths of calico and one of the bombazine." She set the bundle next to the thread and yarns Mrs. Blanchard had already selected. Why had the woman chosen today of all days to brave the store? "Is there anything else I can do for you?"

"Thank you, dear." Mrs. Blanchard dug in her purse. Someone jostled her elbow and coins plopped onto the counter.

Fran slapped them to keep them from rolling off onto the floor. They'd never find them in this crush if they escaped.

"Such a lot of people in here."

"It is the Fourth, Mrs. Blanchard. Every cowboy and rancher and farmer and businessman in Ford County is here to celebrate."

She saw the elderly lady to the front door and hurried on to the next customer. They stood three and four deep all along the counters, laughing, joking, and for the most part under control. Spurs jangled and wide-brimmed hats blocked her view of the back of the store where she'd last seen Wally.

Divide and conquer was the order of the day. Fran manned the counter with the patent medicines, housewares, cloth, and sewing notions, while keeping an eye on the center table of ready-made clothing. Wally took care of the other long counter with the tobacco, foodstuffs, and candy. The demand for new clothes kept Fran hopping, and Wally made several trips to the storeroom to replenish the stacks.

"Hello, darlin'." A sunburned cowboy leaned on the counter. "You sure are a sight for these trail-weary eyes."

Since he was at least the tenth drover in the last hour to pay her a compliment and she was already tired to death, she had to force herself to smile at him. "What can I get you?"

"How about a dance tonight? You will be at the dance, won't you?" He put an extra-thick drawl into his words. "A lady as pretty as you can't be sitting home on the Fourth."

A flutter jumped to life in her middle, not because of this ordinary cowboy but because Vin Rutter had been in first thing to see her and asked her to save him a dance. "I'll be there. If you're lucky, you might get a dance, but you're not the first cowboy to ask."

"Lady, if you're going to be there, there's probably going to be a fight." He winked at her. "There might even be bloodshed, as pretty as you are."

And so it went until she finally closed the front door on the last customer. As the bell overhead jangled, she turned and leaned against the door. Wally dropped into a chair near the cold, potbellied stove and stretched his feet out.

Fran walked slowly toward him. The store was a mess. What had started out as neat stacks of clothing and precise pyramids of canned goods, now looked as if a tornado had blown through. The shelves were nearly bare behind the counters. As unladylike as it was, she was too tired to care, and bracing her hands on the counter near where Wally lounged, she hopped up to sit. "A cloud of locusts couldn't have made a neater job of it." She tucked a strand of hair up into a hairpin.

"I do believe we must've set some kind of record." Though he drooped with tiredness, Wally's eyes gleamed. "We even got rid of almost all those ridiculous pickled beets, though what cowboys would want with them I can't imagine."

"It's like they had buying fever. I sold the most bizarre things today. Patent medicine and scarves and gloves and every last pair of suspenders." Fran laughed, trying to ignore her aching feet. How was she going to get through an entire evening of dancing? "I don't know when I've been this tired."

Wally smoothed his oiled hair, the part still razor straight even after the day they'd put in. "You've done a marvelous job today, Miss Seaton. I'm sorry Hap wasn't here to be more helpful. Why he had to choose today of all days to go over to

Fort Dodge is beyond me. Though, after the row we had last night, I told him he could stay over there for all I cared. Things are going to change around here. I need a partner I can count on, not one who bleeds us dry and sponges off my labor."

Fran hadn't actually been sorry Hap wasn't with them today, though she liked him well enough. Hap Greeley wasn't on speaking terms with hard work, and if he'd have been here underfoot, he and Wally would've been scrapping instead of waiting on customers. For the first time that day the chimes of the wall clock could be heard. Four o'clock. Only an hour to go before the town supper and dance.

"Do you want me to help you count the tills?" Though she longed to head home and soak her feet, she wouldn't miss the dinner and dance for anything. The sooner she got out of here, the sooner she might see Vin.

As she'd hoped, Wally waved her away. "No, you head home and get ready for tonight's festivities. I'll count the receipts. Bat promised me a deputy to see me safely to the bank, and Banker Poulter is holding the vault open for me. I think we must've cleared more than two thousand dollars. Be sure to lock the front door on your way out."

Fran hopped off the counter, her sore feet yelping as they impacted the board floor. "Do you want me to be here first thing in the morning to help clean everything up?"

He put his hands on his knees and forced himself to his feet with a slight groan. "No, I think we'll open at noon tomorrow. You don't need to come in until about ten, I should think. Hap might be back by then, and he can help us. I'm tired of slaving while he loafs around. He can bend his back for once."

She left him counting stacks of bills next to the register, making careful notes in his receipt book. If Wally got Hap to work tomorrow it would be the first time since she'd known either of them.

Rushed for time, she didn't wait for one of her brothers to show up. She wove through the throngs on Front Street and hurried to her house. Nobody was home. She quickly heated water for a sketchy bath, then brushed and restyled her hair.

Vin had been a frequent customer at the store the past week, and she couldn't quell the thrill she got each time he stepped into the mercantile. Though he hadn't asked formal permission to call on her, she knew he would soon. And she had a feeling he wouldn't be intimidated by her brothers.

Donning her best dress, sewn by her and Addie—with Mrs. Blanchard's help—just for tonight, she knew she looked her best. The pale green fabric scattered with tiny white flowers exactly matched her eyes and highlighted her red-gold hair. She didn't need to touch her lips and cheeks with any color—though her brothers would be scandalized to know she even possessed makeup. Bad enough the fit they'd thrown when she'd pierced her ears. She swung her head a little, feeling the tug of the silver and peridot dangling from her lobes.

A knock sounded on the door.

She inserted the last hairpin and went to answer.

Jonas Spooner stood on the doorstep, hat in hand. "Evening, Fran. You sure look nice. I came to take you over to the dinner. I was going to walk you home from the mercantile, but you left before I got there."

She held on to the door. "Did one of my brothers send you?"

He shook his head. "Nope, thought it up all on my own. You don't have someone else calling for you, do you?"

Irritation scratched at her. "No. But I've arranged to meet someone there."

"A man?" His brows narrowed together, and his lips flattened.

"A gentleman, yes." Fran reached for her fan and bag.

"Do your brothers know?" Jonas stepped back as she closed the door behind her then offered his elbow.

She took it with bad grace, and not for the first time noticed the muscles under his shirt sleeve. Where Vin was lean, Jonas was sturdy. And where Vin had all the excitement of the unknown, Jonas was as familiar to her as her brothers. . .and as annoying. "I don't have to get their approval for everything I do."

His shoulders relaxed, and he blew out a long breath. "Fran, I'm tired of arguing with you. Let's bury the hatchet, call a truce. We used to be such good friends."

He was right. They had been good friends, until he messed everything up by declaring his love for her. To tell the truth, she was weary of fighting with him, too. A truce sounded nice. He tilted his head and gave her a smile, making something spark in her heart. He could be endearing, charming even, when he tried. Why couldn't he accept that friends was all they would ever be?

"I'd like that. To be friends again."

"I was hoping you'd say that. Let's have a good time tonight." He tucked her hand more securely into his elbow and gave it a pat. "I'm hungry. Are you?"

The dinner held little appeal for her. It was the dance that occupied her thoughts. When would Vin get there? How many dances could she have with him before people started talking? What would her brothers say?

They strolled up the street, following the crowd toward the church where the supper would be held. They ran into her brother Stuart, and he seemed glad enough to relinquish any responsibility for her to Jonas. Fran searched the dinner crowd for Vin's pale face, but he didn't appear to be among the diners.

As soon as a seat opened up at one of the long benches, someone filled it. Women carried laden dishes to the tables and empty plates back to the kitchen.

"I'm glad I didn't volunteer to serve. This is worse than the crowds we had at the store today."

Jonas found them two seats near the door, and throughout the dinner he saw to her every need and chatted easily with her and those around them. She couldn't help but notice how several of the single ladies serving the dinner stopped to say hello to him and ask if he would be at the dance later. By the time the fourth young lady had stopped to inquire, Fran found herself becoming irritated. Couldn't they see he was escorting her? Brazen, that was what it was.

The minute Jonas finished his slice of apple pie, she took his arm. "Let's go. I don't want to be late for the dance."

Jonas smiled and led her outside and down the way toward the Arden Palace where the dance was being held.

Once inside the building, she scanned the packed seating areas and the dance floor. The orchestra, borrowed from the Long Branch Saloon for the night, sawed away at a reel. Women pivoted and swung, their dresses like bright flowers in a sea of big hats and bandanas. Fran tapped her foot along with the music as she searched for Vin.

Jonas surveyed the crowd. "I better get in before you get mobbed. Dance?"

She nodded, still searching for Vin, until Jonas fitted his arm around her waist and drew her toward him. Her eyes widened. Had she ever danced with Jonas before? She couldn't remember.

Her glance bounced off his, and her breath hitched. Under her fingers, the muscles of his shoulder felt as solid as a draft horse, but his steps were light and fluid leading her in the waltz. Though he maintained several inches of space between them, the iron band of his arm made her feel as if he held her against him. Heat flared in her middle, and uneasy, unfamiliar feelings began sloshing, as if her heart were a bottle of sarsaparilla being shaken.

She tried to concentrate on the steps and rationalize her inner turmoil. When she closed her eyes, she could feel his hand on her back, warm and strong. Her eyelids bounced up. He swung her in a perfect pivot, leading with confidence, as if they were floating.

"You look surprised." He grinned. "Didn't think a country

boy like me could dance, did you?"

She shook her head and gave herself over to the enjoyment of dancing with Jonas. The man had hidden depths. Not that she was interested, she reminded herself, but at least he wasn't murdering her feet like a lot of the cowboys. Passing a group of ladies on the fringes, Fran wasn't unaware of their envious looks.

The music swirled to an end, and Jonas's arms dropped from around her. Why this action should give her such a feeling of loss baffled her, and she squelched it by clapping a smile on her face and following him off the floor. She was a muddleheaded fool, that was what.

They reached the seating area, and her heart gave a jolt. Vin stood there, tall and slim, his pale hair brushed smooth and his clothing immaculate. Though several ladies encircled him, he looked over their heads and locked eyes with her.

Her heart thundered and her mouth went dry.

He threaded through the women and smiled down at her. "Ah Fran, you look delightful."

Jonas's jaw tightened. "Evening, Rutter."

"Thank you for occupying my girl until I could get here, Spooner." He lifted Fran's hand and kissed the air over her knuckles. "There goes the music, my dear. Shall we dance?" He didn't wait for her consent, swinging her into his arms and joining the throng on the dance floor.

She caught sight of Jonas watching her for a moment before being surrounded by females. A strange emptiness grew in the pit of her stomach.

"Am I such a poor dance partner that you should look so sad?" Vin bent and whispered against her temple. His warm breath stirred the fine wisps along her hairline and dragged her mind away from Jonas.

"No, of course not." He was an accomplished dancer, though not in Jonas's class. She gave him her brightest smile. "I've looked forward to being with you all day."

He held her a bit closer. "You stand out like a flower in a cornfield. Have you ever thought of leaving Dodge City? Your face and form"—his voice dipped—"are more suited to society balls in Kansas City or St. Louis, or even New York, rather than this little prairie stomp." His lips drew into a sneer as he took in the cowboys and calico.

Stung that he should think so poorly of the biggest event she'd ever been invited to, she bit her lower lip and tried to see it through his eyes. If he'd been to those cities, she could understand perhaps why he didn't think so much of a cow town celebration.

"Do you think so? Dodge is the biggest city I've lived in. I grew up on a farm near Springfield, Missouri, and came here with my brothers two years ago when herds first started trailing into Dodge."

"I assure you, my dear"—again his breath tickled her temple—"you would make a sensation in a big city. Have you ever thought of traveling?"

Had she ever? Only every night before she drifted off to sleep. "I suppose with your job you travel a lot." She couldn't keep the wistfulness out of her voice. What would it be like to swing aboard the AT&SF and let those clacking wheels take her to all the places she dreamed of seeing?

"You could say I move around a lot."

"It sounds lonely, always moving like that."

He shrugged, and his eyes bored into hers. "Maybe I didn't know I was lonely until recently."

Her breath hitched. "When will you move on, and will you be back through here often?"

"I'm not sure how long I'll stay. I'm expecting to come into a great deal of money in the near future, and I plan to use some of it to travel." A smile tugged his lips. "Maybe when I do pull out of here, I won't be going alone. You dance beautifully." He turned his head just enough that his lips brushed her forehead, leaving her skin tingling.

Vin Rutter was a man who could give her all the things she dreamed of—adventure, travel, excitement. She gave herself over to enjoying the evening.

Vin kept her to himself and refused to allow anyone to cut in, but in the middle of their third dance, a grubby boy snaked toward them through the crowd and tapped Vin on the arm.

"It's time."

Vin's arms dropped away, and he lifted her hand, squeezing her fingers. "I do apologize, but I have an appointment I can't possibly break. I shall turn you over to the tender mercies of these gentlemen." He waved to the men standing on the sidelines waiting for partners. "But I shall expect your heart to remain true to me." He followed the young messenger toward the doors.

After his departure, the spark went out of the evening. Though she laughed and flirted with her partners, nothing seemed as fun. It didn't help at all that Jonas swung past again and again, each time with a different girl in his arms.

Addie slipped another wet-plate into the Chevalier and removed the lens cover to capture the man staring so intently at the camera. She counted off the seconds. The knot between her shoulder blades reminded her that she'd been preparing plates and posing subjects for almost ten straight hours. Every drover in town seemed to have stomped through her studio to commemorate the holiday with a portrait.

The cowboy paid her and sauntered out, and with thankfulness, she flipped the sign in the front door to CLOSED and snicked the lock. Though weary, a thrill ran through her at how her coffers had swollen today. This thrill was quickly followed by a twinge of apprehension. Even with such a boost to her cash flow, the final mortgage payment loomed like a tyrant.

Another tyrant stalked her as well, contributing to her weariness. Ever since spying Vin Rutter at the Arden ten days ago, her nerves had been on edge. Sleep eluded her, and food tasted like sawdust, though she hadn't seen him since that night. Maybe his coming to Dodge was a coincidence. Maybe he was just passing through. Maybe she was worried for nothing.

And maybe he was just biding his time until he confronted her.

If only she could confide in someone. Fran would be her natural choice, but telling Fran meant revealing how gullible she'd been to fall for the likes of Cliff. The pain was too raw. Besides, Fran had been too consumed with a new beau—a mystery man that had her all aflutter—to pay much attention to Addie. According to Fran, the man was more exciting than an Italian count, better looking than Bat Masterson, and more fascinating than a magician. Addie shook her head. Nothing with Fran was ever simple, especially when it came to men.

She supposed she shouldn't throw any stones. Every time she thought of Miles Carr—and she seemed to think about him way too much—her heart did strange things and her mind ran in a dozen different directions. She had no idea what he might feel for her.

When he'd come to her studio for his portrait, he'd been composed and businesslike. He hadn't mentioned their kiss, and she would've rather died than bring it up first. She blushed, remembering the bliss of being held in his strong arms, the way his presence had calmed her fears and made her feel safe. Had it meant nothing to him? Had she let it mean too much to her?

The portrait she'd taken of him was good—better than good—if she did say so herself. Would he mind that she'd printed a copy of the photograph for herself?

Stop these foolish thoughts. You seem to be forgetting that he'd drop you like a hot rock if he knew about your past. You have other things to worry about. Though this was far from the first time she'd given herself a stern talking-to regarding Miles, her heart didn't seem to want to listen any better now than before.

She gathered her things and prepared to leave. If she hurried, she might make it to the church in time to get some of the community dinner, though by now most of the tables were bound to be cleared as the town dance had been underway for more than an hour.

Her hand brushed the camera case at her side. The contents of the hidden compartment reminded her yet again that she needed to avoid getting involved with a man. With the mortgage payment hanging over her head like a sword, she couldn't let her attention be diverted from her work, even by someone as handsome and kind as Miles Carr. She'd been fooled once before, and she wasn't minded to play the fool again. If the bank knew of her past, the manager would call in the loan and put her out of business quicker than igniting flash powder. And there was the complication of Vin Rutter to contend with.

She stepped out onto the boardwalk and locked the door. Dust and noise filled the air as riders, wagons, and pedestrians clogged the street. Everyone was dressed in their best, and red, white, and blue bunting hung from every porch and balcony.

In spite of the high spirits and joviality all around her, a feeling like cold fingers brushed across the back of her neck, and she turned around. The crowd parted for a moment. Her breath snagged in her throat. Vin Rutter leaned against a hitching post, staring at her. His thin lips twitched, and he bowed slightly before the crowd obscured him again.

Shaking, she gripped her camera case. Anger burned bright, incinerating her fear. How dare he come here and by his very presence threaten to disrupt her life all over again? She wasn't minded to play the victim again. Marching toward him, she vowed to get to the bottom of his reason for being in Dodge City and make sure he knew she wanted nothing to do with him or the tangled past.

When she finally made it through the crowd, he had vanished.

Miles strode down the street, alert to trouble but feeling pretty good about how things had gone today. Though Dodge City teemed with people, so far the skirmishes had been few. But like a pot of water on a stove, the air held a sense of impending action, as if something might boil over at any time. The quickly approaching nightfall might bring with it everything the lawmen of Dodge could handle.

As he passed the bank, he stuck his head in. "Everything set here? I'm just headed to the mercantile now."

Ty Pearson lounged against one of the teller windows, cradling a shotgun in his arms. The bank manager, Archie Poulter, jingled some keys or coins in his pocket, his heavy eyebrows overhanging his eyes. "Hurry him up if you can. I can't wait here all evening."

"I'll do my best to chivvy him along." He nodded to the banker and to Ty and headed up the street. His antipathy toward Archie Poulter had been an irrational thing until he learned from Jonas via Fran that the pompous old man had made an offer of marriage to Addie. Then his antipathy had solidified into active dislike.

Miles rapped on the mercantile door and shaded his eyes to peer through the glass. Wally sat at the counter surrounded by stacks of coins and bills. He looked up, frowned, and nodded. Miles turned his back to the door and watched the street as he waited for Wally to round the counter and come let him in.

"Come in, come in. Sorry, I didn't recognize you at first." The little shopkeeper stepped aside to let Miles enter.

Miles scanned the shelves and tables. "Looks like a stampede went through here."

Wally scuffed his way back to his stool behind the counter and tapped some bills into a neater pile. "It feels like it ran right over me, though I shouldn't complain. This is the single best day we've ever had. Nearly twenty-three hundred dollars in sales. I'm about cleaned out for inventory."

"I checked on the way over, and they're waiting for you down at the bank." Miles hooked his thumbs into his belt.

Wally mopped his forehead with a wrinkled handkerchief and made a couple more notes in his ledger. "I'm sorry to keep everyone waiting. It's taken me longer to count the receipts than I thought." He reached for a canvas bag and began lifting stacks of bills into it.

A faint popping sound caught Miles's attention. He strode to the door to see several men running down Front Street. More popping. He wrenched the door open, and the sound got louder. Gunfire? Bat and two of the town policemen charged past.

Shouts echoed. Should he go help, or should he stay with

Wally? His job was here, but what if Bat needed help? More gunshots. So many it sounded as if an army advanced on the west end of town.

"Wally, lock this door behind me and wait here until I get back." Miles drew his gun, checked his load, and hurried after his boss.

Crowds jostled past Miles and headed east, and he fought against them to get through. When he finally found himself on open ground, he realized the ruckus was coming from the livery stable on the far end of Front Street. Bat and two deputies had their guns drawn, watching the scene from cover.

Miles cut across the street to join them, diving behind the edge of the building they crouched beside. "Who's in there, and who are they shooting at?"

The door to the livery rattled. Bat shook his head. "Maybe someone in there shooting off a shotgun?"

The firing stopped. The smell of gunpowder hung in the air, and slowly they emerged from cover. Silence.

"Do you think he shot himself?" one of the policemen asked.

"Or he's out of ammunition." Bat motioned for Miles to follow him. Before they were halfway across the street, smoke began leaking under and around the livery door.

"Fire! Fire!" the two city policemen yelled and ran for the water barrels nearby.

Miles followed Bat. Wrenching the doors open, Miles covered the lower half of his face with his arm. A wall of smoke billowed out into the street, and an orange glow made shadows dance on the wall. Horses neighed and stamped.

"You take the right!" Bat ducked into the first stall on the left.

Miles dodged the hooves of a draft horse and yanked at the halter rope. Removing his hat, he swatted at the face of the animal, backing him out of the stall and shooing him out of the livery.

His eyes streamed water and stung, and his throat rasped on the heavy smoke. Six more horses on his side of the immense barn. Men rushed past him with buckets of water, shouting and splashing, kicking at the straw and soaking the walls.

In the last stall, so near the flames, the horse bucked and plunged, terror-stricken. Miles darted in and got shoved back. He tried to gauge his leap this time and managed to get halfway into the stall before the horse jerked and sidestepped again. The animal pinned him against the side of the stall, grinding Miles's ribs and shoving the breath out of his chest. Already short of breath because of the smoke, Miles saw stars and blackness crowded the edge of his vision.

Of all the stupid ways for a lawman to die.

Addie's sweet face swam in his vision, peeping at him from over the top of her camera, and his vision darkened further, until he could see nothing but swirling smoke and blackness.

Mercifully, the horse yanked back once more on the halter rope and managed to break free. Miles sank against the stall divider, cradling his ribs and gulping in thick, smoky air that made him cough painfully, unable to stand, unable to even crawl to safety away from the thrashing hooves. He felt himself sliding toward the straw, felt the heat of the flames encroaching, but in his dazed state, he couldn't move.

The air this close to the ground was better, and mercifully, someone managed to get the horse out of the stall. The sound of flames engulfing the barn and showers of sparks illuminating the scarves and blankets of smoke overhead prodded him to do something about getting out. Miles rolled onto all fours and got to his knees.

Hands reached out of the smoke and grabbed his lapels, dragging him up and toward the door. Wobbling, clutching at the stall dividers for support, they made toward the lighter square of smoke that must show where the doorway was. He and his rescuer stumbled into the street where other hands hauled them out of the way of the fire brigade.

Miles's knees gave out, and he found himself sitting on the ground, his head hanging, gulping great lungfuls of fresh air. The frenetic activity around him slowed, and the shouting and tumult died.

Bat leaned against the building next to Miles, his hands braced on his knees and his face streaked with soot. Red spidery veins surrounded his piercing eyes, and smoke-induced tears made tracks on his cheeks. "Thought we lost you there," he said through coughs.

Miles rubbed his squashed ribs and groaned. "I thought you did, too." His head swam, and he had a hard time focusing through the tears pouring from his eyes.

Someone squatted before him, holding his shoulders. "Are you hurt?"

Addie.

He coughed, trying to answer her, but finally had to settle for shaking his head.

She disappeared for a moment then returned, holding a dipper and splashing water onto his pant leg in her haste. "Here, drink this." She cupped the dipper around his hands, holding them steady while he tipped it up to take a long, smoke-clearing draft.

Coolness slid down his irritated throat and improved things considerably. He stopped with half the water still left and offered it to Bat, who took it, spitting and coughing before downing the rest of the contents. "What happened?" Miles rubbed his hands down his face.

One of the city policemen flopped down between him and Bat. He held a bucket, but this one would never carry water again. Jagged holes of ripped metal jutted out on all sides. "A prank."

"A prank?"

"Looks like someone threw a handful of bullets and shotgun shells into this bucket then built a fire on top. Left it to burn and ran away. When the fire got hot enough, the bullets started exploding. Ripped through the bucket, the door, and injured a couple of the horses."

Addie gripped Miles's upraised knee. "You mean to tell me these men risked their lives, *nearly died,* because of someone's stupid prank?"

Gratified at her indignation, Miles covered her hand with his and squeezed. Now that he could breathe again, the dizziness abated, and his eyes quit leaking. With a swipe, he ran his sleeve over his cheeks and chuckled. "You once told me, Bat, that this job was never boring."

"Speaking of jobs, did you get Wally to the bank before this little shivaree?" Bat straightened his coat and accepted his hat from a bystander, brushing the crown with his sleeve before setting it on his head.

"No." Miles pushed himself upright, trying to ignore the squashed-bug feeling in his chest. That horse had really worked over his ribs. "I'd best get up there and see to it. Wally and Mr. Poulter are probably champing at the bit." He adjusted his gun belt and jacket and headed up the street with Addie at his elbow.

Dozens of people stood observing and talking. The firemen and volunteers had managed to douse the flames before too much damage had been done, and now they raked piles of charred straw out into the street where others wet it down further.

Addie tucked a strand of hair up behind her ear. "I was headed to my studio when I heard the gunfire. Then someone yelled that the livery was on fire. I got there just in time to see you and Bat disappear into the smoke." She took a deep breath. "I thought you'd never come out of there."

Miles rubbed his ribs. "For a while there, I thought I might not either." Smoke-smell clung to his clothes and hair.

The block where the mercantile sat was nearly deserted. Everyone was either still at the dance or milling around the livery, it seemed.

He checked his watch. Less than half an hour since he'd run out of the store. He glanced at the sun, nearly to the horizon, and swallowed against the rasp in his throat. The sun could've easily set on his life back there in that barn. Seeing Addie's face in his mind's eye when he thought he was dying made him realize how much she had come to mean to him. Perhaps he should say something to her. He stopped walking. "Addie, I. . ." What about Vin and Addie's history with his stepbrother, Cliff?

"Yes?" A breeze stirred her hair, and the sunset gilded the brown strands. She reached out and picked some straw from his shoulder. He stood still, and she brushed her fingers down his cheek, leaving a trail of sensation where she touched him. "Yes, Miles?"

Until he knew for sure, he'd be a fool to commit to anything. And there was always the chance that she'd lump him in with Cliff if she ever found out they were related. Better to keep things impersonal.

"Nothing." He stepped up on the boardwalk to bang on the mercantile door. "Wally? Open up. It's Deputy Carr."

No answer. Perhaps he was in the storeroom. Or maybe he'd gone on to the bank without an escort.

Addie fiddled with her camera case. "I think I'll head to my studio. I have some pictures to develop. Will you be at the fireworks later?" He didn't miss the uncertainty in her voice or the question in her eyes, asking him to explain his odd behavior.

"I'll be around." Her eyes widened at his abrupt answer,

and he tried to soften it. "I'm on patrol tonight."

She stepped away. "Maybe I'll see you there."

He nodded and banged on the door again, rattling the glass panes. "Wally!" Cupping his hands, he peered into the store. He rattled the knob, and it gave in his hand. His gut clenched.

"Addie."

She stopped a few yards away. "Yes?"

"Wait here for a moment, will you?" He entered the store, looked around, squatted for a moment, and went back to the door. "Go get Bat. And be quiet about it."

"Is something wrong?"

"Wally's been killed, and the store's been robbed."

Chapter 11

Addie's camera case bounced against her hip, and she grabbed it up, holding it pressed to her middle as she ran up the street. Plenty of people still milled around the smoldering livery, and at first, she couldn't find Bat in the gathering dusk.

Finally, after she'd about given up hope and decided to head for the jail, she spotted his bowler. He stood talking with Mayor Kelley and the editor of the *Globe*. Mindful of Miles's warning to be discreet, she moved around behind the mayor, caught Bat's eye, and jerked her head away from the group before strolling to an open space in the crowd.

Thankfully, he excused himself after a couple of agonizingly long minutes. "What can I do for you, Miss Reid?"

She swallowed. "Deputy Carr needs you at the mercantile." She kept her voice so low he had to bend close.

"What happened?"

"Mr. Price has been killed, and the store's been robbed."

Bat took a deep breath through his nose, his lips pressed together. Cinders had charred holes in his fine suit, and the odors of smoke and burned straw clung to him, as they had to Miles. He scanned the crowd. "I'll head right there. Go tap

Deputy Spooner on the shoulder and ask him to follow me."

Addie sidled up to Jonas and whispered her news in his ear, and together they sauntered up the street as if they'd both lost interest in the fire. They weren't alone, as others, now that the excitement had abated, headed back toward the town dance.

Addie and Jonas found Bat and Miles squatting beside the body. Though Addie had known Wally must be dead, nothing prepared her for the shock of seeing him that way.

Bat braced his hands on his thighs and rose.

Miles handed him a dented can.

"Not much of a murder weapon." Bat set it on the counter.

A dark red stain marred the label, but not so much that Addie couldn't make out the picture and words. Pickled beets.

"A crime of opportunity?" Miles studied the shelves and counters. "It looks like whoever did this picked up whatever was handy and bashed him in the head. The place is such a wreck, it's hard to say if Wally put up any kind of a fight. I was in here just before the fire, and it looked pretty much like this. I guess they had a banner day with customers."

Bat set the can on the counter and snapped his fingers to Jonas. "You'd better find the town marshal. This is his jurisdiction, but do your best to keep it quiet. The last thing we need is a bunch of gawkers." He turned to Miles, who stood and dusted off his hands. "Get a pencil and paper and start writing things down. When we catch the killer, we'll need to keep the evidence straight for the courts."

Addie frowned, and an idea blossomed in her head. She

relaxed her hold on her camera bag, letting it rest against her hip. "Sheriff?"

"Miss Reid? I forgot you were there. This is no sight for a lady. I trust you won't broadcast this until we've finished here?"

"Sheriff, I have my camera. Would it be helpful to have a picture of the. . ." She waved her hand over Wally's body, sickened but willing to be of aid if she could. "It might help later when the case goes to trial."

Bat smoothed his moustache, his keen eyes studying her. "An excellent idea. You have the equipment you need?"

She patted her case. "Everything's here. I just need some light."

Miles stood on a chair to light the overhead kerosene lamps, as well as the ones behind the counter. Their reflectors magnified the illumination until it was bright enough for her to get a good picture.

With a lump in her throat for Wally, and for Fran, too, when she heard the news, Addie readied the Scovill. Her hands shook, and she had to steady the camera on the edge of a flour barrel, sighting through her loop to frame as much of the store as she could while still capturing the details.

She didn't have to tell poor Wally to hold still for the exposure.

The instant she replaced the lens cover, the door burst open, and Mr. Poulter strode in with Deputy Pearson on his heels. "Really, Price, I've waited as long as I can. You're more than two hours overdue—" He halted, his mouth falling open and his hands reaching out to clutch something solid to steady himself. “Dear me, what happened?”

“Mr. Poulter, you need to leave.”

Pearson took one look at the body, ducked out the door, and before anyone could stop him, he yelled into the early evening air, “The storekeeper’s been murdered! Wally Price is dead!”

“That fool!” Bat charged through the doorway, but the damage had been done.

The dozens of people passing the store on their way back to the dance stopped, and as one, they tried to crowd into the store for a look at the gruesome crime scene. Women shrieked, men shoved and shouted, pushing Bat back into the store.

Addie found herself nearly carried toward the back of the mercantile on a wave of curious onlookers. Someone grabbed her arm, and she tried to wrench free, until she realized it was Miles.

“Go out the back way and get to your studio. Develop that picture and bring it to the jail. Hurry.”

Glass broke, and cans toppled as more people wedged into the store.

Addie slipped out past the store room and into the alley, panting and shaking. She’d never seen anything like it. First the murder, and now a stampede. Bile rose in her throat at the callous disregard of Wally’s life, the cheap thrill the townspeople sought at his expense. Tears burned her eyes, and she clutched her camera. At least she had something she could do to help Bat and Miles track down Wally’s killer.

Bodies pressed in through the doorway, men shouted, women screamed, and Miles battled to keep his feet. His ribs ached, and his head pounded. The curious onlookers gawked and jostled their way inside, flooding the store and trampling the crime scene. At least he'd gotten Addie out safely.

Through the throng, Bat's voice reached him, trying to reason with the crowd, but Miles couldn't tell that it made any difference. Two dozen, three dozen? He grabbed a man and shoved him toward the back door. "Get out of here. There's nothing for you to see here."

The man fought back, taking a swing at Miles. They scuffled, knocking against a cabinet. Glass broke, and Miles heaved the man away from him.

A gun blast went off, and everyone stilled. The crowd parted until Bat stood alone over the body, his pistol in his hand emitting a thin stream of blue smoke. A fresh bullet hole decorated the pressed-tin ceiling. "Now that's enough. I want every last one of you to get out of here right now before I lay this barrel upside a few noggins." His eyes seemed to cut through the onlookers. He nodded to Miles, who drew his gun as well. "You folks back there, head out that door and don't come past the body." He barely turned, keeping his gun pointed slightly up but ready to jerk it down if need be. His body quivered, like a panther ready to pounce. "You up here by this door, get out onto the street." He started shoving people out the door with his gun, and they went, like chastised sheep, until only Miles and Bat remained.

"What happened?"

Bat holstered his gun, his face a mask of disgust. "Mob behavior." He wiped his hand across his cheeks, smearing the soot there. "With the whole town keyed up for the celebration, then the fire, I knew if word of this killing got out tonight, the lid would blow off. People do strange things when they're in a group. Panic's going to spread fast, and I wouldn't be surprised if rabble-rousers didn't make the most of it. Remind me to have a word or two with Pearson. Of all the stupid things to do, running into the street and crowing like a rooster."

The city marshal, Charlie Bassett, shouldered through the door. "What's going on?"

Bat pointed. "It's Wally. Got himself robbed and killed."

Charlie scowled. "I thought one of your deputies was looking after him."

The guilt that had peppered Miles the moment he saw Wally sprawled on the floor stung like buckshot. "I was supposed to walk him to the bank." He waited, his hands fisted, for them to say all the things he'd been thinking himself.

What kind of lawman are you?

Your negligence cost Wally his life.

You're a sorry excuse for a man, trash. You'll never be anything but a waste.

"I just heard about the fire." Charlie squatted beside the body. "I was down at the Alhambra breaking up a fistfight. The only casualty down there was the mirror behind the bar."

The mob had knocked Wally even more askew than he'd

been, and merchandise littered the floor. The marshal, a good friend of Bat's, shook his head. "If I hadn't had my hands full in the saloon, I'd have helped you out down at the livery."

"There's going to be plenty of accusations and blame-shifting over this." Bat blew out a long breath. "We're going to take a beating in the papers."

Miles grimaced. If he would've stayed at his post, Wally would be alive. Should he turn his badge in first, or should he let Bat have the satisfaction of firing him? He stared at the floor. Every hateful accusation his stepfather had ever hurled at him sat like a fistful of rusty nails in his gut. Worthless, useless, no-account. What had ever made him think he could be a lawman?

Bat checked his watch, holding it to the light of one of the lamps. "By now the whole town knows about this. Any evidence here has been ruined. No mystery how Wally died. He's got a dent in the back of his head." Bat searched around him. "Where'd that can go?" He found it behind the counter and showed the bloody label to the marshal. He took it and set it on the floor beside the body. "We'd best go get the undertaker. This is terrible timing. You and I are supposed to leave on the night train, Charlie. We have to transport those horse thieves over to Wichita and testify at the hearing."

"This can't afford to wait. Store got robbed, too?"

Miles spoke up. "Wally said it was more than two grand. I was in here just before the fire at the livery. He was counting the money. I told him to lock the door behind me, but he must not've. It wasn't locked when I got back here, and you can see it hasn't been forced." He pointed to the latch, as normal as a nickel. "I don't know how long I was away. Half an hour maybe?"

Jonas appeared in the doorway, and Bat beckoned him in. "Spooner."

"The undertaker's waiting outside, and the city police are standing guard on the porch. Most of the crowd has taken off toward where they'll be setting off the fireworks."

Charlie tilted his head and appraised Miles. "So you were the last one to see Wally Price alive?"

Miles stilled. "Except for the killer." Was Charlie Bassett accusing him?

The marshal's eyebrows rose.

Bat rolled his eyes. "Easy there, both of you. Miles didn't kill Wally. He was down at the livery helping me."

Jonas stepped farther into the store. "Miles wasn't the last to see Wally alive. I was on the front porch of the Arden when I heard the ruckus at the livery. I headed down Front Street, and when I passed here, Wally was standing in the doorway looking up the street. That had to be after Miles raced out. I didn't pay too much attention at the time, but I did see Wally, and he was very much alive."

Relief coursed through Miles. At least he wasn't going to have to stand trial for murder.

Charlie shrugged. "All right, that clears Miles." He jerked his chin. "Sorry about that, but we have to consider everything."

Miles nodded, his jaw tight. "The door wasn't locked when I got here, so either Wally forgot or the killer got in before

Wally relocked it."

"If I was the killer, I'd have come in the back door." Bat pointed his walking stick to the back of the store. "Carr, you and Spooner go check it out. We'll get the undertaker in here."

Miles and Jonas filed into the narrow hallway that led to the back door. When they were out of earshot of Bat and the marshal, Miles whispered, "Thanks for backing me up."

Jonas nodded. "Good thing I saw him at the door as I ran by or you might be in a real fix." He opened the back door and studied the lock. "No sign of trouble here, but we don't know for sure if it was locked at the time of the killing."

"And I sent Addie through here when the crowd came boiling in the front. She took a photograph of Wally for us, and she's gone to develop it. We should ask her if the door was locked when she tried to get out."

They returned to the store in time to see Wally being covered with a sheet. The undertaker, a rosy-cheeked man who looked more like a fairy-tale gnome than a mortician, lifted the head and shoulders, while another man lifted the legs.

Bat checked his watch again. "Charlie and I have talked it over." He smoothed his moustache with his thumb and forefinger. "Since you are technically being seconded to the city marshal's office for the cattle season, we don't see any reason why you, Miles, shouldn't be in charge of the investigation. We'll be hauling those prisoners over to Wichita and waiting to testify. No telling how long that will take. That leaves you to find Wally's killer."

Miles blinked. "Me?"

The serious light in Bat's eyes compelled Miles, and he couldn't look away. "Tomorrow morning, the papers will be full of how we failed to protect Wally Price. It will be all over town that you were the deputy tasked with seeing him safely to the bank. I think you should be the man to bring the killer in. Take Spooner with you. Until this man is caught, you have no other duties, the pair of you. Use whatever means necessary within the law, and don't be afraid to interpret the law pretty broadly if need be. If you don't bring in the killer yourself, Miles, you'll never have the respect of this town or the cowboys who ride in here. You might as well hang up your badge and get out of Dodge."

Miles swallowed, the weight of responsibility, the weight of his whole future as a lawman now resting on tracking down a killer and bringing him to justice. The rightness of Bat's words rang true. If he couldn't do this, if he couldn't find the murderer, he'd never be able to walk down Front Street with his head up again.

Chapter 12

"Any idea where we should start?" Jonas spoke above the rattle of wagons and music and laughter as he and Miles stepped out of the store. He took a deep breath, trying to ease the tension in his shoulders. How was he going to tell Fran about Wally? She'd be crushed.

"Undertaker's first, I suppose. Then ask around if anyone saw anything."

"The town's chock-full of strangers, even more than usual, what with it being the Fourth and all."

Miles dragged his hand down his face, leaving streaks in the soot. His clothes smelled of smoke and horses, and red rimmed his eyes.

"I think we should take a good hard look at Vin Rutter." Jonas spat the name. Seeing Rutter fawning over Fran and her lapping it up made Jonas's stomach roil.

"Vin Rutter?" Miles stopped, and Jonas collided with him.

Revelers flowed around them, all heading in the opposite direction, toward the prairie on the west side of town where the fireworks display was set to begin around ten o'clock. Riders on horseback and wagons and buggies clogged the street.

Nightfall had brought about a whole new wave of celebrants, and things were livening up.

Jonas nodded. "He's a fellow who hit town a couple of weeks ago. Been hanging around the mercantile, bothering Fran some." Though Jonas tried to quash his jealousy, it still writhed like a ball of rattlesnakes in his chest. "She let it slip once that he had asked how much money the place made. He's been in that store half a dozen times or more, but he never buys anything. He was at the dance for a while, but he left before I did."

Miles braced his hands on a hitching rail. The light from the Alamo Saloon fell across his face. Lines creased his forehead, and the tightness around his eyes spoke of the stress he was under. A muscle worked in his jaw. His chest swelled as he took a deep breath. "It's as good a place to start as any. We'll see if we can track him down after we talk to the undertaker."

Mr. Givens met them on the front porch of his mortuary establishment, wiping his hands on a towel. His eyes shone bright as new pennies behind his round glasses, and his cheeks were rosier than ever. "Come in, come in."

Jonas let Miles take the lead, and they threaded their way through a front room full of coffins. A spidery-legged chill ran across Jonas's chest. He'd never been too comfortable with the trappings of death, and standing in a room full of caskets did nothing to put him at ease.

"I've just started the laying-out process, deputies. Doc Meyer is with him now." Givens entered a back room, and they followed into the brightly lit space. On a table in the center,

Wally Price lay, half-covered by a sheet.

Miles leaned against a counter and crossed his arms. "Anything you can tell us, Doc?"

Jonas dug in his pocket for his pencil and notebook, licked the lead point, and prepared to jot down relevant details.

Dr. Meyer bent over the body. "Probably nothing you don't already know. He died as a result of a blow to the head. I don't see any signs that he put up a fight. No bruises or split knuckles. At a guess, I'd say his attacker surprised him." He pulled out a pipe and tamped it full of tobacco.

Jonas blinked at the clouds of smoke soon wreathing Doc's head. "Ambush?"

"Possibly. Either that or he knew his attacker and had no fear of turning his back." Doc shrugged and tossed a spent match onto a tray. "But that isn't saying much, since Wally knew pretty much everyone in town, and he was a trusting soul. The most I can say is that his attacker was tall. At least taller than Wally, and he's right-handed."

Jonas wrote down the doctor's words. "How can you tell?"

Using the stem of his pipe, he pointed to the wound. "The fracture is above the curve of the back of the skull and it's on the right side of the head." He turned the undertaker around. "If this is Wally, and I'm the killer. . ." He lifted his right hand and made a chopping motion from above.

Miles nodded. "Thanks, Doc. If you find anything else, let us know."

They stepped out onto the street together. Jonas tucked his notebook away, grateful to be out of there. His mind returned to the subject that had occupied him for the past couple of weeks. "Rutter's tall, and I bet he's right-handed."

A cowboy galloped past whooping, scattering people before disappearing up the street. Music spilled out of the saloons and dance halls, and pedestrians clustered on the sidewalks.

Miles rested his hand on his gun and surveyed the street. "So are more than half the men in this town. And you're making an assumption. The killer doesn't have to be a man. It could've just as easily been a woman. Wally wasn't very tall, and he wouldn't have feared turning his back on a woman."

Jonas stepped close to allow a couple to pass by on the boardwalk. "Call it a gut feeling. There's something not right about Rutter. He's too smooth." He scowled. "Fran said he was in acquisitions for the railroad, whatever that means, but I've never seen him at the depot or in the railroad office upstairs at the bank."

Miles turned troubled eyes his way. "Are you sure this isn't just jealousy because Fran seems to prefer someone else? It's a far cry from poaching a fellow's girl—even lying to a girl about your job in order to impress her—to robbing a store and killing a shopkeeper."

Though Jonas knew Miles spoke the truth, he stubbornly clung to his belief. "There's something there that I don't trust, and it has nothing to do with Fran. That man is up to something shady, and I aim to find out what it is. He's been nosing around the store, and Fran might've been the excuse he needed to scout the place before robbing it."

"Okay. It won't hurt to track him down, I guess."

Familiarity with Vin's proclivities led Miles to begin the search south of the deadline in the red light district. A couple of discreet inquiries and a few dollars to a working girl, and he had the information he needed. Fortunately, people tended to remember Vin with his pale eyes and fancy clothes.

Miles's skin itched. He hadn't told Jonas that he knew Rutter, that Jonas's instincts were telling him the truth that Vin was hatching some sort of plan that boded ill. And the longer Miles withheld that information from his friend, the more he encroached on having to tell an outright lie.

And Jonas's motives bothered him. Pursuing a suspect he had a personal grudge against blurred his objectivity. . .though Miles was in no position to judge. He didn't want Vin convicted of murder if he was innocent, but he wouldn't mind finding a legitimate reason to throw Vin behind bars or run him out of town and away from both Addie and Fran. With Vin gone, maybe he could squash the guilt gnawing at him for hiding the truth.

Miles and Jonas entered a narrow, dark, smoke-filled saloon. No piano music, singers, or performers of any kind. This establishment was for serious drinking and gambling. Two steps into the place and Miles longed for fresh air. Stale beer and cigar fumes assaulted him.

A doxy sidled up to him with pouty lips, and her cheap toilet water added to the miasma. "Buy me a drink, cowboy?" Her husky voice slurred, and she put her hand on his arm.

Miles motioned for Jonas to stay by the door and keep watch. "I think you've had enough."

"If I'm still standing, honey, I ain't had enough." She gave his forearm a squeeze, leaned in, and whispered a coarse suggestion.

"Not interested, ma'am." Grimacing, he removed her hand from his arm and walked to the bar.

A cadaverously thin man wiped glasses with a dirty towel. "What'll it be?" He didn't bother looking at Miles.

"Information."

The man's head swiveled, and his focus glanced off Miles before returning to the glass in his hand. "We don't deal in that here. Beer and whiskey we got. Information you'll have to find elsewhere."

"I'm just looking for a fellow. Goes by the name of Vin Rutter. Tall, pale, talks with a Southern accent."

"Askin' after a man in these parts of town ain't exactly healthy. Almost as unhealthy as answering those kinds of questions."

Miles eased back his lapel so the edge of his badge showed. He studied the bartender. "When was the last time you had your liquor license reviewed by the city council? I hear the city's coffers are getting kinda bare. Might be time for some more raids so they can gather in some fines to pay for running the town."

The towel and glass slowly descended to the stained and gouged bar top. "There ain't no call to play rough."

"Then talk straight. Have you seen him?" Miles inclined his head to where Jonas stood by the door with his hand on his six-gun. "My friend's getting tired of waiting."

The bartender leaned close, and for the first time in the dim lighting, Miles got a look at his eyes. One brown and one green. Disconcerting. "He's in the back room playing poker." The bartender jerked his thumb, and the woman who had approached Miles when he came in sidled over. He tried to ignore her bare arms and low-cut dress.

"Rosabelle, take this gentleman to the back room."

Her eyebrows lifted. "He don't look like no high roller to me."

"Do as I say, woman," the bartender growled, and Rosabelle scowled right back, but she did as she was told, leading Miles past several closed doors to a cramped room near the back.

Miles glanced back down the hall at Jonas and jerked his head. Jonas disappeared out the front door. He'd cover the back to make sure Vin didn't bolt out that way.

Rosabelle didn't bother to knock, just shoved the door open and stepped aside to let him enter.

Six men sat around a green felt table, cards, cash, and chips covering the surface. On a low settee in the corner, a woman sprawled, snoring softly.

Vin sat on the far side of the table, eyes gleaming over his cards. He lifted his glass and tossed back the contents, then froze, sighting Miles.

Heads turned. Miles recognized some of the other gamblers. "Evening, gentlemen."

"This is a private room." A burly teamster lifted his chin, jutting his wild beard over his cards.

"Sorry to interrupt. Just need a word with one of your opponents." Miles stared at Vin, whose mouth had thinned to the point his lips disappeared.

"I've waited too long for a chair to open up at this game. I have no intention of leaving it, especially not when I'm on such a hot streak." Vin fanned his cards then picked up some chips. "I call."

The bearded man scowled, stared at his cards, and threw them facedown on the felt. "Take it."

Vin's long, pale fingers raked in the pile of bills and coins and separated them with lightning-quick dexterity.

"Deal him out." Miles glared at the dealer, a bare-armed girl with sallow skin and stringy hair. She regarded him soberly and skipped Vin as she tossed out the pasteboards.

Vin's jaw tightened, and he blinked slowly.

Miles stood his ground. "Up to you, Rutter. Either you come with me, or I have to shut the whole game down and run you all down to the jail."

"Here, what for?" The teamster bristled.

"I'll think of something."

The gamblers all scowled at Vin. Tension mounted until all at once Vin relaxed.

"Thank you, gentlemen, for a most profitable evening." He shoved his chips toward the dealer who counted them up and exchanged them for cash. Carefully folding the money, Vin inserted it into a gold clip and pushed the bundle deep into his trouser pocket. "Let's take our discussion outside, shall we?"

Miles stepped aside to allow Vin to precede him and accidently kicked the leg of the woman on the settee. An apology flew to his lips, but the woman didn't even stir. Though she snored, dead to the world, her eyes were partially open, rolled back a bit in her head. Disgust and pity tangled in his belly. Drugs or drink or both.

Vin led him out the back door and stopped when he spotted Jonas waiting in the alley. "A pincer movement." He leaned against the wall, cool and bored. "To what do I owe the pleasure, gentlemen?" He glanced at Jonas. "Surely this isn't about Fran?"

Was his cool exterior a front to hide the fact that he'd bashed Wally Price over the head and robbed him, or was he nonchalant because he had nothing to fear from answering their questions? Miles couldn't tell.

"It's nothing to do with Fran, but it is to do with you hanging around the store asking questions." Jonas stepped closer.

The alley was dark, and Miles glanced up and down the narrow passageway. "Why don't we continue this conversation up at the jail?"

"The jail?" Vin straightened. "What is this about?" His drawl diminished.

Jonas shoved Vin toward the front of the building. "At least let's get out of the dark here so I can see your face. Get moving."

Light from the saloon's front window bathed the porch, and Miles positioned Vin so he could see his face. Vin's fishy, pale eyes locked onto Miles. "What is this about?" he asked again.

"Where were you tonight between six and seven?"

"Why?"

"Just tell me."

"Am I under arrest?"

"Not yet." Miles examined Vin's clothes as best he could for any telltale evidence that he'd killed Wally. "A shopkeeper got murdered tonight. Mr. Price from the mercantile. You've been seen hanging around there, and tonight I find you in a high-stakes poker game. It's well known around town that particular game has a steep buy-in. Where'd the money come from, and where were you at six tonight?"

"Well, I can assure you I wasn't murdering Price or anyone else. There are more ways of acquiring stake money than robbing someone."

Though, in Miles's experience, it was a favorite method of members of the Walker Gang. He set his jaw. "If you don't have an alibi, I'm going to have to run you in. You were seen leaving the town dance not long before the murder, so where did you go?"

Vin studied his fingernails, completely relaxed. A knowing smile dragged at his lips, and his eyelids lowered to half-mast. "I came straight here. At six o'clock, I was sitting down to the first hand of the night." He indicated the saloon. "I had to wait two weeks for a chair to open up in that game." He smirked at Jonas. "The opportunity came at a most delicate moment. I do hope Fran wasn't too upset when I left her."

"Anyone else see you here?" Jonas never took his eyes off Vin. He had a stillness about him that some might be foolish enough to interpret as indifference, but Miles recognized it as steel-strong control, keeping a tight lid on his temper.

"Everyone at the poker game, I expect."

Miles wanted to bash the smug look off Rutter's face. "You haven't explained how you came by the money to get into the game."

A gleam shot into Vin's eyes. "As I told you, there are plenty of ways to get cash in this town. It's all in knowing where to look."

Dread slithered through Miles. The knowing gleam in Rutter's eyes set up a gnawing worry. "We're going to have to verify your alibi."

Vin shrugged. "Go ahead. Everyone in there will vouch for me. As for the money, I parlayed a small stake into a big one playing poker at the Alhambra today. You can check with the bartender there. I bought a round of drinks for the house when I cashed out for the day."

Miles glanced at Jonas. Vin's alibi for the time of the murder was solid.

"If that's all, gentlemen, I believe I'll be going. I have a few things yet to accomplish tonight."

Jonas's hands fisted until Miles thought he might hear the knuckles crack. "Rutter, we're going to track your every move. And I'm warning you, stay away from Fran Seaton."

Stepping just in front of Jonas, Miles rested his hand on his gun. "You're free to go for now. Don't make any plans to leave town just yet."

"No worries there, my dear Miles. I haven't finished what

I came to do." He sketched a wave and sauntered away toward Front Street.

Jonas stared after him. "You two sound as if you know each other."

Miles's chest tightened. "We've crossed trails before." He tried to refocus the attention on the investigation. "Let's head back into the saloon and check his alibi. After that, you can go meet Addie and walk her over to the jail. I'll meet you there after I check on Vin's story about hitting it lucky at the Alhambra this afternoon."

Addie wiped her hands on her apron and studied the still wet print in the light of the red lantern. Even with rosy illumination and the unfortunate subject matter, she knew the picture was flawless. Every board in the floor, every wrinkle in the clothes, every letter on the canned good labels stood out in sharp detail.

Careful not to bang into anything in the crowded space, she rolled her head and shook her arms, forcing herself to relax. Developing photographs was a precise and tedious business, as the knot between her shoulder blades and the band of tension around her forehead testified. Though she wanted to snatch the picture off the drying line and race with it to the sheriff's office, she had to wait until it was dry enough to move without damaging it.

She checked her timepiece, holding it up to the glow of the lantern. Nearly ten. She grimaced. Darkroom work always took longer than she wanted.

Arranging jars and draining solutions through filters and funnels, she tidied her workspace. Chemicals were unforgiving and demanded to be cared for correctly, something that Addie had no trouble with, being neat by nature. Touching her finger to the edge of the print, she judged it not quite ready.

With a sigh, she swept aside the heavy curtain and opened the door to the studio. The light from the studio lamps dazzled her for a moment after the low, red light of the darkroom. She blinked, feeling like a burrowing owl.

"I thought you were never going to come out of there."

She jerked.

Vin Rutter stepped from the front room into the studio.

Her heart lodged in her throat then dropped to stampede around her chest. "What do you want?"

He produced a wicked little cheroot and a match. With a *scritch*, he struck the match against his boot sole. It flared to life, and he lifted it to the cigar, puffing and filling the air with acrid smoke. "That's hardly a gracious greeting."

Her mouth went dry as flash powder. "How did you get in here?" She was sure she had locked the front door.

He patted his pocket. "Oh I have plenty of talents. A simple lock like that didn't deter me for long." He came closer, crowding her between a plaster pedestal and the darkroom door. "It's good to see you again, Addie. You're as lovely as ever." His cold, pale eyes raked over her face and form. "I've been asking around town about you."

"I can't imagine why. And put that cigar out. It's a hazard in here, and it smells terrible."

He stared at the glowing end of the cheroot. "I can remember a time when you didn't complain about the smell of a good cigar. Someone we both knew and loved had a fondness for them."

"I don't wish to discuss anything from that time in my life. Anyway, that cheroot isn't even remotely a good cigar." She wrinkled her nose and waved her hand in front of her face.

"Ah, I see you've gained some spirit since last we met. I always thought there was more lurking behind those guileless eyes than you let on."

"Mr. Rutter, if that is your real name, I want you to leave. I can't imagine why you sought me out, but we have nothing to discuss." She lifted her chin, praying he would go. If anyone saw them together, it could open the door to a lot of awkward questions that would eventually reveal all her secrets. Then she'd be forced out of town again, and she couldn't face that.

He held up his hands, palms outward, and spoke around the cigar clamped in the corner of his mouth. "Addie, is that any way to treat Cliff's best friend?"

"Don't talk about him." A bitter shudder rippled through her, and she gripped the edge of the pedestal.

"Is he still so dear to you that you can't bear the sound of his name?" A chilled laugh came from his thin lips. "Or is it another reason that makes his memory painful? You've certainly kept your past association with him a secret here in Dodge. I haven't heard so much as a whisper, not even from that chatty friend of yours at the mercantile. Is your reticence caused by shame, or are you truly mourning the loss of your lover?"

"We were never lovers." The idea made her skin crawl. "If he indicated otherwise, you can add it to his long list of lies."

Vin rose from the settee and circled the studio, touching drapes and running his hand over the back of a wicker chair. "You've done quite well for yourself here. No one would suspect you were practically run out of Abilene without a penny to your name. I really am impressed. It must've taken quite a lot of money to get started again. And without the help of your uncle now, too. You must be lonely." He tilted his head and smiled, trying to coax a response from her.

The calculating look in his lizard-eyes put her nerves on alert. "Vin, I have no desire to relive any of that, especially not with you. Cliff Walker robbed me of everything. I lost my home, my business, and my only family member. I've rebuilt here, and I want my new life to be free of reminders of the past. That includes you. I don't know why you came to Dodge, and I don't know why you're still hanging around, but hear me clear. I want nothing to do with you or anyone else even remotely related to Cliff. Leave me alone." She moved toward the front room.

He followed her to the reception area and leaned against the doorjamb. Crossing his arms, he raised his hand to adjust the cigar and blew a cloud of foul smoke toward the ceiling. "He really did love you, you know, whatever his other faults."

"I asked you to put that nasty thing out." She jerked up the heavy, canvas window shade.

"You were all he talked about when we were on the road."

"When you were out robbing banks and trains and

stagecoaches, you mean." Addie peered out the window. The street had cleared considerably while she'd been in the darkroom. The fireworks were scheduled to begin soon, and it seemed most folks were already assembled at that end of town.

"Addie."

He spoke from so close behind her, she jumped. An army of ants ran through her veins. She moved to the other window and snapped the shade up to allow lamplight to spill into the street. "Vin, leave me alone. You and your ilk have done enough harm to me and mine."

"Perhaps I'd like to make amends. Smoke the peace pipe, as it were."

She whirled and shoved him backward. "I don't smoke."

He grabbed her wrists and hauled her close, breathing cigar fumes across her skin. His eyes bored into hers, and his grip stung. "Enough. I'm tired of sparring with you. I had intended to go slowly, tread softly, but something happened tonight to let me know I might need to cut my time here in Dodge City short. So the kid gloves come off. I want to know where it is."

"I don't know what you're talking about." *Though she knew very well. It was the only reason he'd be sniffing around.*

"Don't play games with me. I want that money."

"I don't have it." She gritted her teeth and strained away from him. He smelled of smoke and liquor and cheap perfume.

"Then where is it?" The words hissed from his slash of a mouth like steam.

"I never had it. I don't know where it is, and even if I did, you would be the last person I'd tell." She tried to wrench her arms from his cold, hard grasp, but his strength made a mockery of her attempts.

"You must have it. I've searched everywhere else, all our hideouts, all the places we stayed after the last robbery. He was devoted to you. You played a pretty part at the trial, pretending to know nothing of his real identity, all dewy-eyed, protesting your innocence. It was a beautiful performance. But you can't fool me. I know you have that cash, and I'm not leaving Dodge until I get it." He loomed over her.

Since the trial and Cliff's execution, she'd had nightmares about someone coming after her, seeking the treasure she didn't have. "Vin, I don't know where it is." The quiver in her voice gouged her soul. Hadn't she vowed never again to be the victim of a low-minded man, and here she was, cowering? She straightened her spine and swallowed. He might be stronger of body, but she would be stronger in mind and spirit. She would not beg.

The glass in the door rattled, and the knob twisted. Vin's hands dropped away, and he stepped back as the door swung open.

Addie had never been so glad to see anyone in her life. It was all she could do not to launch herself into the arms of Jonas Spooner.

"Any trouble here?" His sandy eyebrows lowered, and his eyes went stony. "Addie, are you all right? I saw the shades were up and figured you were waiting for someone to walk you out."

"Thank you, Jonas. I'm just about ready to go." She rubbed her stinging wrists. "Mr. Rutter was just leaving."

The deputy stepped farther into the room, leaving space for Vin to get by. The two men eyed one another until Vin shrugged, readjusted his cheroot, and headed for the door.

As he passed Addie, he whispered, "I'll be back."

Chapter 13

Addie sagged into an armchair in her waiting room, swallowing hard and trying to calm her racing heart.

Jonas closed the door, twisted the lock, and came to squat beside her. "What's going on, Addie? Was he causing you trouble?"

The urge to spill the entire story pressed against her throat, but the price tag of unburdening was too high. If Jonas knew, he would despise her, and it would only be a matter of time until he told Fran. . .and Miles. Her mind quailed at the thought. "No, no trouble."

His eyes flicked to her reddened arms. "Addie, you can trust me, you know."

She stood and untied her apron. "I know, Jonas. You're a good friend. If I ever have a problem you can help me with, I'll come running. I promise. Can you walk me down to the jail? The photograph I took should be dry now."

Jonas stood, opened his mouth to say something, but thankfully closed it, not pressing the issue.

She hurried to the darkroom, tucked the photograph into her camera case, and blew out the lamps. Jonas waited while she lowered the window blinds.

"You should lock that door while you're in there working alone at night." Jonas tested the knob.

She slipped the key into her pocket and frowned. The lock had proven no obstacle to Vin. She would need to see about bolstering her defenses with a sturdier model, though she couldn't really spare the money.

"The picture turned out all right?" Jonas steered her down one set of steps, across a side street, and up onto the next stretch of boardwalk.

"Yes. Poor Wally." She kept her hand on her camera case. "I can't imagine anyone killing him. He was such a nice man."

"Money's a powerful motivator. The store did a great business earlier today. There are more than a few men in town who would kill for that kind of money, and they wouldn't care if Wally was a nice man or not."

They approached the end of the block, the same end where Price and Greeley's Mercantile sat. Lamplight shone through the windows. "The marshal posted a couple of deputies. With Wally dead and Hap out of town, the place is defenseless. Looters would ransack the place like buzzards on a carcass."

As they drew abreast of the opening, Hap Greeley himself stumbled out, colliding with Addie and nearly knocking her off her feet.

She yelped and grappled with her camera case, clinging to Jonas's arm to regain her balance. "Mr. Greeley."

He raised trembling hands to his face, shoving his glasses up and wiping his eyes. His shoulders shook, and he gulped.

Blinking, he seemed to notice them for the first time.

"It's terrible. Poor Wally." Hap dragged out his red handkerchief and rubbed his bulbous nose.

Addie put her hand on his arm. "I'm so sorry."

Hap nodded and shoved his glasses up to swipe his eyes. "I just got back into town and heard the news. Couldn't imagine why the store was lit up at this hour." He jerked his thumb toward the doorway where two city policemen stood. "I just can't believe it. It's like a bad dream. The store is such a mess."

"Sorry about the ruckus in there. Folks sort of stampeded through the place when they heard about the killing. We got them out as soon as we could, but not before they trampled stuff pretty good." Jonas shook his head. "Did you see anything in there that would tell us who did this?"

Quivering, his eyes still moist, Hap dropped onto the bench beneath the window. He cradled his head in his hands. "Poor, poor Wally."

Addie looked at Jonas, who seemed at a loss how to deal with the devastated man. She blew out a breath and joined Hap on the bench. "Hap, we're going to find out who did this. In fact, Jonas and I were just on our way to the jail to take some evidence in."

Hap straightened, his eyes locking onto hers. "Evidence?"

She smiled encouragingly and patted her camera case. "Yes. I don't know if it will make any difference, but I did photograph the crime scene. I just developed the picture, and we're taking it to the sheriff. I hope it helps find who did this to Mr. Price."

The mention of his former partner's name sent him into

another bout of the shakes. "Even if you do find the killer, it won't bring Wally back. He wasn't just my cousin. He was my best friend."

Jonas shifted his weight. "Hap, I know this is a hard time for you, but you have to pull yourself together. Come down to the jail with us. I know Miles and Bat will want to ask you some questions."

"Questions?" He scrubbed his nose with the hankie again. "But I wasn't even in town today. I don't know who did this. If I did, I'd shoot him myself." His big hands fisted around the red cloth, and his ashen cheeks bloomed with righteous color.

Jonas took his elbow and got him to his feet. "You never know. Anything you can tell us might be helpful, and it's better than sitting here wallowing."

Hap rolled these words around for a minute. "You're right. If I can do anything to help, I will." He rumbled along behind them toward the jail, sniffling and occasionally muttering, "Poor, poor Wally."

Addie realized her sleeves were still rolled up and unrolled them, buttoning the long cuffs to hide the marks where Vin had squeezed her wrists. Though she had been waiting for him to make his move, she hadn't expected him to accost her so forcefully. Cliff had never laid a hand on her, never given her any indication of his violent side. But Vin Rutter was apparently a cat of a different color. Though he wore the trappings of civilization with his nice suit and cultured voice, pure meanness lurked close to the surface.

What would it take to convince him she didn't have the

stolen money? Railroad detectives had searched her home in Abilene and gone over every inch of the studio looking for the cash, more than thirty thousand dollars in bills and gold coins. Though she and Uncle Carl had protested, they were helpless to stop the search. By the time the jury reached a verdict, their future in Abilene was over.

Addie shook her head. That wouldn't happen here. She couldn't let it. Though Dodge was a wide open, volatile town, she loved it and wanted to stay. She'd made a dear friend in Fran, and she was succeeding at her business, fulfilling her dream of being a good photographer. And there was Miles to consider. Her feelings for him had grown in spite of her efforts to quell them, to be reasonable. She wanted her life and future to be in Dodge City. Vin had no part in that, and she refused to let him destroy her dreams. Somehow, she would convince him she didn't have the money, and he would leave town.

They approached the jail shared by the city and county law officers. The upstairs of the two-story building was dark, but the door stood open on the first floor. Behind them, the first boom and explosion of light from the fireworks blazed across the sky.

At the first explosion of fireworks, Miles looked up from his notes. "Finally getting started. I have a feeling nobody in town is going to get much sleep tonight." A faint glow flickered across the window as the firework faded. Another blast soon followed. "I heard they had enough rockets to last for more than an hour."

Letting his feet slide off the corner of the desk, Bat straightened in his chair and yawned. "That's just the ones the volunteer fire department is lighting. There will be plenty of others throughout the night. How long did Miss Reid think she would be?"

Miles shrugged, feigning nonchalance, though his mind had returned to her again and again while he worked on writing down everything he could think of regarding the investigation so far. "She said she would hurry."

"A fine woman, Addie Reid. A man could go farther and fare worse." Bat tugged the corner of his moustache. "Yes sir, a smart man wouldn't let much grass grow under his feet where Addie was concerned. Some young jackanapes might ride up the trail and throw his loop at her."

Prickly warmth hitched its way over Miles's chest. "You thinking of courting Addie?" He wouldn't stand a chance against someone as handsome and fascinating as Bat Masterson. *Whoa there, pard, where did that come from?*

"Me?" Bat's eyes twinkled. "I was just making a general observation, not a declaration of intent." A smile twitched his moustache, and Miles winced, realizing he'd risen to the bait. "I was just thinking what a nice couple you two would make."

Miles's muscles relaxed by increments—muscles he didn't know he'd tensed. Shaking his head, he returned to his notes. He was going to have to confront his feelings about Addie sooner or later, but for now, he needed to focus on finding Wally's killer. After that he'd deal with Vin and telling Addie about his relationship with Cliff. If, after all that, she still wanted to be with him—and he hardly dared hope she would—then he'd—

The door opened, dragging him from his thoughts, and Addie entered the jail followed by Jonas and Hap Greeley. Miles shot to his feet a fraction before Bat. He reached up to loosen his tight collar only to find the top buttons weren't even closed.

She lifted the camera case strap over her head and shoulder, freeing a few wisps of hair from the knot at her neck. They drifted down and teased her cheeks, and he had to check himself to keep from reaching out to tuck a strand or two behind her ear.

Her slate eyes locked with his, and his tongue quit working. All he could think about was how beautiful she was to him, how courageous and talented, and how much he wanted to protect her from Vin. How much he wanted her to be innocent in all of this.

Jonas cleared his throat, and the sound broke the spell and allowed Miles to look away. His friend dragged a chair from beside the door. "Here you go, Addie. Do you want some coffee?"

"No, thank you."

Why hadn't he thought of that? While Jonas took care of her, Miles stood there like some plaster pillar. He shoved aside a stack of papers and perched on the corner of the desk as she unbuckled the case.

"I've got the picture in here." She lifted a four-by-six-inch print from a compartment at the bottom of the box. Must be where she kept the extra plates for the camera.

He took the photograph from her and passed it first to Bat, though he itched to snatch it back and study it for clues. "Thank you. I'm sorry you had to see such a terrible thing."

"I only hope it helps catch the killer."

Hap took a staggering breath. "Poor Wally."

Jonas stepped close to Miles. "He's pretty worked up. Guess I might be, too, coming home to news like this. I don't know how much help he'll be, rattled as he is."

Miles nodded. Known for his excess of emotion, Hap wouldn't be any different in grieving his cousin. "Take notes for me, will you?"

Jonas nodded and dug in the desk drawer. He came up with several sheets of torn paper, remnants of the Wanted posters. Miles's palms grew damp. *Please, God, don't let him use one with Cliff's name or face on it.*

Bat looked up from the photograph. "This is excellent, Miss Reid. Of course, knowing your work as I do, I expected nothing less." He smiled at her, and Miles quelled a thrust of jealousy. According to the ladies about town, Bat was considered quite handsome and a prime catch. He glanced at Addie to see what effect the sheriff's blue eyes and charming manner might be having.

Addie merely nodded. "I got it here as quickly as I could."

"A shame we weren't able to keep people out of the store until we had time to look things over more thoroughly." He smoothed his moustache. "Pearson's ears are probably still burning from the dressing-down I gave him." He handed the picture to Miles. "I'd best head toward the fireworks. I promised the mayor I'd stay handy in case there was trouble down there."

"Don't you want to stay and question Hap?"

Bat shook his head. "I believe in hiring capable men. You're in charge of the investigation." He tipped his hat to Addie. "Miss Reid, it's been a pleasure."

Miles blinked at this vote of confidence and stared after Bat's back as he stepped out of the jail. The responsibility pressed against his chest, but a thrust of pride battled for space there, too. "Addie, I'm sorry to bore you with all this, but I can't spare anyone to see you home just yet. If you can wait until I'm done here with Hap, I'll see you safely to your boardinghouse."

She nodded. "I'd like to stay, especially if you have any other questions about the photograph."

Jonas handed her the sheets of paper and the pencil. "How 'bout you take notes for me then. Miles always makes me write everything down, but my penmanship isn't much better than his."

Addie took the implements, cleared a space on the desk by setting a stack of papers on the floor, and poised the pencil over the sheet of paper.

Shifting his attention, Miles tried to clear his mind of everything except asking the right questions. "Hap, you feel up to answering a few things?"

The storekeeper nodded. "I'll do whatever I can, but like I told Deputy Spooner, I was out of town since yesterday, so I don't know how much help I'll be."

"I understand. Have you noticed anyone hanging around the store? Anyone you didn't know?"

Hap pinched the bridge of his nose. "I'm in and out of there all day. Lots of folks come through the store, some are buyers and some are lookers." He glanced at Jonas and shrugged. "A lot of them come in to see Fran. Our business has really grown since we hired her."

Jonas nodded, grimacing.

"Do you recognize the name Vin Rutter?"

Addie jerked, her hand coming up to cover her lips. It stood to reason, with her history with Cliff, she might know Vin's name and might even have met him. Maybe having her here wasn't such a good idea. Though what harm could she do to Miles's investigation? Vin already knew Miles suspected him in the crime.

Hap's chair creaked as he shifted his weight. "I don't know that name. Who is he?"

"Tall, lean fellow with really pale eyes. He's been hanging around the store asking questions. Jonas here overheard him asking Fran about how much money the store made." Low thuds came from outside, the fireworks show punctuating the discussion.

Hap's watery eyes shone. "He must be the man then, the one who done in Wally." He surged to his feet. "You'll arrest him, right? Is he still in town? Why aren't you chasing him? Is there a posse forming? I want to ride with them."

"Easy, Hap. We're looking into it. He's been questioned, and he has an alibi for the time of the murder." The poker players had corroborated Vin's claim that at the time of the murder Vin was flashing a roll of cash that would choke a cow.

Jonas tapped Miles's shoulder. "What'd they say down at the Alhambra?"

Rubbing the edge of his fist against his thigh, Miles rolled his eyes. "Just what Vin told us. He hit a hot streak at poker and raked in a bundle. Stood a round of drinks for the whole place and left. That was about three o'clock."

"And we already know he was at the town dance for a while." Disgust laced Jonas's words. He slammed his fist into his hand. "I wish it had been him."

"We can't arrest him just because we don't like him. His alibi is solid."

Hap stood and paced the small space between the desk and the door. His movements were jerky and sharp, so unlike his usual genial self, and with each ricochet from the fireworks, he flinched. "We were best friends, me and Wally. Lifelong friends. And where was I when he needed me most? Over at the fort chewing the fat with the quartermaster." He wrung his hands. "If I was any kind of a partner, I would've stayed to help out on our busiest day."

"Why didn't you?" Jonas voiced the question Miles had been going to ask.

A sheepish frown tugged down Hap's face. "I was peeved. Wally and I had a fight." He shrugged and shuffled again between the door and the desk. "I know, that's nothing new. We've always fought, from the time we was kids. I was sore at him for something. I can't even remember what now." He stopped and blinked hard. "I'll never forgive myself. My best friend gets murdered, and my last words to him were said in anger."

A huge sigh lifted his chest, and he fought for composure, his cheeks and throat quivering. When he mastered himself, he continued. "I figured I'd punish Wally for the fight by leaving him high and dry on the Fourth. I knew the place would be swamped with customers, and I guess I thought he might be more appreciative of the work I do around there if he got a chance to miss me when things were busy."

Miles glanced at the picture beside him on the desk. Hap was so worked up at the thought of Wally dead, he wondered if it was wise to show the poor man the photograph. "Sit down, Hap." Miles stalled for time by going to the water bucket. He brought a dripping ladleful.

Hap sank onto the chair, grabbed the dipper, and slurped, spilling water down his shirtfront and swiping at his lips with the back of his sleeve. "Thanks."

"I have something I want you to look at. You need to tell me if you see anything that might be out of place, anything that might help us identify who did this to Wally." Miles picked up the photograph, glanced at it, and handed it to Hap.

He sucked in a huge breath. His jaw dropped open, and his Adam's apple bobbed. "Who would do such a thing?" he whispered. His hands shook so hard, Miles thought he might drop the photograph.

"Take your time. Look it over carefully."

"He's seen the store," Jonas said. "That's where he was when Addie and I came by on our way here. There are still two city policemen down there to stop any looters or busybodies."

"Everything is such a mess. This never should've happened."

The big man's shoulders shook, and he lurched out of his chair again, as if his body couldn't sit still with all the sorrow pushing at him.

Guilt that he hadn't been there to protect Wally rose up as far as Miles's neck, and he swallowed it down. Bat had told him not to blame himself, but it was proving harder than he thought.

"I think that's enough." Addie rose and rounded the corner of the desk, brushing past Miles. She reached for the photograph. He gripped it, and she tugged again until, reluctantly, he let go. She passed it to Miles, and her look accused him for distressing Hap so much. "I'm so sorry, Hap." She patted his arm.

At her touch, he seemed to pull himself together. "I need to go. I need some fresh air."

Miles nodded. He couldn't think of anything else relevant to ask, and Hap was in no condition to think rationally anyway.

At the door, Hap turned around, a frown creasing his forehead. "I still don't understand how this happened. Wally had made arrangements for a deputy to walk him to the bank. How was it no peace officer showed up to look out for him? He was killed just after closing time, wasn't he?"

Miles gritted his teeth and forced himself to tell the truth. "Hap, I was the one supposed to get Wally to the bank safely, but there was a fire down at the livery. I told Wally to lock the door and wait for me to get back, but by the time we had the fire out and I made it back to the store, Wally was dead."

Hap's chest rose and fell, and his ham-sized hands drew into fists. "You? You let Wally get killed?" His eyes spread wide, and with a quickness belied by his bulk, he lunged.

Miles jerked his head backward, narrowly escaping a haymaker to the jaw. He scrambled off the corner of the desk, toppling stacks of paper and leaping away from the onrushing shopkeeper. "Hap, stop!"

Addie skittered out of the way, taking another sheaf of pages with her.

Jonas leapt around and encircled Hap with his arms. "Enough! Hap, calm down."

With Jonas's weight on his back and his arms squeezing so hard they shook, the bull rush slowed. Not until Hap's shoulders relaxed did Jonas loosen his grip.

Hap sank to his knees. He braced himself on his palms, gasping for air, great, choking sobs wrestling their way out of his throat. The Wanted posters, letters, and paperwork strewn across the floor crunched and rustled under his weight.

Miles's own chest rose and fell faster than he would like to admit. The speed behind the attack still had him rattled.

When Hap had control of himself once more, he pulled himself upright, digging for his handkerchief. "I'm sorry. I'm so sorry. I don't know what came over me." He struggled to his feet. "It's just so terrible. I—" Hap dove through the open doorway into the night.

Jonas tugged his jacket sleeves down, and Miles rubbed his palm across the back of his neck. "That is one rattled man."

Addie spread her hands. "Look at this place." Papers littered the floor, Hap's chair was overturned, and an inkwell had given up the fight all over the desktop.

"Great." Miles jammed his fingers through his hair. "I have to clean up this mess before Bat gets back. If he sees this, Pearson won't be the only deputy in his doghouse. It might not look too great, but it looks better stacked up than spilled all over the floor."

"I'll help." Addie set her camera case on a chair and bent to a stack of papers that had fanned all the way underneath the desk. "Where does all this stuff come from?"

Miles scooped up a handful of scrap paper and tossed it onto the ink puddle. He couldn't deny a thrust of satisfaction when India ink obscured half of Cliff Walker's picture on one of the scraps. Lifting the waste bucket, he crumpled a paper up to protect his fingers and swiped the drippy mess into the metal container. "This blotter will never be the same."

Jonas snorted. "Good thing it was there at all or you might find yourself sanding and refinishing the desktop." He edged past Addie, his arms full. "Bat never throws anything away. Newspapers, flyers, Wanted posters, circulars, advertisements. And he jots notes all the time. I told him he had a future as a writer if he ever gave up lawing."

They tidied the worst of it, but it couldn't really be called clean. Miles shoveled another sheaf of papers onto the corner of the desk. "What this place needs is a good fire."

Two city policemen came into the office for the night shift, freeing Miles and Jonas.

Jonas lifted Addie's camera case. "I think we've done enough. We can still take in the last of the fireworks if we hurry."

Miles gladly turned his back on the jail and followed Addie

and Jonas onto the porch. "I wonder where Hap got to. I've never seen a man cry like that. Men don't do that where I'm from. A man caught crying. . ." He shrugged. "He'd never live it down. He'd lose all respect."

A firework burst on the night sky, red and blue stars of color. They watched it together until it faded away. Miles offered Addie his arm.

Jonas fell into step on her other side. "Hap's an emotional man. I guess that's why he and Wally always fought so much. Hap is as likely to cry or yell as laugh. He wears his emotions where everyone can see them."

Addie settled her camera case on her hip and threaded her hand through Miles's arm. He tried to ignore the thrill her touch gave him. It might be foolish, but he clung to her innocence, needing it to be true as much as he wanted it to be true. "I suppose. Everybody's different, but all that emotion makes me uncomfortable."

Chapter 14

The smart thing would've been to ask to be taken home, but Addie was loath to miss a chance to be with Miles for a while longer.

Refusing to examine her reasoning, she strolled between the two deputies, eager to embrace at least a little of the holiday festivities that she'd missed by working all day. But by the time they reached the edge of town, the last firework had been lit and the crowds were dispersing. Scores of people came toward them, some to their homes and more toward the establishments waiting to help them celebrate further.

"Sorry, Addie, looks like we missed it." Miles guided her to the side of the road and out of the traffic.

"That's all right. It's been a very long day." She stifled a yawn.

Miles and Jonas watched the passersby, alert to trouble, lawmen even when they were supposed to be off duty.

Warmth spread through her, and a bit of pride, too. Miles was a good man, honorable and true. Perhaps, if she told him about her past, he would understand. It was only a matter of time before someone connected her with the trial of

Cliff Walker. Coming clean first would be better than being found out. And somewhere in town Vin Rutter lurked like a mountain lion, ready to pounce.

When the majority of the revelers had dispersed, they followed, walking up Front Street toward her studio and her boardinghouse beyond. They passed a saloon and the brightly lit Arden Palace, and as they walked in front of the drugstore, someone shouted.

"Addie!" She barely had time to brace herself before Fran launched herself into Addie's arms. "Isn't it terrible? Wally's been killed!"

Addie hugged Fran and patted her shoulder. "I know. I'm so sorry."

Fran's brothers stepped off the Arden porch, casting uneasy looks at one another. "Evening, Jonas, Miles." Linc Seaton shrugged and jerked his head toward Fran. "She's been crying pretty much since she got the news. We were just flipping a coin to see who got to take her home."

Fran snorted and dabbed her eyes. "Who *had* to take me home, you mean."

The brothers shared a guilty look. One of the twins slapped Jonas on the shoulder. "Now that you're here, you wouldn't mind walking her back to our place, would you?" A grin split his face.

Jonas nodded. "Be glad to."

The Seaton brothers scattered like quail.

Fran stared after them, her cheeks wet. "Like schoolboys let out early for summer vacation. Only too glad to be rid of me."

Jonas took her hand. "That's all right. I never mind seeing you home. You know that. Though I'm surprised. I thought you might be with someone else. Men were lining up to dance with you the last time I saw you."

Fran lowered her chin and studied her crumpled handkerchief.

Addie glanced from her to Jonas. Something had shifted there. Fran usually bristled like a hairbrush when Jonas was around, but tonight, she seemed shy and uncertain. Was she softening toward Jonas at last?

"My escort had to leave. Then I got the news about Wally, and I haven't been able to think of anything else." Fran dabbed her eyes again.

Jonas caught Addie staring at their linked fingers and shrugged. "We've declared a truce. We're friends, just like we used to be."

Miles's eyebrows rose. He appeared about to say something but must've thought better of it and closed his mouth.

Addie, too, chose to say nothing, but her thoughts swirled skeptically. Could two people be friends when one was so obviously in love with the other? Her heart went out to Jonas, and for a moment, she wanted to shake Fran. Everything a woman could want in a man was right in front of her, and she couldn't see it. Jonas's heart was hers for the taking, but she spurned it, hankering after a girlish, gossamer fantasy. Imagine settling for something as tepid as friendship when love—true, honest, glorious love—was within her grasp.

Two riders galloped up the street, scattering pedestrians

and whooping into the night air.

Miles took Addie's elbow. "Let's get moving. Things are getting rowdy."

They walked a block in silence. She couldn't blame Miles for being preoccupied, here at the outset of a murder investigation. At least she'd been able to do something to help him, taking that photograph. They'd have a record preserved for when he found the murderer and the case went to trial.

Thoughts of Wally brought Hap to mind. His and Wally's fights had been common knowledge around town, but Addie had been surprised to realize how close they were. Hap's emotions had been so raw her heart had gone out to him.

She remembered the bewilderment and shock when Uncle Carl died. The fear of facing life without him, of having to run a business all alone.

To hear Fran tell it, Hap didn't do a lot around the store, relying on Wally to take care of the details. Hap had been more interested in shooting the breeze, swapping stories and tall tales, making the customers feel welcome enough to come back over and over.

Miles guided her up the steps onto the boardwalk in front of the gunsmith's, and out of habit, Addie's eyes strayed to her own studio's front windows. The shades were drawn just as she had left them. Thankfully, her signal earlier that evening had worked. She didn't know how she would've gotten rid of Vin if Jonas hadn't come by. She would have to have a new lock installed tomorrow, or she wouldn't feel safe in her own place of business.

A patter of unease scampered across her skin. Something wasn't right. She blinked. A dark outline showed around the edge of the door.

"What is it?" Miles looked down at his arm where her grip had tightened.

"The studio. I think the door is open. I know I locked it when I left."

Miles stopped, guided her into the recessed doorway of the gunsmith's, and pushed Fran in after her. "You girls wait here, and if you hear any gunfire, keep your heads down." He motioned for Jonas to catch up and drew his pistol. Moonlight raced along the barrel, and his face hardened. He was so intent and alert, he seemed a stranger, and Addie caught a fresh glimpse of the lawman steel she'd captured in his portrait.

Jonas drew his own weapon. "Is there a back way out of the building?"

Addie shook her head. "No, I nailed the back door shut because it is in the darkroom. I didn't want someone opening it at the wrong moment and ruining developing pictures."

Fran clutched Jonas's arm. "You'll be careful?"

His eyebrows rose, and his eyes gleamed. "I will." He pushed her farther into the doorway. "You wait for us to come and get you, you hear? Don't follow us, even if you think it's safe."

He and Miles disappeared into the studio before Addie could warn Miles to be careful. Her hands found Fran's, icy cold, and her heart thundered. "I *know* I locked the door." A sick, breathless, swoopy feeling settled into her stomach.

Please, God, protect Miles and Jonas.

Time stretched out, though only a few moments had passed since they had entered the studio. Though many businesses along Front Street were doing a lively business, spilling noise and light onto the boardwalks, the silence from the studio deafened her. Visions of Miles and Vin coming face-to-face in the dark made her insides quiver.

"I hate it that we can't see what's going on." Sheltered in the doorway of the gunsmith's, the front door of her place was out of their sight. There had been no light around the window shades. Did that mean whoever had been in there was now gone? The unsteady feeling increased, and she closed her eyes, reminding herself to take deep breaths. Fran's hands stayed clutched in hers as they waited what seemed a long time, though Addie had no way of measuring other than her racing heartbeats.

Where were they? Had the intruder somehow overpowered both deputies? Were they hurt or hostage? Her imagination grabbed the reins and took off at a gallop. Maybe it wasn't Vin. Perhaps Wally's killer was hiding out in her studio, and somehow he'd done to Miles and Jonas what he'd done to the shopkeeper.

Addie nearly went right up in the air when someone touched her arm. Quelling a scream, her eyes popped open, and her knees buckled.

"It's all clear." Miles holstered his gun. "But you'd better come inside."

Fran stepped out of the doorway first. "Is Jonas all right?"

"Yes. He's still in there looking around."

Addie found her voice. "What happened? Did you find someone in there?"

"No, whoever it was cleared out." The gravity in his expression sent her heart plummeting.

Fran headed toward the faint light spilling out of the now wide open studio door, and Addie followed, her footsteps ringing on the boardwalk, but her mind not registering the impacts.

Miles stopped her at the threshold by putting his hand on her arm. "Addie, I'm really sorry."

She pushed past him, needing to see what had happened. The worst case would be if someone had stolen the Chevalier. She nearly collided with Fran, who stood in the center of the front room with her fingers over her lips. Jonas, in the doorway to the studio, held a lantern high. Addie recognized it from the darkroom, though he'd removed the red glass shade so yellow light spilled over everything.

Her reception room was in a shambles. Stuffing protruded from long slashes in the upholstered chairs, and not a single picture remained on the walls. Broken glass crunched under her feet, grinding into the rug. Her two Boston ferns had been uprooted and lay in bedraggled heaps of dirt and fronds, stomped to death beside their smashed planters.

"Oh no," Fran breathed. "Your beautiful portraits."

Mangled frames wrenched from the walls lay in discarded heaps, glass shattered and photographs ripped into random fragments. Miles took Addie's hand, but she could hardly feel his touch. Her breathing sounded harsh in her ears, but she couldn't seem to get enough air.

Jonas moved the lantern to reveal more damage. "It's worse in here." He backed up a few steps into the studio proper. "I'd light more lamps, but I couldn't find any others that hadn't been broken." The smell of kerosene drifted from the studio, mixed with the tang of developing chemicals so familiar to Addie.

With dread, she allowed Miles to lead her. The weak light from the lantern and the skylight revealed devastation reminiscent of a tornado. Her eyes went first to the center of the room. The beautiful glossy Chevalier lay in a heap of splintered wood and ripped leather. The lens lay faceup, a sunburst of cracks spidering across it. The legs of the tripod had been snapped like kindling. Bits of glass winked back from the floor, all around what was left of her portrait camera.

Slowly, Jonas toured the room. The painted canvas backdrops had been gouged with a knife, leaving long ribbons of fabric hanging. Shards of mirror decorated the settee, and the prop box would never hold another prop again. A puddle seeped through the open doorway to the darkroom.

"The darkroom?" Her question rasped out of her dry throat. The chemicals, the glass slides, the pans and equipment. . .

"There, too." Miles's hand tightened on hers, and she realized he still held it.

Fran picked up the parasol, her favorite accessory, and fingered the bent and broken ribs. "Who would do this? Was it drunks out of control?"

Miles shook his head. "Whoever did this was fast and thorough. I don't think anything escaped destruction. This doesn't feel like random vandalism. This feels personal."

Jonas stepped closer, throwing the perimeter of the room into shadow, blanking out at least some of the horror. He nodded his agreement with Miles. "It's so methodical. Almost as if the person was looking for something, and when they couldn't find it, they went into a rage and busted the place up."

Vin.

The realization echoed through her head. He hadn't believed her about not having the gold, and the minute she left the studio undefended, he'd snuck back in to search for it. When he didn't find it, he decided to pay her out for denying him.

"Any idea what someone might be looking for?" Miles bent an intent gaze on her. "Did you keep anything of value here? Can you tell if anything's been stolen?"

Jonas used his toe to nudge the pile of kindling that had once been a fabulous camera. "There's such a mess in here, maybe the vandalism is to keep us from noticing whatever was stolen. Can you tell if anything is missing? Where do you keep your money?"

She shuddered and clasped the camera case at her waist. "I put the day's receipts in here to take to the bank tomorrow. The Chevalier"—she pointed—"was the most expensive thing I had here." At least she had the money she'd made today, but how far would that take her? The bank manager would be furious when he saw the damage. Her collateral had disappeared.

Though she tried, she couldn't focus on anything but

the gaping loss. How was she going to make the mortgage payment? How was she going to take portraits when her camera was ruined? How could she explain Vin, Cliff Walker, the money he'd stolen and hidden somewhere, and everything else to Miles?

Fran put her arm around Addie's shoulders. "It's too late and too dark to sift through everything tonight to see what might've been stolen. Tomorrow will be soon enough."

"Fran's right." Jonas nodded. "We should get you girls home."

They crunched their way through the broken glass toward the front door. Miles motioned for Jonas to bring the lamp closer. "Look at that." He pointed to the latch. "It wasn't forced. Either someone had a key, or someone picked the lock."

"Just like the mercantile. That door wasn't broken or kicked in either."

"You think the two are related?" They put their heads together.

"I don't know, but it's awfully strange that they both happened today." Jonas scanned the street. "I don't have any reason to link the two except that neither place had a damaged lock. It's possible Wally let whoever killed him into the store. This. . ." He gestured to the doorknob. "Who knows?"

Chills formed in Addie's middle and radiated outward until she trembled. The sense of violation, of trespassing on not only her property but on her peace of mind, overwhelmed her.

How could he do this to me? What have I ever done to him? And why was I naive enough to hope that he would take me at my word? He wouldn't find the cash, because I don't have it. I've never had it. I wish I'd never even heard of it.

Addie let Fran guide her into the house, grateful she'd allowed herself to be talked into spending the night. The last place she wanted to be was her boardinghouse, alone with her thoughts.

Fran lit a lamp beside the door and pushed Addie into a rocking chair. "You poor thing. Your teeth are chattering."

Stove lids rattled, a match scraped, and the pump handle squeaked as Fran filled up the kettle. She disappeared into her bedroom and emerged with a shawl, which she draped around Addie's shoulders. "I know it's a warm night, but you're shivering. You just sit quiet. Tea will be ready in a jiffy." She yanked open a drawer, rattling the cutlery, and with quick movements, she sliced some bread. "I'll be right back." Hoisting the trapdoor to the cellar, she disappeared, reemerging with a plate of butter.

Addie clutched the soft, woolen shawl around her shoulders and tangled her fingers in the fringe, though she knew it wouldn't bring any warmth. The cold she felt was so deep inside, it would take something hotter than a blacksmith's forge to melt it.

You have to tell him. You have to tell Miles about Vin.

The teakettle whistled, and Fran dragged it off the stove. "Here," she said as she held out a mug of fragrant tea, "drink this."

"Thanks." Addie whispered the word and cleared her throat. "Thank you."

"What a rotten thing to have happen. I'm so sorry, Addie. It's just been a miserable day all around." Fran blew across the top of her own cup. "I can't decide what to dwell on first. If I think too long about Wally, I'll just break right down and cry. Then there's your beautiful studio, all smashed up. Who would do such a terrible thing? Not to mention Jonas. I will never understand that man."

Sipping the hot tea, Addie strove to sound normal. She grasped onto something to divert her mind from the depredations inflicted on her poor studio. "What happened with Jonas?"

"He asked me if we couldn't be friends. Like we used to be." Fran toyed with a sugar spoon. "And I said I'd like that. I am tired of fighting with him. We used to be so close, until he changed."

Addie knew she shouldn't meddle, that they should be left to sort it out themselves, but perhaps because her own life was in such a mess, she felt the need to do what she could to straighten out Fran's. "You better be sure of your feelings, that there's no hope that you could ever return Jonas's love. Otherwise, once you get those foolish notions about romance out of your head and face reality, you might find you've lost the most precious thing you've ever had."

Fran gave her a not-you-too look. "I *am* facing reality. I know what I want, and it isn't Jonas. Can you imagine me and Jonas together?"

"Yes. Everyone seems to see it except you. You two are perfect for each other."

"You can't be serious. Jonas is so. . .so. . ." She stopped, frowned, and finished, "He's too good to be interesting."

"I take it the mystery man you've been going on about for the last week or so isn't a good man?"

"I didn't say that." A wistful look came into her eyes. "He's not bad, just. . .mysterious. It's exciting." She picked up her tea and challenged Addie. "Is it wrong to want a little adventure? To want something other than to be a housewife, producing a new baby every year or two, a slave in my own house? I want to travel, to see the world and do something exciting. I think Vin could do that for me."

Addie's teeth rattled on the rim of her teacup. "Vin? Did you say Vin?" *Please, God, don't let it be him.*

Fran chewed her bottom lip and nodded. "His name is Vin Rutter, and he's the most interesting man I've ever met. I don't know what it is about him, but he's got this. . .I don't know, presence? And he's so charming."

Her heart sank. That rat. That utter and absolute rat.

Fran, now that she'd divulged his identity, burst open like a sack of beans. "He's tall and slim, and he's got this sort of swagger to him." Her expression softened, and her voice got dreamy. "And his eyes are so pale. The first time I saw them, I thought of icicles, but now that I know him better, I don't think of them as cold. He comes into the store every day, just to see me."

"Fran, I don't—"

"Jonas told me to stay away from Vin, but he's just jealous." Fran hugged herself. "I get all churned up whenever I see Vin, and my heart does cartwheels. That's how love is supposed to feel, all giddy, like you're flying. I don't feel that when I'm with Jonas. I just feel. . .ordinary."

Addie remembered that swooping feeling, like her heart had grown wings. The moment she first saw Cliff Walker, she knew her life would never be the same. And here was Fran, about to make the same dreadful mistake.

"Is that love? Is that enough to carry you through a lifetime? I have a feeling that real love burns like a candle with a steady flame. What you're describing is more like a firework, bright lights and sound that burst across the sky but fade away to a few floating cinders before you can blink. Real love is lasting. It will stand the test of time. I think real love is recognizing in someone else everything you need to be complete."

Even as she said the words, Addie knew she'd found that in Miles. The spark had been there from the moment they first met, and in every encounter since then, the realization had grown. He was everything she wanted and needed, and her feelings for him burned steady, like a candle, obliterating anything she might've felt for Cliff.

"You make it sound so boring." Fran refilled her cup. "Do you think Hap will sell out now? He's going to be devastated when he gets back from the fort. I wonder if anyone has ridden over to tell him. Surely someone did."

Typical of Fran to change the subject if things weren't going the way she wanted. Addie sighed and let her get away with it for the moment.

"Hap already knows." His collapse on the jail floor pressed

on her heart. "Devastated just about sums it up. He was in a bad way when I saw him. Crying. . .sobbing, actually. I had no idea it would hit him that hard."

Fran's eyes filled up and glistened. "Oh, I knew this would happen if I thought about Wally at all. Poor Hap. They scrapped all the time, but they really were best friends." Groping for her handkerchief, she sniffed. "He'll want some help with the funeral arrangements."

Addie set her cup aside. "Fran, we should talk about Vin."

"No, we shouldn't. At least not tonight. I know you were hoping I'd choose Jonas, but that's not going to happen. Vin is completely different from Jonas, and he's so charming. You'll understand when you meet him."

She understood right now, but how much could she tell Fran without jeopardizing their friendship? Would Fran turn on her—like her friends in Abilene had—when she found out about Cliff and the trial and the stolen money? Or would it merely fuel Fran's thirst for adventure, pushing her into Vin's arms? And how soon after she told Fran would the entire town know? The bank would undoubtedly call in the loan right away, not that she had any way of paying the note back now that the studio was in ruins.

Her mind scampered from one fruitless thought to another, while weariness poured over her. Listening to Fran rhapsodize about Vin made her stomach lurch. Had she sounded the same way about Cliff once upon a time? Regardless of what it might cost her, she had to save Fran from making the same mistake.

"Fran, about Vin—"

"No, we're not going to talk about him any more tonight. I'm being selfish. You've been through a terrible time this evening, and I'm prattling on. You're going to go straight to bed. Don't worry if you hear something in the night. It will be the boys coming home late." She pushed herself up from the table. "You can borrow one of my nightgowns."

Before Addie quite knew where she was, Fran had her tucked into bed. A wave of sleepiness engulfed her, but she shoved it away to make a promise to herself.

First thing in the morning, I'm going to sit Fran down for a long talk.

Miles let Jonas precede him into the room Miles rented at the Western Hotel. He followed and dropped down onto his bed and flopped backward across the quilt. The room wasn't anything to brag about, but it was cheap.

Jonas scrubbed his palm across his short hair. "I'm tired, but my mind is too full to sleep just yet. I figured we could talk about the case or something."

"Seems like it's one thing after another." Miles pressed the heels of his hands against his forehead. "And I'm no nearer finding Wally's killer than I was when I first knelt over the body, and now there's this new thing at Addie's. With Bat and Charlie out of town and half the county deputies sorting out that horse thief situation. . ."

Jonas didn't reply. Turning up the lamp, he reached for Miles's Bible lying on the dresser, but instead of opening it, he laid it back down and walked over to the window to stare through the opening in the drapes. The tension around his eyes told Miles he had plenty on his mind, too, and it might not be related to their jobs.

Miles frowned. He didn't want to pry, but if Jonas wanted to unload, he was willing to listen. "Anything you want to talk about? Fran maybe? You two sure were quiet tonight."

Jonas didn't turn away from the window, and he didn't answer for such a long time Miles thought he might be mad. Finally, Jonas sighed. "I've loved Fran for about as long as I can remember. Since we were kids. I always thought she'd be mine, you know? I never figured it any other way." He shrugged and shook his head. "Last night, I couldn't sleep, thinking about her. I wrestled with God, asking Him why He didn't change Fran's heart when I knew I'd be a good husband to her."

Pushing himself upright, Miles rested his forearms on his thighs and waited. Jonas was always so open about his relationship with God, something Miles admired.

"God made me realize that if I truly loved Fran, then I had to want what was best for her, what would make her happy." He pivoted and sat on the sill of the open window. "I don't know if you've noticed, but Fran has been anything but happy when I'm around lately." He grimaced. "I wanted her to be something she obviously can't be. And I needed to realize that I can't force her to love me. If friendship is all she can give me, then I need to be happy with that."

"How's that working for you?"

Jonas grunted and gave a wry grin. "It hurts worse than

getting gored by a longhorn. But I'll survive."

Laughter drifted up through the open window, harmonizing with piano music from the saloons and the occasional lowing of cattle in the pens near the depot. Nighttime in Dodge City.

Miles shrugged out of his vest and gun belt. "I admire you, Jonas." He spoke softly, not used to voicing feelings. "I wish I had your courage."

"What are you talking about? You're one of the bravest men I know. Bat thinks so, too. He told me when he was thinking about hiring you that he thought you had a lot of sand."

Miles tucked that compliment away to savor it later. "There's brave and there's brave. I don't seem to have any trouble facing down rowdy drunks or chasing horse thieves, but there are some things that scare me rigid."

"Such as?"

The need to tell someone, to share his burden with someone who would understand, surged through Miles. "There are things I should've told you, that I should've told Bat, before he hired me. If he knew the truth about me, he would send me packing."

It was Jonas's turn to wait while Miles marshaled his thoughts. Now that he'd begun, though he was tempted to retreat, he forced himself to get it out, to be as courageous as people thought he was—as he wanted to be.

"I spent my growing up years with the Walker Gang. Cliff Walker was my stepbrother. My mother married his father when I was about five." He sat up straight and looked Jonas in the eye, not flinching from whatever judgment he might see there. "I got out when I was sixteen, almost ten years ago, after my mother died and before Cliff took over and started robbing trains. I turned my life over to God, and I've tried to put all that behind me, but it keeps following me."

Jonas pursed his lips in a silent whistle and raised his eyebrows. Crossing his arms, he studied Miles until he wanted to squirm. "Is that all?"

"All? Isn't that enough?"

Miles couldn't have been more surprised when Jonas chuckled. "I thought you were going to tell me something really bad. Sounds like you were a kid stuck in a bad situation, and you escaped as soon as you could. You should tell Bat about it, though he won't care. Bat hasn't exactly been a choirboy, you know."

"There's a little more." Actually, a lot, and he needed to get it out tonight.

"Go ahead, but I don't think it can be as bad as you think it is."

"It's about Addie."

"If you're coming to me for advice on women, you might as well know I'm not exactly a font of knowledge, but you're welcome to get it off your chest."

"Before she moved here, Addie was Cliff Walker's girl."

"What?" Jonas shot upright off the windowsill.

Miles put up his hands, motioning Jonas to sit down again. "And I haven't told her that I knew him—that he was my stepbrother."

"How is it that you know this? Did Addie tell you?"

"No, it was Vin Rutter. Rutter was Cliff's best friend and a member of the gang. He was arrested at the same time as Cliff, but he got off because someone messed up on the warrant. For some reason, he followed Addie here to Dodge, but I don't know why. Vin never does anything that doesn't benefit himself somehow, so whatever his reason for hanging around, it can't be good. I haven't seen him in ten years, but he hasn't changed."

This time, his revelation made Jonas rub his hands down his cheeks and stare at the ceiling, blowing out a long breath. "That explains why it seemed you two knew each other when we questioned Vin and why you haven't gone ahead and pursued Addie, though it's plain that you're in love with her."

Miles jerked, but before he could protest, Jonas rolled his eyes. "Don't try to deny it. I've been there. I *am* there. From one hopeless case to another, trust me, you're in love."

In love. "I don't have time to be in love. I have to solve Wally's murder."

Pacing the area between the window and the door, Jonas clasped his hands behind his back. "Vin's been hanging around Fran a lot. She's fascinated with him. But she wouldn't take a twenty-four-carat suggestion from me right now, so I can't warn her off. It would be like throwing kerosene on a fire."

"I'd much rather find a way of dealing with Vin that kept the girls out of it. I'd hate for it to get around town that Addie had been tied up with Cliff. And please don't talk to Fran about this until I can sort things out with Addie. Her past is her secret, just as my past is mine, and she should be allowed to choose who she talks to about it."

Jonas stopped pacing. "You've been carrying around a lot of burdens. I stand by my earlier assessment. You're one of the bravest men I know."

"I sure don't feel like it. Have you ever tried not to be something you've been your whole life?"

"Every day."

That answer, when Miles expected a denial, made him blink.

"Every day I have to let God be in charge and change me. It's when I try to do the changing, or when I get bucky and refuse to change, that things get fouled up." He clapped Miles on the shoulder. "Get some sleep. You're going to need it. We've got quite a few mysteries to solve."

Miles closed the door after his friend. When he put his head on the pillow, he thought he'd have trouble getting to sleep, he had so much to think about and work through, but as his eyelids grew heavy, he realized that in sharing his troubles with Jonas, he'd lightened his burden.

Would he experience the same easing of his troubles when he confessed everything to Addie?

Chapter 15

Fran eased out of bed at sunup, careful not to disturb Addie. Indignation at the destruction caused in Addie's studio burned through her. As if Addie didn't have enough troubles. Whoever did it should be horsewhipped.

She took pains with her hair and dress, anticipating seeing Vin sometime during the day. A line formed between her brows as she studied her reflection. Jonas disapproved of Vin, and his motive was plain, but from what Addie said, she disapproved of him as well. The way Addie had spoken of love being a steady flame, a recognition of something in the other person that she needed to complete her. . .

Fran sighed and smoothed her eyebrows. Every time she ran those words through her head, though she wanted to see Vin's face in her mind, it was Jonas's features she saw.

A cold biscuit sufficed for breakfast. Anything more would necessitate building a fire and making enough noise to rouse the house. She slipped outside, breathing in the cool morning air that already held a harbinger of the heat of the day still to come. Odd on a Friday morning not to see more bustle and signs of life, but Dodge City drooped, victim of the celebrations of the previous day.

She used her key to let herself into the store, swallowing hard and bolstering her courage. "Just get in, get the book, and get out."

The store looked like cattle had stampeded through. Goods lay strewn and toppled on the floor and across the tables and counters. What on earth had happened in here?

Though she didn't mean to look, her eyes went to the floor in front of the cash register. She yanked her gaze away from the place where Wally had breathed his last and scuttled behind the counter. Though she didn't have a lamp and the early morning sunlight barely penetrated the front windows, she knew exactly what she was looking for. But as she groped on the shelf below the register, her hands found only bare wood.

Stooping, she reached well back under the counter and was rewarded with only dust on her fingertips. She stood and put her hands on her hips, searching the disheveled area, but didn't find what she sought.

With a shrug, she skirted the center of the room and let herself out, careful to lock the door behind her. It was in there somewhere, but she didn't have time for a thorough search. Time to go face Jonas at the jail.

"Morning, Miss Fran." Ty Pearson tipped his hat and leaned on his broom on the front porch of the jail.

"Good morning." She tilted her head. "Bat's got you sweeping today?"

A dusky red tinted his neck. "Yep, I'm on jail duty. Somebody's got to do it." He shrugged and jabbed at the porch with his broom.

She'd heard from Jonas in the past that sweeping out the jail was reserved either for a prisoner or someone Bat was peeved at and wondered what Ty had done to earn Bat's disapproval. "Is Deputy Spooner in yet?"

"He's in there."

Jonas met her at the door. He wore a guarded expression, and tiredness lurked around his eyes.

A twinge of guilt pricked her. He was handsome, in a steady, solid sort of way. She tried to imagine her life without him and drew a blank. He was always there, like the sun coming up in the morning, like the breeze that blew across the prairie. Though she wasn't in love with him, she didn't want him to go out of her life. She wanted the friendship he'd offered yesterday, and yet, that, too, left her strangely dissatisfied.

"I didn't expect you so early." He brushed his hand down his vest front.

"Do you want me to come back later?"

"No, don't go." He swept some papers off a chair and turned it so the back rested against the front edge of the desk. "Miles isn't here, but I can take you through some questions. If he thinks of anything else, we can find you again. How is Addie this morning? I realize now we left you off at your door kind of abruptly last night."

"She was still sleeping when I left, and don't worry about last night. You had plenty on your plate, and we went right to bed after we had a cup of tea." *And quite a talk about you.*

"Let's get started then." He dug in his pocket and withdrew a small notebook. "I wrote down some questions for you last night."

"Did you sleep at all?" The words popped out before she could stop them.

He shrugged. "A few hours." Pages rustled as he thumbed through the little booklet until he found the page he wanted. "Now, I want to walk you through yesterday at the store, who came in, what they bought, who was hanging around."

She settled herself in the chair and crossed her ankles, resting her hands in her lap. "I thought you'd want to know that, and I stopped by the store this morning to get the receipt book, but I couldn't find it. The store is a mess."

He nodded. "A bunch of folks forced their way into the store to get a gander at what had happened. They ended up shoving each other, and some goods got damaged. You couldn't find the receipt book?"

"It wasn't under the counter. That's where Wally would've put it when he finished counting the money."

"Probably got stolen along with the cash. Whoever did it probably scooped everything off the counter into a bag or a sack." He licked his pencil and held it over his notebook. "Try to remember who was in the store. If you don't know the name, a description will do. Pay particular attention to anyone who might've had an altercation with Wally."

She chuckled. "The one most likely to have an altercation with Wally was out of town. Hap was over at the fort, and we were rushed off our feet serving customers. There wasn't time for disagreements. We were practically shoving packages at people to get to the next customer in line."

Starting with opening the store in the morning, she went

through the day, describing regulars, cowboys, ranchers in town for the Fourth. "I know I'm missing a lot of people, folks Wally waited on while I was busy, and I didn't know everyone, not even half."

"It's all right. This just gives us a place to start."

"Do you really think the killer was in the store yesterday, that he was one of the customers?"

"It's possible. That's why it's important that you try to remember as much as you can."

She taxed her memory. "There were so many people. I can't possibly remember them all. That's why I wanted the receipt book."

"Was anybody upset?"

"No more than usual, I guess. You always get a few difficult customers. A couple of cowboys got a little rowdy. You know how they do. But Wally smoothed things over, convinced them to take it outside. It was all very good-natured."

Jonas consulted his notebook. "What about Vin Rutter?"

She stiffened. "What about him?"

He wiped his hand down his face. "I meant, was Vin in the store yesterday? In the morning maybe? I know where he was in the afternoon."

"You don't think Vin had anything to do with this?"

"We've checked his alibi for the time of the murder. If he's involved, it isn't directly." His tone left no doubt that he thought it possible if not probable that Vin was somehow tied to Wally's death.

"You questioned him?" She knotted her fingers, striving

to hold on to her temper. "You had no call to do that, Jonas. I thought you were my friend. Vin didn't kill Wally, and I won't let you accuse him." Defiance bloomed in her chest. If everyone wasn't careful, they'd drive her to do something drastic where Vin was concerned, like elope or something.

The color drained from Jonas's face as his expression tightened. "I'm beginning to think you don't know me at all. Especially if you think I would frame a man for murder out of jealousy. I asked you a straightforward question. Was Vin in the store yesterday morning?"

She nodded. If he thought she was going to help him implicate an innocent man, he had another think coming.

"Did he buy anything?"

She shook her head.

"Nothing?" His jaw tightened and his eyes narrowed.

"Not from me."

"What did he want, then?" The patient tone in his voice, as if she were a badly behaved toddler, grated.

"He just wanted to talk."

"About what?"

"It's not relevant to your investigation."

"I'll be the judge of that." He leapt up and pinned her by putting his hands on the edge of the desk on either side of her and leaning close. "When are you going to get it through that beautiful head that I'm trying to protect you? Stop being so stubborn, or I'll have to throw you in a cell for obstructing an investigation." His eyes gleamed like ice chips, and his lips were only inches from hers. With a growl, he pushed himself away, and her breath started again.

She swallowed. "He asked me to save him a dance. I told him I would." Shrugging, she twisted the drawstring on her handbag. "And he asked if business was as good as we expected, since it seemed there were a lot of people in the store. I didn't have much time to talk to him, and I think he realized that, because he said he'd see me later at the dance and left."

"Did he say anything else to you? Did he talk to Wally at all?"

"I don't think so."

"It's important, Fran. I wouldn't ask if I didn't have to. It isn't as if I *like* hearing about you and another man. I'm doing the best I can here." The bleakness that entered his eyes and voice rubbed a fresh, raw place on her heart.

Her shoulders sagged. "There was one other thing. He asked about Addie."

"Addie?" Jonas's eyebrows rose.

"Yes. He said he was thinking of getting his portrait taken and was Addie as good as he'd heard. I told him she was the best in town, but not to take my word for it. I told him to stop by there and see for himself. She had lots of her work hanging up in her front room." Remembering the devastation from the night before, she bit her lip. "Though all that's ruined now."

Jonas snapped the notebook shut and shoved it in his pocket.

"Whatever you're thinking, it's wrong, Jonas."

"You couldn't possibly know what I'm thinking right now."

"Then why don't you tell me?" It disturbed her to know

he was right. For much of her life she'd known exactly what he was thinking, but now, she hadn't the faintest idea. The niggling suspicion that Addie might've been right—that Fran had lost something precious forever—irked her.

"All right." Jonas hauled her to her feet, his hands hard on her arms, his eyes demanding that she look at him. "I'll tell you, though you won't like it. I think you've let your romantic notions color your good sense. A stranger starts hanging around asking questions about the kind of money the store is taking in, and the next thing you know, your boss is murdered and the place is robbed. Now you tell me this same man was asking questions about Addie, and lo and behold, her place is ransacked that same day. Even a simpleton could see the connection."

Tears smarted her eyes. When she struggled, he let her go, hanging his head and turning his back on her. She wanted to reach out to him, to return somehow to the familiar relationship she'd found so irritating only days ago, but when she touched him, he moved away.

She left the jail trying to convince herself that she'd made the right choice. Vin was her ticket out of there, her ticket to a life of adventure. If Jonas couldn't understand that, then there was no friendship between them anymore.

Chapter 16

Miles shouldered the shovel and broom he'd borrowed from the hotel and headed to the photography studio. The morning sunshine almost hurt his eyes. There were probably a lot of revelers who wouldn't welcome the daylight, but he needed it. Everything always looked worse at night. In the daylight, despair dissipated, or at least diminished to a manageable level.

Lord, help me to help Addie. Help me find out who did this to her. Help me find who killed Wally, and whether the two are related. And above all, help me to be the man You want me to be, to act with honor and not let fear keep me from doing the right thing.

With a brisk knock on the photography studio door, he let himself into the reception room. Though daylight had improved his outlook, it shone cruelly on the havoc wreaked here. Nothing had survived the devastation except the window and door glass. He frowned. All that plate glass would be hard for a vandal to resist. Why hadn't it been smashed, too?

A scrape and thump from the other room drew his attention. "Addie?" He headed that direction.

Sunlight streamed through the skylight, illuminating dust motes in the air and cascading over Addie. Though she'd put her hair up, strands were already finding their way out of the pins and framing her face. She straightened from bending over the pile of debris in the center of the room that had been the big camera. "Miles." Telltale tear tracks left damp streaks on her cheeks. She swiped at them and wiped her hands on her skirt. "What are you doing here?"

Lowering the shovel and broom, he surveyed the room. "I came to help." He indicated the tools. "Where would you like me to start?"

She took another swipe at her cheeks. "You don't have to do that. You're too busy."

"I'm here, and I'm not too busy. Jonas is questioning some of the people who were in the store yesterday. If we can discover if anything was stolen here, it might give us a lead into who did this. Now, what do you want me to do first?"

Her bewilderment at the chaos surrounding her made him want to hug her and assure her everything would be all right. But how could he make such a promise? Perhaps a little physical labor would help him marshal his thoughts.

He couldn't shake the feeling that the mercantile and the photography studio were somehow linked, but how? And what role did Vin play? He had a solid alibi for the time of the murder, and so far this morning, Miles hadn't been able to run him to earth. All he knew was that Vin was still in town. His horse was at the livery, and Miles had checked at the depot. Vin hadn't boarded the night train.

She looked around the room. "I guess it would be best to see what can be salvaged."

"Leave the heavy stuff for me, and don't throw anything out. If we sort as we clean, maybe you'll be able to discover if anything is missing." His boots crunched on broken glass, bits of plaster, and wood with every step. He put his hands on his waist and considered the shattered furniture, mirror shards, and the camera carcass. "Wait here. I'll be right back."

He ducked outside and around the back of the building to the rear door of the Alhambra Saloon.

One of the bartenders opened the door to his knock.

"Hey, Jethro, I need some crates. Do you mind if I take some of these?" He pointed to the pyramid of beer crates stacked in the alley. About twice a week a wagon went through and picked them up to be put on the train and sent back to the distilleries for reuse.

"Take some. Boss won't care."

Miles grabbed three and returned to the studio. "We can use these to sort stuff."

"Thank you." Addie took one of the boxes and began placing shards of looking glass in the bottom. The sadness in her eyes tore at him, as did the droop to her shoulders.

"Be careful. You could get a nasty cut." He took another box and stacked the camera into it. A shame. Such a nice piece of equipment, and she was so gifted with it. Miles used the side of his boot to scrape together a pile of broken glass.

She scanned the room, brushing her hands against her skirt. Finally, she shrugged. "I don't think anything is missing, just destroyed. All the props are here and the equipment." Returning her attention to the settee, she lifted another jagged piece of mirror and dropped it in the box. It shattered, and she gave a suspicious sniff.

Seeking to distract her from tears if he could, he said the first thing that came into his mind. "If this is some random vandal and not a targeted attack, why not bust out the front windows?"

She stopped and turned, her eyebrows bunching. "I've no idea. Maybe he ran out of time? Maybe he didn't want anyone to suspect anything too soon? I wouldn't have known until this morning that anything had happened if I hadn't seen the door open last night. But you can bet that someone would've seen or heard something, and certainly someone would've noticed if the front windows shattered."

The precariously growing stack of broken furniture shifted and crashed to the floor, startling both of them.

She squeezed her eyes shut and pinched the bridge of her nose.

"You said he."

"What?" She tucked a strand of hair behind her ear.

"You said he, not they. You think this was the work of one man?"

She shrugged and poked at the bits that used to be a stool, possibly the one she'd had him sit on for his portrait. "He, they, does it matter? The studio is destroyed." Emotion thickened her voice, but she blinked a few times, marched to the darkroom door, and wrenched it wide. A cry escaped her throat, and she turned away.

Miles crossed the room, his hand going to his sidearm. Shoving her aside, he peered inside, ready to confront anyone who might be hiding there. His mind boggled. Even in the reduced light, the destruction awed him. Glass lay in glittering snowdrifts amid globs of sodden paper and dented metal trays. A cabinet had been overturned, and photographs and papers soaked up whatever had been in the bottles that lay broken everywhere. Over all, a pungent chemical smell bathed the air. He relaxed and let his hand drop away from his gun.

Sobs reached his ears. Addie stood a few feet away, her head bowed, arms limp at her sides. Her shoulders shook, and a tear fell from her cheek to the wood floor and splattered.

Instinctively, he gathered her into his arms and pressed her head into his shoulder. "Shhh, Addie. I'm so sorry." If the fury of the destruction bludgeoned his senses, what must it be doing to her?

"He didn't leave me anything at all." The words, muffled against his shirtfront, tore his heart. "All my Uncle Carl's work was in there. All his slides. Everything he managed to save from the Abilene studio."

That explained all the glass. He rubbed his chin on the top of her head, holding her close, trying to take some of her sorrow. Her light scent drifted to him, reminding him of the last time he'd held her, and he felt a heel even thinking about kissing her when she was in such distress.

Rubbing small circles on her shoulder, he let her cry. Anger burned hot in his belly. He would find out who did this, and he would pay.

Addie soaked in the comfort of Miles's embrace even as she soaked his shirtfront with her tears. Though mortified at breaking down so thoroughly in front of him, she couldn't seem to help it.

The loss of Uncle Carl's work was like losing him all over again. He'd spent the better part of twenty years accumulating a body of work—portraits, still-life photographs, experiments with development techniques and exposures, and hardest to bear, all his war photographs—and now everything lay in splinters. All because of her.

She didn't doubt for a minute Vin Rutter was responsible for the vandalism. But if she hadn't fallen for Cliff Walker, none of this would've happened. She and Uncle Carl wouldn't have had to move away from Abilene, Uncle Carl wouldn't have been put under such strain with a heavy mortgage and the shame of all but being run out of town, and Vin Rutter would never have shown up again to harass her.

A victim again, at the hands of one of the Walker Gang.

The realization dried up her tears. The sobs slowed to a few hiccups and sniffles.

Miles pressed his handkerchief into her hands, and she dabbed and swiped. He kept his arms around her and his chin against her temple, and she savored the contact. When she had herself well under control, she tried to step out of his embrace, but he held on.

With one hand he tipped her chin up, and she looked deep

into his brown eyes. Questions lurked there, ones she hoped he never asked. Something else tinged his expression, something that reached out to a vulnerable place in her heart and stirred it to life. Heat curled through her.

Run away, Addie. You can't love him. Your life is too broken.

But as his lips lowered to hers and her eyes fluttered closed, she realized that being with Miles was beginning to mend the broken places in her heart. The comfort of his arms around her and the warmth of his kiss wrapped her in a feeling of peace and safety that she'd never felt with any man before.

He ended the kiss long after he should have and long before she wanted him to. Her skin tingled when he brushed his fingertips against her temple, trailed them down her cheek, and rested them at her throat. "Addie, I'm sorry this happened to you, and I'm going to do everything I can to find out who did this. Is there anything you can tell me to help narrow the search?"

It was on the tip of her tongue to blurt out that she knew who had done it and why, but her fingers tightened, and she realized she had placed her hand over his badge. Deputy Marshal, Ford County. Miles Carr stood for everything Cliff Walker had despised. Would he think her a fool to have fallen for Cliff's charms? Would he, as his fellow peace officers had up in Dickenson County, assume she had been in on Cliff's crimes? Pointing the finger at Vin meant opening all those old wounds. She swallowed her confessions. "No, there's nothing I can tell you."

He eased her out of his arms and stepped back, leaving her

feeling more alone than ever. "I guess I'd better be on my way then. I'm supposed to meet Jonas down at the jail and see what he found out about business in the mercantile yesterday. I'll check back in with you later."

"If I'm not here, I'll be at Fran's. I promised I'd stay with her at least one more night. She's coming to help with the cleanup."

"That's good. I was going to suggest it myself, that you might be better off with her for the next little while. Don't try to move the heaviest stuff. Jonas and I will help you carry that out later." He tipped his hat and left.

Rubbing her upper arms, she tried to talk sense into herself. *What you need is to take another look at those photographs of Cliff and get your head on straight about Miles.*

Even as she thought it, her heart decried the comparison. Miles was nothing like Cliff. Miles hadn't misled her, deceived her, or used her. He'd been honest from the first. She could trust him.

Then why didn't you? You had the perfect opportunity to tell him the truth about Vin and Cliff and why the studio got ransacked, but you held back. Ashamed to be truthful with him about your past, afraid he would reject you.

"Oh hush up," she whispered. "Get to work. You've got more than enough to think about without swooning over Miles or wrestling with the mess Cliff made of your life a year ago." The mess Vin had made was more than enough to be going on with.

Though she repeated this dictate to herself several times

over the next few hours, she couldn't get Miles out of her mind. . .or her heart.

Miles spent the rest of the day questioning people who had visited the mercantile on the Fourth. Just finding some of them was proving difficult, since some folks had come to town only for the day and returned to outlying ranches and farms, and others were sleeping off the effects of the previous night. Still, tracking down the customers gave him a good excuse to continue his search for Vin, though that, too, proved fruitless.

Not a single person he questioned raised any warning flags or produced any solid leads. Housewives, ranchers, cowboys, ordinary citizens who had seen nothing out of the ordinary. By evening, Miles had nothing to show for his questions but a headache and a nagging sense of futility.

"The more I look at it, the more it looks like a crime of opportunity." He tossed his pencil down onto the paper-strewn desk and rubbed his temples.

"What about the door? It wasn't locked." Jonas tipped his chair back to lean against the wall and propped his boots up on the corner of the desk.

"Wally probably forgot to lock it behind me when I ran up the street. He was concentrating hard on the cash and ledger book. Or maybe a last-minute customer came in to get something, and he opened the door for them, forgetting to lock it when they left and allowing the robber inside."

"Without that receipt book, we can't know if he had a late customer."

"And we wouldn't know anyway unless this customer had a charge account. According to Fran, if you pay cash, Wally doesn't write down your name."

"Do you think the killer might've been a charge account customer, and that's why he took the receipt book?"

Miles planted his elbow on the desk and his chin on his fist. "I don't know. It was right there with all the money. If the killer swept the money into a sack or a bag or something, stands to reason the book would go, too."

"And we're no closer to finding the killer."

"I'm not licked yet. There's one other trail we can follow."

"What?" Jonas sat up and dropped his feet to the floor.

"The money. Somebody's flush right now when they were spare yesterday morning." Miles stood, stretched, and reached for his hat.

"Money isn't easy to track in this town. Too much gambling." Jonas rose and checked his gun.

"Every place that has gambling has a gambling boss. We'll ask them which way the money's flowing. I figure we should start with Luke Short over at the Long Branch."

They found Luke sitting in the lookout chair at the Long Branch. To those who didn't know him, his slight frame and quiet manner seemed to put him in the no-account column. Miles knew better. Luke Short was one of the toughest, sharpest-eyed, intelligent men Miles had ever come across. Which made him perfect as a gambling boss for the busiest saloon in Dodge.

"Hard to say." Luke never took his eyes off the faro table. "Lotsa cash floating around this week especially. Four herds hit town the day before yesterday, and most of the cowhands are still here. Money is changing hands faster than fleas swap dogs."

"What about cowhands that have more money than you'd figure they would, even just getting paid off?" Miles pitched his voice low to get under the music and chatter.

"Nobody's come in with more money than I'd expect them to have. Several riders have lost their whole pay and gotten a little unruly about it, but nothing I couldn't handle." He patted his sidearm.

"Any big winners?"

"Just that fellow we talked about before, Vin Rutter. He hit a hot streak in a poker game and fleeced a few swellheads. Walked out with a pocketful of money. Too bad he didn't switch to faro. I could've gotten some of it back." Though he didn't smile, a half-humorous, half-predatory gleam lit his eyes. "I was dealing while he was in here, but he wasn't of a mind to buck the tiger."

Miles flicked a glance at the oil painting of a tiger that graced the wall over the faro table—an advertisement to all that the saloon offered faro, the same way the longhorns mounted over the bar indicated a patron could get a full meal in that establishment if desired. Several cowboys crowded around one of the faro tables, even this early in the afternoon. He shook his head. If faro was played fair and square, the odds were even between the house and the gambler. Which didn't suit the house at all. Consequently, there wasn't a faro game west of the Mississippi that wasn't rigged, crooked, or otherwise tilted in the favor of the gambling establishment. "If you hear anything you think might be helpful, let us know."

"I will. It's a bad business, what happened to Wally. I'll keep my ear to the ground."

Miles stepped out into the evening air, and Jonas joined him. Whenever they went into one of the saloons, they always split up. No sense bunching targets if things were going to get unruly.

"Where to next?"

"Might as well keep working in a straight line. The Saratoga and the Alhambra."

Checking in with the bartenders and gambling bosses netted them no new information.

As they crossed Front Street toward the river, a gaudily dressed young woman hurried toward them. She might've been pretty if not for heavy makeup and a world-weariness in her eyes that made her look old before her time. "Scottie sent me to get you. That fellow you're looking for is down at the Lone Star. Weird-looking man. Pale eyes, like a fish." One of the straps holding up her dress slipped, baring her shoulder, and she yanked it up. "Scottie said for you to hotfoot it down there, because this fellow was drinking pretty fast, and he was packing a gun."

Miles locked eyes with Jonas. Bat was zealous about enforcing the law of no guns inside city limits, and rightly so, considering his brother had been gunned down disarming a drunk. What was Vin thinking?

Jonas nodded. "Thanks, ma'am. We'll head right down there."

The girl led the way but stopped on the porch of the Lone Star Dance Hall, so named to appeal to the hundreds of Texans who came through each season. From the looks of things, they were doing a roaring business for so early in the day. They entered the barn-like structure, and the girl blended into the crush.

"Mighty crowded." Jonas sidestepped a bowlegged cowboy and a giggling woman who looked to be staggering more than two-stepping. A haze hung in the air from cigar and cigarette smoke, and men stood three deep at the rail waiting for a dance. "You see him?"

"Nope." Miles grabbed an empty chair along the wall and stood upon it to survey the crowd. Wide-brimmed hats, fancy dresses that didn't cover enough of the dancing girls, in a couple of cases a pair of enormous, wooly chaps. Music, the stomping of boots, laughter, and clapping. Then he spied a familiar figure over by the bar.

Miles hopped down and nudged Jonas. "Swing around thataway, and I'll come at him this way." He waited until Jonas had time to thread his way through the crowd to come up on Vin's left.

"Gimme another."

Coins clinked onto the bar, and Scottie, the bartender, slopped whiskey into a glass. Miles noted the bulge under Vin's jacket. The girl had been right. Drunk and carrying a gun.

Vin tossed back the drink and smacked the bar. "Another."

Miles put his hand on Vin's forearm and pressed it into the bar. "I think you've had enough." He jerked his head at Scottie before slipping his hand into Vin's coat and relieving him of a pistol.

" 'Bout time you got here." Scottie grabbed the bottle and headed toward the other end of the bar to serve waiting customers.

Vin's thin nostrils flared. He wheeled around, blinking. "Deputy." He lurched slightly, corrected, and leaned against the bar.

"Vin, I think you'd better come along with me."

His eyes narrowed. "Where?"

"Down to the jail. You're under arrest for carrying a gun inside city limits." Miles latched on to Vin's elbow. "Let's go."

"Jail? I don't think so."

"I do think so."

Vin leaned close and hissed into Miles's face, "I'm not leaving until I get drunk as a skunk. I'm in mourning." His whiskey-soaked breath wafted around Miles.

"Mourning? For what?"

"I'm mourning the demise of my brilliant plan. I arrived too late. The cupboard is bare." He waved his arms in an exaggerated swoop, and the force of the motion carried him staggering sideways.

Miles grabbed his arm.

The patrons of the dance hall seemed to realize that an arrest was in progress, and they formed an interested ring.

"We'll talk about it at the jail. C'mon."

"I'm not going anywhere with you." Vin's hand jerked into his jacket, where he groped under his arm. Blinking, he lifted aside his coat to look at his shirt.

"Looking for this?" Miles patted the pistol he'd taken off Vin, now safely tucked into his waistband.

Jonas handcuffed the prisoner, and between the two of them, they got him to the jail. He collapsed on the bunk in the first cell and began snoring.

Miles tossed the key into the top drawer of the desk. "I don't know what else Vin might have been planning, but he did accomplish one thing."

"What?" Jonas scowled through the bars at the prisoner.

"He got drunk as a skunk."

Mr. Poulter lifted a shred of canvas that had once been part of a lovely backdrop and let it fall from his fingers. "Why didn't you come to me first thing this morning? I had to hear about this from Heber Donaldson."

Heber stood in the doorway, a supercilious smirk on his face.

Addie took a deep breath and counted to ten so she wouldn't fly right over there and smack it off. He couldn't wait to spread the news of her misfortune, she bet.

At least most of the damage had been cleared away, though the empty place where the Chevalier had stood mocked her as much as Heber's smirk. Her muscles ached from the hours of cleaning, and she knew she was too tired to be rational about business matters.

She had been locking up before heading to Fran's house

when the banker had arrived with Donaldson on his heels. It was hard not to imagine buzzards circling over a dying animal.

"I'm afraid the bank will have to call in the loan." Poulter dusted his hands. "Without equipment, you have no way of paying off the loan and the bank has no collateral. You will have to close immediately and surrender whatever can be salvaged to satisfy the note."

His eyes drifted to her waist, and her hands instinctively covered the Scovill's case, as if to shield it from his mercenary eyes. Though his words were no more than she'd expected, hearing them was like a hammer blow.

"We had an agreement, Mr. Poulter, that I expect you to honor. I have until the end of August to pay the balance on the loan, provided I continue to meet the mortgage payments on time between now and then." She'd fought this battle in her head all afternoon, and she was more than prepared. "Unless or until I miss a payment, you cannot call in the loan."

"But, my dear"—his patronizing tone smeared over her, making her want to shudder—"you have nothing with which to earn the money. I knew I never should've extended the loan to a woman. They just don't understand business."

Donaldson snickered. "She'll understand soon enough." He sneered. "You thought you'd bested me when you stole that Arden commission, but who's laughing now?"

Addie stood her ground, determined not to cry or show any weakness. "This building is mine for the time being, and I want you both to leave. If you don't, I'll have you arrested for trespassing."

Poulter snapped to attention, indignation contorting his features and blood suffusing his cheeks. "How dare you! Nobody talks to me that way, young lady."

"Don't they? Well, it's high time, don't you think? Now get out. We have nothing more to discuss until the end of next month." She held on to her bravado, even as she smelled the smoke of her bridges burning.

Chapter 17

Addie looped her camera case over her head and adjusted the strap across her chest. "Thank you for letting me stay over again last night." She'd been so bludgeoned by her encounter with Poulter and Donaldson, she'd practically stumbled to Fran's place and collapsed into bed. She hadn't even heard Fran come in.

Fran pinned her hat on her upswept hair and checked her reflection one last time. "You know it's no trouble. Are you headed right back to the studio this morning?"

"No, I have to go to my boardinghouse. I need a change of clothes."

"I am sorry I wasn't able to help you clean up yesterday. Hap corralled me as soon as I was finished at the jailhouse and demanded an inventory of the store so we can determine just how much money was stolen. It took much longer than I thought it would, mostly because Hap doesn't have a clue how to run the store. He'll probably need me there for most of the day today, too. He's so distracted, and he keeps breaking into tears."

"Don't worry about that. You have an obligation to Hap to

get the store open as soon as possible. I won't be at the studio much today in any case, at least not until I've talked to a few people. I have to raise some money and fast. I'm only sorry we don't have time for a talk, because, Fran, we need to discuss Vin. There are some things you don't know about him. Some things that you won't like hearing."

Fran's jaw set, and a steely look invaded her green eyes. "How are you planning to raise money to restore the studio?"

Addie sighed. "Fine, but we're going to talk about Vin sooner or later. As for the money, I guess I'm going to have to look for an investor or two. I need to get back into business fast, or I'll lose too many customers to even think of meeting the mortgage payment."

"Where are you going to look for investors? You know if I had the money I'd give it to you." Fran threaded her hand through the strings on her bag. "And my brothers, too. Maybe you could ask Linc, though I don't know as he has any cash to spare." In a flash Fran went from angry and stubborn to generous and caring.

"Don't worry, and don't ask your brothers." Addie linked her arm with Fran's and gave it a squeeze. "I'll find someone." She spoke with more confidence than she felt. So many of the men in this town who had money chose to invest in businesses of a tawdry nature. She didn't want to link her studio to any of that, which cut down on her options considerably.

"How was Hap when you left him last night?" Addie shielded her eyes as they stepped outside. She needed to remember to get a hat from her room.

Fran shook her head. "He's in a terrible state. I never realized what an anchor Wally was for poor Hap. And the funeral is the day after tomorrow. If it wasn't for the church ladies, I don't know where we'd be. They've handled all the arrangements. Hap just wanders around picking things up and setting them down. He won't even come to the front of the store where it happened. Said he can't bear to walk over the place where Wally died. The longer he stayed in the store, the more upset he got. Truthfully, I was glad he finally left me to it. It's looking more and more like he won't be able to keep the place going alone. I imagine he'll either sell up, or like you, he'll be looking for a new partner."

"Poor man. And he's all alone. If he was married, things might be easier for him. He would have someone to take care of him and help him through his grief."

"Up to now I was always glad neither of them was married. No bossy wife coming into the store to tell me how to do my job, but now, I think you're right. I wish Hap had someone. Right now he looks like a calf that got separated from the herd and can't find its way home."

Addie parted ways with Fran at the mercantile and walked the remaining blocks to the boardinghouse, her mind spinning with her to-do list. She mounted the stairs and opened the front door. "It's just me, Mrs. Blanchard."

Her landlady, usually knitting away in her rocker at this time of the morning, wasn't in the parlor. Shrugging, Addie lifted her hem and trotted up the stairs, relieved not to be dragged into a long chat session with Mrs. Blanchard, who would insist on knowing every last detail of the break-in at the studio. Word had spread yesterday, and people had knocked on the studio door and rattled the knob, trying to get a look inside.

She turned to head along the hallway to her room at the end and nearly collided with her landlady.

Mrs. Blanchard grabbed her by the arms, her breath coming in gasps. "Miss Reid, oh thank the Lord you're all right! I was on my way right this minute to the marshal's office." White ringed her eyes, and her hands made quick, jerky movements like a scared bird.

"What's happened?"

"Your room. Oh my stars and garters, your room. It must've happened last night when I went over to my sister Gertrude's house. The only one here was Marley Jacobs, and he was so drunk he couldn't have hit the ground with a hat. He never heard anything at all."

Addie's throat closed up, and she plucked Mrs. Blanchard's bony fingers off her arm. Fearing what she would find, she forced herself to open the door to her room.

Chaos.

She stood, frozen, in the doorway.

Mrs. Blanchard nudged her aside to look as well. "I was just coming in to change the towels, and I found all this."

Every drawer hung open, every cupboard door gaped wide. The bedclothes were strewn on the floor, and the mattress had been dragged off the frame. Long slashes eviscerated the pillows, and goose down dusted every surface. The mirror from the washstand lay in shards on the rug, joined by pieces of pitcher and bowl.

Mrs. Blanchard wrung her hands. "Everything's ruined. Look at my drapes." The dusty-rose velvet hung in ribbons, all the silvery fringe ripped away and long rents sliced into the panels. "I'm so glad you weren't home when this happened, but who's going to pay for this? The bedding, the china, even the wallpaper." She waved to the wall beside the door.

Addie stepped farther into the room and turned to view the damage.

WHERE IS IT?

The letters, nearly a foot high, had been carved into the wall, marring the muted cabbage rose and ribbon pattern. Addie's hand went to her mouth, and tears stung her eyes. The violence in those slashes, the vindictiveness and malice, made her insides quake.

"Addie dear, who would do such a thing? And what were they looking for? What is 'it'?"

It was something she didn't have. *It* was something she didn't know how to get. And *it* was something she wasn't willing to die for. Up until now, even with the vandalism of the studio, she'd not really feared for her safety. But this, the invasion of her room, the destruction of her personal items, and especially that message hacked into the wall. . . She swallowed. This felt like more than anger. It bespoke an unbalanced mind. Had he been drunk? If she had been here when Vin ransacked this room, she had no doubt but that he would've killed her.

"You know, don't you? You know what he was looking for.

I can tell by your expression that you do." Mrs. Blanchard grabbed Addie's arm.

Her hands shook, and she took short, jagged breaths. "Mrs. Blanchard, please don't let anyone else into this room until I get back. I'll go report the break-in at the jail." Once more she peeled the woman's fingers off her arm.

Her landlady returned to wringing her hands at her waist, balling them in her apron. "Addie, I don't like to do this, but you can't stay here anymore. For the first time in my life, I don't feel safe in my own home. First your studio, now your room? I have an obligation to my other boarders, too. It's obvious that whoever did this didn't find whatever he was looking for. That means he'll keep looking." She blinked, her lips quivering, but her head high. "I don't want him looking for it here ever again, whatever it is."

Addie's throat tightened, and her heart dropped down to her stomach. How many more shocks could she take before she lost her mind? A glance told her the few dollars she'd stashed under her mattress had disappeared. Penniless, homeless, and thanks to Vin, the only possessions she owned that hadn't been destroyed were on her back.

"Addie? You understand why I can't have you here?"

"I understand." And she did. She understood that she would never be free of her past until she brought it into the present. Vin couldn't be allowed to terrorize people this way, no matter what it cost her to admit to being Cliff Walker's girl. She would put an end to this today.

"I probably shouldn't have hit him." Jonas flexed his fingers. "I just couldn't take it anymore."

Miles stared down at the unconscious form now sprawled across the bunk in the first cell. "I'm surprised you stood it for as long as you did. He had no call to say those things about Fran. He's a sloppy drunk, and he's mean afterward." And more slippery than a pickled onion. Vin's alibi for the time the studio was ransacked was as unassailable as for the time of the murder. Luke Short had verified that Vin had been in the Long Branch from ten o'clock on the night of the Fourth until dawn. Which left Miles exactly nowhere as far as solving the crime.

Cowboys on a tear didn't make sense, because they would've broken the front windows. Robbery wasn't the motive like at the mercantile, because nothing had been stolen, only destroyed. He jangled the cell keys, spinning them on the ring while his thoughts spiraled.

Jonas gripped the bars and rested his forehead on his hands. "What's Fran thinking of, hankering after someone like this? Can't she see he's no good?"

"I doubt Vin Rutter has shown this side of himself to her. You've seen him around town. He acts cultured and smooth. Whatever fascination Fran has with him will wear off soon. She's like a rabbit, mesmerized by a rattlesnake."

"But will she realize the danger before the snake strikes? I've tried to warn her, but she won't listen to me. I didn't break your confidence or Addie's, but unless one of you tells Fran about who Vin really is, I'm afraid for her." Jonas straightened and let his hands fall away from the cell door. "I've already lost all chance of winning her love. Now I just want to keep her safe."

Miles shoved his hands into his pockets and stared at the floor. If he hadn't been such a coward about trying to hide his past, maybe he could've saved people he cared about a lot of heartache. But no more. "Keeping Fran safe is more important than trying not to hurt her feelings. I'll talk to her. At least while Vin's in jail he can't be causing anyone any harm."

His mind blanked at what Addie would say when she found out. But keeping her safe from Vin was more important than her feelings. . .or his. He'd have to tell her the truth.

He nearly dropped the keys when the door opened and Addie slipped into the jail. She stopped just inside the doorway, clutching the strap of her camera case. Her eyes glistened, and she blinked, sending a couple of tears tracking down her cheeks.

In two strides he was before her. He grabbed her by the shoulders, checking for an injury. "Are you hurt? What's wrong?"

She shook her head, gulped, and swiped at the tears in an angry, little-girl gesture. "I wasn't going to cry." Which seemed a silly thing to say, since she clearly was crying.

"What happened? Are you still upset about the studio?" That was understandable.

"No. I mean, yes, of course I am. But that's not all. I need to report another break-in. And. . ." She gulped another big breath of air. "I know who did it."

His eyebrows rose? "Another break-in? At the studio?"

"No, not at the studio. At my boardinghouse."

Jonas swept a pile of papers up into his arm and offered her a chair. "Here, Addie. You look about all in. Sit down and tell us what happened."

Miles let his hands drop away, and she sank onto the chair. Her camera case knocked against the desk, and absently, she tugged it around to let it sit in her lap. "I spent last night with Fran at her place, and this morning when I went to my room at Mrs. Blanchard's to get something, I found that someone had broken in." She clutched the camera case, her knuckles going white. "Sometime after seven last night, someone got into my room and tore it apart. All my things are ruined, the furniture is broken, the drapes and bedding destroyed."

Jonas perched on the edge of the desk and touched her shoulder. "And you know who did it?"

She nodded and moistened her lips. "The same man who broke up my studio."

A low moan came from the cells, and Vin sat up, rubbing his jaw and scowling.

Addie's eyes widened and her jaw fell open. "You've arrested Vin? But—" She stopped. "How did you know?"

Miles's thoughts spun. "Slow down and tell me what happened and what Vin has to do with it."

"Mrs. Blanchard says sometime after seven last night someone broke into my room. If anything, it looks worse than the studio." She shuddered and renewed her grip on the camera case. "So much hate." Her blue-gray eyes trained on the prisoner. "How could you? What did I ever do to you?"

"Me?" Vin grimaced and touched his swollen left eye. "I've never been to your boardinghouse, and I certainly wasn't there last night."

Addie shot out of her chair. "Don't try to deny it. I got your message. Why won't you believe me when I tell you I don't have what you're looking for?"

"Message? What message?"

"Don't play ignorant with me. The message you carved into the wall of my room. 'Where is it?' Not exactly subtle. I knew it was you the minute I saw it."

He scowled, wincing. "You've got a problem."

"I'll say I do. I'm being preyed upon by a malicious, yellow thief."

"Maybe, but it isn't me."

"Addie." Miles put his hand on her arm.

She shrugged it off. "I don't know how you figured it out so quickly, but thank you for arresting Vin. I want to file charges."

"Addie, we arrested him early last night."

"Did someone already report the break-in?" She tore her eyes away from her tormenter and looked up at Miles. "Is there a witness? Mrs. Blanchard said the place was empty except for Marley Jacobs, and he was sleeping off a drinking binge. Did someone see Vin leaving?"

"No, what I'm trying to tell you is we arrested Vin last night at about six. He was carrying a firearm inside city limits. If your break-in didn't happen until sometime after seven, it couldn't have been Vin who did it."

Vin put his head back and laughed, making Addie want to reach through the bars and slap his face. "Hoo hoo!" He wiped his eyes and dragged himself off the floor to sit on the bunk. "This is great. All of you trying so hard to pin something on me, and every time I've got an alibi. I never thought I'd say this, but"—he waved at Jonas—"thank you for arresting me last night." He tipped his head back and laughed again.

"Shut up, or I'll black your other eye." Jonas stepped forward, his hands fisted and a dull, red flush climbing his cheeks.

Miles jammed his fingers through his hair. How had things unraveled so quickly?

Chapter 18

Addie groped for the chair and sank into it. If what Miles said was true, then Vin couldn't have been the one to break into her room. But if it wasn't Vin, then who? One of Cliff's other gang members? A chill shot through her. Vin was right. She did have a problem.

The door crashed open, and Addie jumped. Fran marched into the jailhouse. "Jonas Spooner, you rat, what's the idea of locking Vin up? Have you lost your mind?"

Addie pressed her fingertips to her temples. She loved Fran dearly, but now was not the time for histrionics. "Fran, please."

Fran didn't stop until she stood toe-to-toe with Jonas in front of the bars. "This is outrageous. Did you think I wouldn't hear about this?" Jamming her hands on her hips, she looked into the cell. "Oh Vin! What have they done to you?" Her jaw dropped. "Jonas? You hit him? How could you?" She rounded on the deputy.

Miles inserted his arm between Fran and the bars. "You need to step back."

"No, not until you tell me what happened here. I want this man released. He hasn't done anything wrong, other than make Jonas jealous." Hectic color decorated her cheeks, and her eyes snapped fire.

Jonas said nothing, but neither did he move to open the cell door.

"Fran"—Addie rose—"it isn't what you think."

"It's exactly what I think. It's shameful of Jonas to abuse his office this way. I never would've suspected it of you. It's so unlike you to use violence."

Addie tried to catch Miles's glance. Everything was coming apart at the seams, and Fran's dramatic protests weren't helping.

Vin grinned through the bars. "Fran, my sweet, how lovely of you to be concerned. I shall come and find you the minute I get out of this. . .establishment. Then we can be together."

Jonas started forward. "Now see here, Rutter. If you come anywhere near—"

Fran slapped his hand off her arm. "I can take care of myself, Jonas Spooner, and don't you—"

Miles tried to speak over the argument. "Let's all calm down and talk this over—"

"Hush up!" The words barreled out of Addie's mouth and everyone froze. Before they could gather themselves, she continued. "Fran, sit down." Pointing to the chair she'd just left, she marched to the cells and grabbed her friend's wrist. "You're going to sit still and listen to a few home truths about Vin Rutter. Then you're going to apologize to Jonas and go home."

Fran gasped, but Addie was mad clean through and tired to the point of recklessness. She dragged Fran to the chair and pushed her into it. "Now, listen to me, all of you. Fran Seaton, you're treating a decent man shamefully. Jonas has never had anything but your best interests at heart. The reason Vin Rutter is in jail has nothing to do with you. He's in jail because he broke the law." She poked Fran in the shoulder. "I have news for you, the entire world doesn't spin around you. It's time you dropped these girlish fantasies about a white knight riding in to rescue you from your life and realized the best man for the job is standing right here."

"Um, Addie. . ." Jonas shuffled his feet, his face going even redder.

"Don't. You've been too patient with her. It's time she got a dose of reality before she does herself some real harm."

"I don't have to sit here and take this." Fran gathered herself, but Addie pushed her back down.

"Yes you do. I've been too patient with you, too. I've let you weave dreams about a man I know is bad, and all because I was afraid to tell the truth. Afraid you'd think less of me. I've let you change the subject and skirt the topic every time I bring it up, but no more. I can't stand by any longer. Your precious Vin Rutter is a former member of the Walker Gang, a liar, and a criminal." She took a deep breath and forged on. The time for hiding had ended. She didn't dare look at Miles, afraid of the disgust she would see there. "I was once romantically involved with Vin's saddle pard and boss, Cliff Walker, the leader of the gang."

Fran's eyes widened, and Jonas stepped forward.

Addie held up her hand. "I didn't know about the gang

or the killing or stealing. Cliff kept me completely in the dark, using a fake name and telling lies on top of lies. He was handsome, smooth, fascinating—all the words you've used to describe Vin. I let my head be turned. When the U.S. marshals showed up at my door, I was stunned, and I didn't want to believe them." She swallowed, remembering. "They were convinced I was an accomplice. The marshals badgered me for hours, trying to get me to admit to being part of the gang. They were trying to find the money Cliff and his gang stole during their last train robbery."

Her knees wobbled, all the humiliation, the exhaustion, the confusion, and the hurt piling back. "They questioned me and Uncle Carl extensively, and in the end, they had to let us go. But not before all of Abilene knew and became convinced of our guilt. Our photography studio was burned, people called me names, and eventually, they ran us out of town. It ruined my uncle's health, and my reputation."

She walked to the cell and glared in at Vin. "And Vin was one of the gang members. He was arrested with Cliff, but the sheriff released him. Cliff was tried and executed for robbery and murder. I thought I was done with all of that, that I could put it all behind me and start a new life here, but a few weeks ago, Vin showed up looking for the stolen money. The cash has never turned up, and Vin is convinced I have it or I know where it is." She gripped the bars until her hands shook. "I'm telling you all now, I don't have it, I don't know where it is, and I wish I'd never heard of Cliff Walker or any of his gang."

She let her hands fall away and turned on her heel to

approach Fran once more. "I should've told you before, when you first mentioned Vin, but I was afraid. I was afraid I would lose your friendship if you knew I'd been the girlfriend of a killer. I'm sorry I didn't tell you, but I'm telling you now. Vin Rutter is rotten clear through. He's a liar, a thief, and probably a killer himself."

She swayed. "When my studio was ransacked, I thought it was Vin. He came to my studio after the gold once before." She glanced at Jonas, whose face looked carved from stone. "The night of Wally's murder, when you came in and Vin left. He'd been pestering me to tell him where the money was. And this morning when I saw the destruction in my room, I thought it must be Vin still searching. But if he was in a cell here last night, he couldn't have broken into the boardinghouse." She swallowed. "But if he isn't the culprit, then there is someone else out there looking for the money. One of Cliff's gang members or someone who has heard about the trial."

"Addie." Miles put his hand on her arm, but she eased away, still unable to look at him, afraid to see the disgust in his eyes.

"No, Miles." Her breath hitched in her tight throat as she fought for control. "You deserve to know the truth. Here I am accusing Fran of mistreating Jonas, but I'm to blame as well. The night the Arden Palace opened, I took advantage of your chivalry. I spied Vin in the crowd, and I was afraid of him. I used you as a shield, hoping he would leave me alone if he saw me with another man—and a deputy at that. And I haven't been truthful with you about my past. At first, I thought it wouldn't matter. I was trying to get a fresh start here in Dodge

City and forget about Cliff and everything he'd done to my life. I thought if I ignored it, it would go away." A bitter laugh surprised her. "Then, when I realized I was. . .becoming fond of you. . .I didn't want you to know about Cliff because I was afraid you'd despise me."

"Addie, I wouldn't—"

She straightened her spine, the strength of resolve coursing through her, giving her courage. "I'm not going to be Cliff's victim anymore. He's had far too long a reach—all the way from the grave—holding on to my life. Well, no more." She squared her shoulders. "Fran, I'm sorry I had to speak so harshly to you, and I'm sorry I didn't tell you the truth about Vin sooner. Jonas loves you, and I know you love him, if you'll just grow up enough to realize it. He's worth a hundred Vin Rutters."

Fran stared hard at her, her face pale and her hands knotted in her lap. Her chin was tilted at a dangerous angle, and she looked from one face to another.

Addie's shoulders slumped. Telling the truth had cost her Fran's friendship, just as she had feared. Her only consolation lay in the fact that at least Fran knew about Vin now. Any choice she made wouldn't be made out of ignorance. She wouldn't fall into the same trap Cliff had laid for Addie.

She risked a look at Miles, who stood with his hands jammed in his back pockets, staring at the floor. Though she had never admitted to herself how much she hoped he wouldn't care about her past, that he would somehow say it didn't matter to him, that he loved her anyway, his posture and his refusal to look at her made her face reality. She had been foolish to hope. When he did look at her, his eyes were so tortured, she couldn't bear it.

Jonas shifted his weight. "Fran, hows about I walk you home? I think Miles and Addie might have some things to talk over."

Fran rose, cold and fiery all at once. "Leave me alone. I can find my own way home." She skirted Addie without a glance and stalked to the cell bars. Her glare could've started the corn-husk mattress on fire. "Vin Rutter, you're pathetic. I don't want to see you again. Whenever you get out of here, I'd advise you to keep on riding." She marched to the door but paused to deliver one parting shot. "I don't want to see *any* of you again."

Miles winced when Fran slammed the door on the way out.

Jonas closed his eyes for a moment and tilted his head back, and Addie sank onto the chair Fran had vacated and put her face in her hands.

"What a little spitfire." Vin eased back onto his bunk. "I love the women in this town."

Anger flared through Miles. "Be quiet. You've done enough harm here."

Jonas's fisted hands shook. His throat worked against his collar, and his jaw muscles bulged. "I believe I'll go get some air." He met Bat at the door coming in.

"Boys, what progress have you made on finding Wally's killer?" He slung his bag under his desk and leaned his cane against his hip to remove his leather gloves. "Hap's on his way over to look at the picture again. Maybe something will jar loose. Hello, Miss Reid." His piercing eyes bored into Miles.

Great. The boss was back early. Miles could hardly catch his breath from one crisis to the next. What he wanted to do was sweep Addie out of here and find someplace quiet where they could talk. Where he could tell her how much he loved her, how he admired her bravery in telling Fran the truth, and where he could confess to his own relationship with Cliff Walker. Then he wanted to come back to the jail and haul Vin outside and run him out of town. After that, he'd come back and admit to Bat that he had made no headway on the case, that he was related to Cliff, and that he would turn in his badge if Bat wanted him to.

Oh, that was a great plan. Turn his back on everything he'd ever dreamed of being and doing and hope Addie would overlook the fact that he was a coward, a liar, and jobless.

Jonas hovered near the door, but he stepped aside when Hap Greeley entered.

"Sheriff, I'm willing to look again at the picture, but I don't know what I can tell you." The big shopkeeper removed his glasses and rubbed them with his red handkerchief. He looked terrible, as if he hadn't slept or bathed in days. His clothes bagged, and his thinning hair ran amok. Bloodshot eyes held a world of inner turmoil. "I can't stay long though. I have to take care of some of the details for the funeral tomorrow."

Bat snapped his fingers. "Where's the picture, Miles?"

Miles frowned and looked at heaps of papers covering every

flat surface. He sorted back to the last time he had seen it. "It was on your desk."

"I don't want to know where it was. I want to know where it is." The sheriff lifted a sheaf of pages and ruffled them. "Did you start a file? Why are all these reports and fliers mixed up?"

Jonas shrugged. "There was a little accident with one of the piles. They fell onto the floor. I scooped them up the best I could."

Bat's moustache twitched, and his eyebrows came down. "Well, both of you, get your hands in here and sort through this mess. I want that picture. Hap, you have a seat. I'm sure it's around here somewhere."

Addie rose, and Miles thought she might make her escape, but instead, she took a pile of papers and leafed through them. "When was the last time you had it?"

Miles considered. "I guess the last time I saw it for sure was the night you brought it over here. That's when Hap—when the papers fell off the desk. Since Hap didn't see anything in the picture that would tell us who killed Wally, I didn't give it another thought." Wanted posters, newspapers, arrest reports, telegrams, receipts, train schedules, his fingers flew through the papers. He could feel Bat's eyes on him, judging, assessing. The cane started tapping, and a trickle of sweat beaded at Miles's temple and ran down his cheek.

Hap throttled his handkerchief and mopped his red face. "I hope you find out who did the killing. Poor Wally must be avenged."

"Jonas, did you show the photograph to Fran when

you questioned her?" Miles scrabbled to catch a cascade of newspapers determined to slide onto the floor.

"No, I didn't get a chance. She kinda left abruptly."

The longer they looked, the more desperate Miles became. Losing the photograph was just another black mark against him. What had ever made him think he could be a lawman? He couldn't even run an investigation without losing evidence.

Addie set aside another bundle of pages. "Sheriff, you really need to invest in another filing cabinet. Your papers and the city marshal's are all mixed up, and there're enough old newspapers here to fill a wagon."

Bat grimaced and spread his hands. "I know it. I'm terrible about such things. Never seem to get around to throwing out the old stuff."

Jonas kicked an empty ammunition box over beside the desk. "Maybe we can throw out some things now and whittle this down. I imagine the photograph is on the bottom of one of these stacks."

After half an hour of sorting while listening to Hap moaning, Miles was ready to put a match to the entire works. Vin remained mercifully quiet, no doubt not wanting to be noticed by Bat. Eventually, the scarred and battered desktop emerged. Miles's shoulders sagged.

No picture.

"Why are you pawing through papers when you should be out finding Wally's killer?" Hap rose, his sweaty, balding head almost brushing the ceiling. "I didn't see anything helpful in that photograph, and you're wasting time."

Miles gritted his teeth.

"Now Hap, don't worry." Bat took a cigar from his vest pocket and clamped it between his teeth. "I'm sure the boys are doing all they can to find Wally's killer."

"But what about opening the store again? With a killer on the loose, I won't feel safe. What if he comes back? You don't have any leads." He swiped at his pate with the handkerchief, his face quivering. "You can't even hold on to a single piece of evidence."

"Hap, take it easy. I'm sure we'll find it. And if we don't, we'll have Miss Reid make us another copy." Bat kept calm, no doubt trying to stem the emotional river flowing from Hap before it burst its banks. The man had a crazed edge to his voice, so near the breaking point he shook.

Miles cleared his throat. "As to that, I don't think she can. The photography studio was ransacked, and all the plates and equipment destroyed."

Bat's eyebrows rose. "When did this happen?" He directed the question to Addie.

"Late on the Fourth. Sometime after the murder but before the end of the fireworks show. But—"

"Why didn't you report this to me?" Bat's eyes pinned Miles. He dug a match from his pocket and lit it, holding it to the end of his cigar and creating clouds of blue smoke.

"I would've reported it, but you'd already left on the night train by the time the vandalism was discovered."

A sinking feeling, like bogging in quicksand, floundered in Miles's chest. The harder he struggled to do things right, the more of a hash he made of it all. Exactly as Jonas had described when he tried to change without God's help. *God, I could use some of that help right now.*

Then tell the truth and don't hold anything back. The only way to be free of a lie is to tell the truth. "What have you done about finding Wally's killer?" Bat stroked his moustache.

"We questioned folks who were in the store the day of the murder, but nobody seems to have seen anything. We've also been putting out feelers looking for the money. Luke Short is keeping an eye out, as are several of the other gambling bosses. So far, nothing's turned up."

Bat nodded. "That's what I'd have done, too. What about the break-in at Miss Reid's? Any leads there?"

Miles fisted his hands. "It's not just her studio. Last night someone ransacked her room at Mrs. Blanchard's place. Addie came in to report the crime, and I haven't had a chance to go over there and take a look yet."

Vin rose off the bunk and came to the bars. The swelling around his eye had darkened. "How much longer will you detain me?"

"What's he in for?" Bat frowned. "Anything related to the case?"

Hap jerked and his watery stare bored into Vin. "Did you kill Wally?"

"I didn't kill anyone. I've been harassed by the deputies, questioned, followed, and suspected of everything from murder to spitting on the sidewalk, but I'm innocent, and it's killing them." Vin smirked at Miles.

"We arrested him for carrying a firearm inside city limits. He's been here since last night." Miles swallowed. "He's a former member of the Walker Gang who's been hanging around for a few weeks, and he's made himself a bit of a nuisance with Miss Seaton and Addie here. Addie thought it might've been Vin who tore up her place, since he's been so troublesome, but he was locked up when the second break-in occurred."

Bat motioned to Jonas. "Turn him out." He leveled a stare at Vin. "You strike me as a man who enjoys making trouble for others and not paying for it. I'd recommend you make yourself scarce in Dodge City. We don't hold with your kind around here. If you venture into this county again, I'll make a punchboard out of your hide."

Miles shook his head at the quick summing-up. Bat was astute, no mistake. He'd described Vin perfectly and on short acquaintance.

Jonas rattled the keys as he opened the cell door. Vin gathered his hat and coat and marched out with his chin high.

When he'd departed, Bat jerked his head toward the door. "Spooner, I suggest you follow our friend there and make sure he gets on the train or forks his horse."

With a nod and a slight smile, Jonas left.

Addie had her arms crossed at her waist, tapping her toe. "Sheriff, about the picture. . ."

"That's a grievous loss. I'm vexed that we can't find it." Bat removed his hat and smoothed his hair. "And now we can't even get a duplicate made." He turned to Hap. "I apologize. It's sheer negligence, and I share a part in it for keeping such a derelict office. We'll keep looking. Perhaps it will turn up."

Hap nodded, hanging his head. "It's all so terrible. I'm absolutely lost without Wally to take care of all the details. I imagine I'll have to sell up. I don't know that I could go on trading there anyway, not where Wally was killed. I don't think the horror will ever fade. If only I'd been in town, maybe I could've stopped it. It's too bad about the picture."

Addie blew out an exasperated sigh. "That's what I've been trying to tell you. I've got the glass plate here." She patted her camera case. "If I can get some chemicals and get into my darkroom, I'll make another print."

"What?" Hap's eyebrows rose nearly as high as his voice. "You mean—"

"Don't lose hope, Mr. Greeley. Miles and Jonas and Sheriff Masterson are doing their best. I'm sure they'll find out who killed Wally." She removed the camera and flipped open a little compartment in the bottom of the case. "See, the slide's intact. It won't take me long once I get set up, and we'll have another picture for you to examine. Maybe this time something will stand out."

Her face glowed with such conviction, Miles wanted to hug her. She'd suffered so many blows, and yet, here she was, still standing.

Bat nodded. "Carr, go with Miss Reid and see what you can do to help her. I'm going to go talk to Luke. He might've come across something. You were smart to enlist his help. I don't put much importance on the picture, but I don't like loose ends. If the case comes to trial, we'd best be able to lay our hands on the photograph or the defense might argue that we've handled the evidence poorly. Don't want the killer to get off because a jury thinks we can't do our jobs."

A lot of white showed around Hap's eyes behind his glasses, and he twisted the handkerchief until Miles thought the fabric would rip. He caught Miles looking at him and took a deep breath, as if trying to calm himself. "I hope you can find something, anything. This not knowing is driving me to distraction." He checked his watch and wiped his head once more. "I need to be getting along. There are some things to see to for Wally's service and all."

Miles plucked his hat off the peg by the door. "Addie, where can we get the chemicals and such that you need? The pharmacy?"

She glanced up from repacking the case. "The quickest way will be to go to another photography studio, though I don't know that any of my competitors will be interested in loaning me the chemicals." She looked down at her hands. "With all that's happened at the studio and at my boardinghouse, I can't afford to pay for new supplies just yet."

"What about a place to do the work?"

"I could develop the print in someone else's darkroom, but I prefer my own. I was able to salvage most of the pans and trays I'll need."

"Let's go then."

"Wait." Bat grabbed a piece of paper and a pencil. "I'll write you a requisition for what you need, just in case anyone gives you any trouble over getting the supplies." He scribbled a few lines and signed his name. "There, that should smooth the way."

Addie glanced at the paper and tucked it into a pocket. "We'll be back as soon as we can."

Miles stopped at the door. "Bat, there are a few things we need to talk about later. And I apologize for misplacing that photograph. I don't seem to have made any headway with this case."

Bat settled his hat and picked up his cane. "I think you're doing a fine job on the investigation. It was a rotten set of circumstances to begin with. Too many strangers in town and too few clues to go on. It's lucky Miss Reid can give us another copy of that picture, but I wouldn't put too much stock in it changing things. Unless we come up with a witness, or some of the cash shows up, it's likely the killer is already out of town."

Miles nodded, discouraged by the lack of progress but encouraged by the vote of confidence from his boss. He'd been half-afraid that Bat would fire him on the spot for not having made an arrest already.

Addie was half a block up the street before he caught up with her. "Where're we headed?"

"Donaldson's. He's the closest, though he won't be glad to see me."

They entered the shop, and Miles couldn't help but compare the place to Addie's before the break-in. No welcoming reception area, just a bare counter in front of a dividing curtain. No bell rang out over the door, and no one appeared from the back of the studio.

Miles rapped on the counter. "Donaldson? You in?"

Heber Donaldson emerged from behind the limp drape. "What can I do for you?" he began with a hopeful smile. His expression darkened when he saw Addie. "Miss Reid, what do you want?"

Putting himself slightly in front of Addie, Miles addressed the pompous photographer. "We're here to get some chemicals for developing a picture. As you might've heard, Miss Reid's studio was vandalized. She's in need of some supplies, and while you're at it, a little courtesy would be appreciated."

Addie's hand pressed against his back. "It's all right, Miles. I didn't expect a warm welcome." She offered the note from Bat. "Heber, the sheriff wrote this requisition. You'll be reimbursed for everything."

He took the note, running his hand down his beard and scowling. "What is it you need?"

"Chemicals for developing a dry-plate, and a few pieces of equipment."

He nodded. "Those supplies ain't cheap. I'll be making careful notes of everything you take."

Miles held onto his temper. "Just get the stuff. We're in a hurry."

Twenty minutes later, Donaldson all but shoved them out the door with his bad grace. Miles carried a crate of clinking bottles, and they made short work of getting to Addie's building.

"I'm afraid things are still a mess. I don't know if I'll ever get all the glass swept up." Addie produced the key and let them inside.

Miles surveyed the room. The plants had been swept up and the photographs in their frames all stacked against the right-hand wall. The rug at the front door had disappeared, and the drapery in the doorway had been removed.

"This is as far as I got. The front room and the darkroom. Fran was coming to help later today." She bit her lip. "I suppose I've lost that friendship forever. I spoke too harshly to her." Blinking quickly, she lifted her chin. "I just couldn't have her thinking Vin was her hero when I know what a skunk he really is."

"I didn't even know she was in love with him until recently."

Addie led him into the studio. "I don't know that she was really in love with him. More like she was in love with the idea of him. In love with love. I feel badly for Jonas, so patiently waiting for her to grow up."

"Where do you want me to put these?" He indicated the bottles and jars in his arms.

"This way. Put them on the bench in the darkroom. Be careful though. Some of those are quite dangerous, especially if you don't know what you're doing." She set down the jug of water she carried—special filtered water from Donaldson's for mixing chemicals.

He skirted the stacks and boxes of debris in the studio and entered the little room. The narrow workspace looked better than the last time he'd seen it, but even his untrained eye picked out the barren places on the bench and shelves. He put the crate on the work surface, carefully set out the containers in a row beside some dented trays, and returned to the studio.

"I lined up the supplies. Anything else I can do?" He tucked his fingers into his back pockets.

Addie unbuttoned one of her cuffs and began rolling it up in precise folds. Her slender wrists and delicate hands drew his attention, and he forced his gaze away. "It's really a one-person job." She started in on the other cuff. "The room's so small I'd be tripping over you in there. But"—her lashes flipped up, and he caught a glimpse of worried blue-gray eyes—"I'd really appreciate it if you stayed in the studio. With all that's happened, and Vin not responsible for the vandalism here. . ." She spread her hands and shrugged.

"I don't blame you. I won't leave." He reached for a broom. "I can work on some of the clean-up."

"Thank you." She hoisted the gallon jug again. "Please don't come into the darkroom once I've started or the print will be ruined. I'll do my best to hurry, but it takes awhile." She flashed him a smile that sent his pulse galloping and disappeared into the darkroom.

He grabbed a broom. *Don't be a fool. Once she learns you're related to Cliff, any hope you have of winning her is gone. Keep your mind on business. Protect her as you would any other citizen and forget about anything else.*

Talking to himself didn't change his feelings one bit. He still hoped and prayed she would forgive him, that somehow she could see past the man he had been to the man he wanted to be, the man he felt he could be with God's help and her by his side.

Jabbing with the bristles at a stubborn line of broken glass along the base of a plaster pedestal, he scowled. She was right. She might never get to the end of all the broken glass scattered through this place.

He leaned the broom against the wall and took hold of the pedestal. Something stung his hand, and he yanked it back. Examining his palm, he noted a bright red dot at the base of his thumb. One of the corners of the pillar had broken off, and a jagged piece of wire protruded from the crumbled edge. Frowning, he horsed the pillar out of the way, careful not to grab the wire again. Maybe he could patch it for her somehow.

The pile of junk in the center of the room grew as he added broken furniture and props. Maybe he and Jonas could get a wagon from the livery and help her clear out the room so she could start fresh.

Chapter 19

Fran scowled and leapt back as the box of coat buttons slipped from her fingers and crashed to the floor. Shiny, black, wooden circles skidded and rolled across the floor, racing toward the most inaccessible crevices and hiding places. Tears burned her eyes, and she smacked the counter. Why was she even bothering to continue the inventory? Her life was in ruins and here she was chasing buttons and counting hay rakes. She pressed the heels of her hands to her eyes and calculated the revelations that had brought her to this place.

Addie hadn't trusted her enough to tell her about Cliff Walker and had shamed her in front of everyone at the jail.

Vin Rutter had used her and manipulated her, and she'd fallen for his lies like a naive schoolgirl.

Her boss had been murdered, and her job was in jeopardy if Hap didn't keep the store open.

Jonas despised her for a fool.

Her throat tightened, and fresh tears pricked her eyes. Though each part hurt, the last one ached most. Addie had been right in that, at least. Fran had let herself get carried away with girlish fantasies and driven away the most precious thing she'd ever had. The look in Jonas's eyes when she'd stormed out of the jail—disgust, resignation, repulsion—made her feel as small and foolish as she had been acting.

The front door rattled. Ignoring it, she swiped at her cheeks. Whoever it was would have to go to the store up the street. Hap hadn't given her leave to open for customers, and she wasn't in the mood to fill orders anyway.

The knob jiggled, and the person knocked. Couldn't they see the sign in the window? Fran headed for the storeroom, but before she got halfway down the aisle, the front door opened.

"I thought I might find you here."

Her stomach flared like a blacksmith's forge, heating her blood. "Did you just pick that lock?"

"It's one of my many talents."

"That figures. A criminal like you. What are you doing out of jail?"

Vin closed the door behind himself and leaned against it, snicking the lock. "I was released, though I've been commanded by our illustrious sheriff to vacate the county." He'd dropped the smooth, Southern accent. Now he sounded like the common outlaw he was.

"If Bat ordered you to go, why are you still here?" She crossed her arms at her waist.

"I came to see you." He straightened and started toward her, his stride as smooth as a panther's.

"I can't imagine why. We have nothing to discuss." Skirting the end of the counter, she stepped behind the solid, wooden barrier, wanting to keep something between her and this. . .

rat. . .skunk. . .coyote. . . No word seemed bad enough.

"I have something to do before I leave this town." He followed her progress along the counter, staying opposite her. "I wanted to give you something to remember me by."

"You cannot be serious. You have nothing I want or need, nor do I want to remember you." The man not only had no scruples, his arrogance took her breath away.

"What you want isn't relevant. It never has been. That was always your mistake, thinking any of this was about you. You were so easy to manipulate. A very pretty pawn, but a pawn nonetheless. And you're still a pawn in my game. Miles and Spooner have blocked me at every turn, but I'm not finished yet. I have one more hand to play before I depart."

His words hit like darts. "You're out of your mind. Now get out. I wouldn't want to be you if Bat finds you still in town."

"Not to worry, what I have in mind won't take long." His face hardened. How had she ever thought him handsome? His lizard eyes glittered, making her flesh crawl. "I have no intention of leaving empty-handed." His bold leer raked her face and form, and he laughed.

For the first time she knew real fear. Malice flowed off him in waves. "There's no money here. We were robbed, remember?"

He placed his palms on the counter and leaned toward her. "It's not money I'm after. It's something better."

She pressed her shoulders and hips into the shelves behind her and shot a glance at the door. The smirk dragging his lips sideways left her in no doubt of his intent. Her heart thundered in her ears, and her mouth went dry. She judged the distance to the door and knew she wouldn't make it. He would be on her before she went two steps.

"Ah, I see you understand at last. That's one of the most appealing things about you, Fran, your delightful innocence. Though I shall rectify that condition soon enough. Now, don't be tedious enough to try to run. It's undignified."

She groped behind her for a weapon. Fear and anger warred in her, surging and making her mind blank. "If you touch me, I'll scream." Her hands closed on glass, and her fingers gripped the neck of the bottle, the ridges and size telling her it was Dr. Pettigrew's Cure-All Tonic.

"Who will hear you, my love, after I gag you?"

"You don't love me. Why are you doing this?" She edged toward the door, keeping the bottle behind her back.

He kept pace, cutting off her escape route. "Of course I don't love you. This isn't about love. It's about revenge. Revenge on Spooner for punching me. Revenge on Miles for blocking my attempts to get near Addie. Revenge on Addie for keeping the money from me." With each statement his voice rose and his eyes got wilder. "Killing Spooner wasn't enough. I want what he treasured most."

"What?" Her heart stopped. "Killing Spooner?" The words came out a strangled whisper.

"That's right." He sneered and advanced around the counter, grabbing her arm and hauling her up against him. "The sheriff set Spooner on my trail—I suspect to make sure I left town quickly—and he followed me to my lodgings. I had to get rid of him. I'm only sorry he won't be around to learn about what I did to you."

His breath scraped her cheek, but she barely felt it. Jonas was dead? "You lie." He couldn't be dead. Not Jonas. "You're a liar."

He laughed again, a slimy, sickening laugh—the snake. "I am an accomplished liar, that's true, but in this instance, I assure you, I'm telling the truth. It gave me great pleasure to kill him."

"Let me go." She paused between each word, forcing the syllables through her clenched teeth. His grip on her arm stung, but she knew it was only a precursor to what he intended.

"Soon." He dragged her a couple of steps. "I think the storeroom."

She went limp, hoping to catch him off guard. Tears she didn't have to fake flowed down her cheeks. "My brothers will avenge my honor. Bat and Miles will hunt you down and shoot you like the rabid dog you are."

"Stop sniveling. You might even enjoy it."

She wanted to throw up.

He dragged her down the center aisle, bouncing her hip off the corner of the clothing table and yanking her after him in spite of her yelp of pain.

It's now or never, Fran. If he gets you into the storeroom, you're a goner.

She braced her feet and swung her arm up. The bottle of patent medicine connected with his temple and burst in a cascade of glass and pungent fumes. Vin dropped like a stunned ox, sprawling on the floor and knocking over the bean barrel.

Thousands of rock-hard navy beans shot across the floor.

Had she killed him?

She shook with violent tremors, turning from him and pressing the back of her hand to her mouth to stifle the sobs crowding her throat. She didn't care if she had killed him. Part of her hoped he was dead for killing Jonas. Good riddance.

Weariness weighted her limbs, and she realized she still gripped the neck of the broken bottle. She needed to get outside, to call for help, but her legs refused to move.

Jonas was dead?

A hand grabbed her ankle, and she screamed. Vin struggled to sit upright, glass shards raining off his shoulders. Though she tried to kick away from him, he hung on. In a blink, he lunged up toward her. "You're going to pay for that!" He reached into his coat and withdrew a pistol, ratcheting back the hammer and aiming it at her face.

The door crashed open, and Vin spun his gun toward the sound, dropping his grip on her ankle.

Fran froze. "Jonas!"

Two guns crashed simultaneously, drowning out her scream. Splinters flew from the doorframe. Vin rocked backward and collapsed, a bright red blossom spreading on his snowy shirtfront.

A haze of blue smoke drifted toward the pressed-tin ceiling, and Fran blinked.

Jonas. Blood flowed from a cut over his eyebrow, but there he stood, living and breathing.

The bottle neck slipped from her fingers and shattered at

her feet. She raised her hands to cover her face, giving in to sobs.

"Fran?"

She found herself cradled in his arms. He pulled her hands away from her eyes and peppered her face with kisses. She clung to him, and when his lips found hers, her response rocked her to her core. The kiss bore no resemblance to the platonic pecks he'd placed on her cheek from time to time. Instead, it was a giving, a receiving, promises, and apologies. It took her breath away.

Breaking the kiss, he crushed her to himself and whispered against her hair, "He didn't hurt you, did he? I was so afraid I'd be too late."

She leaned back in his arms. Though his face was as familiar to her as her own, she couldn't stop herself from touching his features, drinking in the sight of him. She brushed her fingers near the cut on his brow. "What happened?"

He winced, though her touch was light. "He ambushed me in an alley. I wasn't paying enough attention. He must've thought he knocked me clean out. I was dazed, but I could hear him. He told me what he wanted to do to you." His voice thickened, and he held her tighter. "He didn't hurt you?"

She wrapped her arms around his neck and buried her face. "No, no, I'm fine." And she was, better than fine. "I'm so sorry, Jonas. I'm sorry for everything."

"Shhh, we'll talk about all that later. For now, just let me hold you." He stroked her back and rocked gently.

Fran absorbed his comfort, his presence, and his love, and

in that moment, the last remnants of her childish fantasies slipped away. Here was everything she wanted and needed to be complete.

Miles dumped another dustpan full of broken glass into a crate and straightened. Sliding his timepiece out of his pocket, he checked it. Again. The darkroom doorknob rattled. At last.

Addie poked her head out of the doorway. "I'm almost done. You can come in now if you want."

He shrugged through the curtain, getting hung up on the shredded fabric for a moment.

"Sorry about that. I put the drape up over the door just in case someone accidentally opened it at the wrong time. It blocks out the light, but it's a nuisance, too, especially now that it's all ripped up." Addie raised the red shade on the lantern and blew out the flame. "You can leave the door open. The light from the studio skylight will be enough."

Two clear prints hung clipped to a line over the workbench. Strong chemical smells pricked his nose, and he resisted the urge to sneeze. "Everything went all right?"

"Yes. I made an extra, just in case." She poured liquid from a tray back into a bottle. Her slender hands moved with such grace, his heart pounded. A hank of hair slipped onto her cheek, and she used her wrist to push it back, but with little success.

He reached out and tucked the silky strands behind her ear. At his touch, she stilled. "Addie, we need to talk."

She nodded. "I'm sorry I didn't tell you before. About Cliff, about Vin." Her throat lurched, and she looked down. "I'll understand if you don't want to have anything to do with me now."

Wanting nothing more than to take her into his arms and tell her he wanted everything to do with her for the rest of her life, he forced himself to grip the edge of the counter. "Addie, you don't owe me any explanations, but I sure owe you one. Vin Rutter told me a few weeks ago about you being Cliff's girl. He thought I already knew. You see, I've known Vin and Cliff for a long time."

Blinking, she shook her head, frowning.

"It's true. I'm sorry I never told you. I was. . .ashamed." He touched her arm.

She stiffened. "How is it that you knew Vin and Cliff?"

"My mother married Cliff's father when I was a kid. Cliff was my stepbrother." There, it was out. And despite all it would cost him, he was glad. Though painful, telling the truth did set him free of the weight of guilt and shame he'd carried for so long. "Addie?"

She was silent for what seemed a long time, a myriad of thoughts and emotions playing across her face. Finally, her shoulders sagged. "Was it the money?"

He frowned. "What?"

"Was it the stolen money you were after? Is that why you paid attention to me, pretended to care about me?" Her hands shook. "Is that why you kissed me?"

"No." He grabbed her upper arms and forced her to look at

him. "I didn't know about the money until you told me about it at the jail this morning. That's the truth."

"The truth?" She reeled back. "How can I believe that? You're part of the Walker Gang. You, Vin, Cliff, you've done nothing but lie to me. I can't trust anyone, least of all you."

Though it was no more than he'd expected, her declaration was a dagger to his heart and hopes. "Addie, I can't tell you how sorry I am."

"Go away."

"Can't we talk about this?"

She sniffed, and he felt more of a heel than ever. "There's nothing to talk about. Just tell me this one thing."

"Anything."

"Are there any more of you?"

"Any more of who?"

"Walkers. Can I expect a visit from anyone else in the Walker clan intent on ruining my life?"

He knew she was lashing out because she'd been hurt, because she'd been buffeted beyond bearing, but her words hit like body blows. "For the record, I'm not a Walker. I'm a Carr. My father was an honorable man. My mother was tricked into marrying Cliff's father. She regretted it from the first, and finally took her own life to escape his cruelty. I left soon after she died, and I never went back. You aren't the only one to have your life blighted by the Walkers. I know you won't believe this, but I love you, Addie Reid, and it has nothing to do with Cliff, Vin, or any stolen money."

He knew he should stop, but the words poured out anyway.

"Before you start hurling accusations and holding grudges, perhaps you should remember that you weren't exactly forthcoming about your relationship with Cliff either. A lot of trouble could've been averted if I'd known what Vin was after when he hit town."

Unable to stand the hurt in her eyes—knowing he'd caused it—he ducked through the curtain.

The brightness of the sun streaming through the skylight dazzled him, and he only had an impression of a large shadow in the doorway to the front room before a gun blast slammed into him and knocked him back into the darkroom.

Addie could hardly see for the tears pouring from her eyes. Miles's words had opened all the old wounds, tearing away half-healed scabs and making her heart bleed anew. Cliff once more reached from beyond the grave and stirred up a tornado of devastation in her life.

She jerked at the boom of a gunshot and knocked the bottle of carbonate of soda over onto the counter. A poof of white powder shot up. Before she could right it or comprehend where the shot had come from, Miles careened backward through the doorway, scrabbling at the curtain for a handhold, but falling heavily to the floor, a shred of fabric ripping away in his hand.

"What happened? What is it?" She knelt beside him, touching his shoulder, and her hand came away wet.

"Stay down." The words came out clipped as he rolled to

his side and drew his gun.

"Is it Vin?"

"Shh."

"Carr? That you? The girl in there with you?"

She recognized the voice, but why he would be shooting a gun in her studio baffled her.

Miles struggled to his knees, checked his gun, and gently pushed her behind him. "Get under the workbench."

"You're bleeding."

Another shot ripped through the curtain and shattered the lantern. Ruby glass rained down.

Miles shrugged off her hand and shoved her under the bench. He used the barrel of his pistol to edge the curtain aside, and the instant the cloth moved, a bullet ripped through it.

Addie screamed and ducked back, hitting her head on the underside of the workbench.

"What does he want? Why is he shooting at us?" Addie's skin rippled as if someone had trailed an icicle down her back.

"Hap Greeley! What are you doing?" Miles edged around until he was beside the door. His left arm hung limp, and blood soaked his sleeve, dripping down his fingers and splashing to the floor.

"I want that picture and the plate." The voice was Hap's, and yet it wasn't. He sounded. . .crazed, out of control. "Throw out your gun and come out of there."

Miles shook his head as if to clear it and blinked. "That's not going to happen."

"You will! You have to!" A shot whipped through the

curtain and thudded into the back door—the back door she'd nailed shut and blocked with a filing cabinet.

Addie's fingernails bit into her palms. "Why does he want the picture? Is he crazed?"

Peeking out again, Miles returned fire for the first time. The acrid smell of burnt gunpowder filled the room. "He's tucked in behind that pillar. I can't get a good shot. I should've thrown that thing in the alley when I had the chance." Sweat beaded on his forehead, and his skin had a pallor that appalled her.

"Hap." He raised his voice, but his chest rose and fell sharply with the effort. "Is there something in that photograph that proves you killed Wally?" He swayed and pinched his eyelids shut.

Hap's answer was another bullet.

Addie inched toward Miles. "You have to let me stop that bleeding."

"Stay back. Someone will have heard the shooting. Help's coming if we can hold him off." He sent another barrage into the studio, the bullets thudding dully. "Need to reloa—" His gun slipped to the floor, and he sagged after it into a heap.

Addie grappled with his broad shoulders, trying to drag him out from in front of the door and under the workbench. She could barely budge him. The slickness of the blood pouring from his shoulder didn't help. She had to get him out of here, or he would bleed to death. "Hap."

"That you, girl?"

"Miles is shot. He needs a doctor." She tore at her sleeve, ripping it away from her shoulder. As quickly as she could, she folded it into a pad and pressed it against the wound. Red soaked it immediately.

"Throw out that plate and whatever pictures you made. No tricks, or you both die."

Her mind whirled, stalling, trying to find a way out of this, anything to hold on until help came. "Were you the one who broke up my studio? And my room at Mrs. Blanchard's?"

"You gave me no choice. I had to have that plate. Now throw it out here along with that gun."

Anger flared through her. How many times in her life would she be a victim? Well, not this time. She pressed her knee against Miles's wound, knowing she must be hurting him but needing both hands to rip a strip off her petticoat. She wrapped his upper arm as best she could, praying it would be enough to stop the blood.

Her mind raced. "Hap, can't we talk about this?" She placed her hand on Miles's chest, reassured by the heartbeat throbbing there. If they got out of this alive, she was going to throw herself into his arms and beg him to forgive her. *Please, God, give me the chance.*

His gun lay on the floor near the curtain. She'd never shot a pistol in her life and wasn't certain she even knew how to load one properly. Miles had been reaching for more bullets on his belt when he keeled over. How many times had Cliff offered to teach her to shoot, and she'd laughed it off as unnecessary?

Well, if she couldn't use a gun, what could she use? She inched out from under the workbench and knelt, coming eye-to-eye with the bottles and pans of developing chemicals.

Quietly, she lifted a glass tray off the workbench, careful not to slosh its contents over the side.

"No tricks now, girlie. Throw out the gun and come out of there."

She put as much fear into her voice as she could, allowing a sob that wasn't all pretense to escape from her throat. "Hap, I'm too scared. You hit Miles, and he passed out. He landed on his gun. It's underneath him somewhere, and I can't find it. Please. I can't get it for you."

He growled and snapped another shot through the doorway. The bullet narrowly missed her, and she screamed, almost dropping the glass basin. Wood chips flew as the filing cabinet took another direct hit. "All right, I'm coming out. I have the plate with me."

She stepped over Miles's legs. *Please, God, don't let him die. Please help me. I need to tell him how sorry I am. I need to tell him I love him.*

Edging the curtain aside, she tried to still the tremors in her hands. The liquid sloshed and rippled.

Hap rose, pushing over the pillar. It crashed to the hardwood, and bits and chunks of plaster flew off and skittered across the floor. "Where is it?" White ringed his eyes behind his spectacles, and his hands jerked as if he was a puppet with no control over his movements.

"It's here. In the tray." Addie raised the shallow container.

"Bring it here." He motioned with his gun for her to come to him.

She sobbed, hoping she looked at least as frightened as she

felt. "I can't. I'm scared. Come take it." She held the tray flat on her hands, keeping her fingers away from the edges.

Through the doorway into the reception room, she glimpsed a crouched figure at the front door. Another dark shadow passed behind the glass in the door.

Hap growled and started toward her. When he was only a step away, she flipped the tray, sending the contents cascading over him. He screamed and grabbed his red, sweaty face. Scrabbling at his eyes, he dropped the pistol, howling in pain and rage.

Addie leapt away from his staggering form, and the front door crashed open. Bat and Deputy Pearson tackled Hap and wrestled him to the floor, and Addie's knees gave out. Jonas caught her before she hit the floor.

Chapter 20

Miles stirred, wishing whoever was pushing a red-hot poker through his arm would lay off.

"Easy, Miles. I'm almost finished."

Gentle hands restrained him when he tried to rub at the pain. He cracked one eyelid, which seemed to weigh a ton. "Doc?" A blurry face slowly came into focus. "Where am I?"

"You're at the jail." The sawbones knotted a bandage on Miles's left arm. "The bullet went clean through. You lost a lot of blood, but you'll be fine."

A gasp caught Miles's attention, but he couldn't see who was there. He made out the bars of one of the cells. He was on a cot inside. Someone in the next cell moaned.

"I'd better see to my other patient. You rest quiet, you hear?" The doctor rose, and Addie came into view.

She had tears on her cheeks. Had she been crying for him? She knelt beside the cot and took his hand. It felt pretty good. She brushed the hair back from his forehead, and that felt even better. Her eyes were so sad, he wanted to hug her, to kiss away the hurt, but he couldn't muster the energy.

Something clanked in the next cell. "Now Hap, stop that.

I have to bathe your burns."

Miles jerked his thoughts away from Addie, and the events of the day came rushing back—getting shot, being pinned down in the darkroom, fighting to stay conscious. "Addie?" His dry throat rasped.

"Shhh. Rest now. We'll talk later." She lifted his head and held a glass to his lips. "Doc said you'd be thirsty and tired, and that you're not to worry about anything."

Cool water. The best he'd ever tasted. His head touched the pillow again. There was so much he needed to say to her. So much he needed to know. But darkness crowded around the edges of his vision, and he knew he was going to succumb again.

"Stay. Stay with me, Addie." He gripped her hand like a little child.

She leaned close and brushed a kiss on his forehead. "Forever, Miles, if you'll let me."

When next Miles woke, it was nighttime. His shoulder felt like a mountain lion had been chewing on it, and something tugged against his hand when he tried to move. He opened his eyes and looked down.

Addie sat on the floor beside his cot, asleep with her head resting on their clasped hands. Contentment like he'd never known filled him, and he knew he must be grinning like a simpleton. She had stayed, and if he hadn't been dreaming awhile ago, she had promised forever. With his right hand he reached across and touched her glossy, brown hair.

She stirred, raising her head and locking clouded blue eyes with his. Her cheeks were flushed, and her hair had come out of its braid to lie in ripples on her shoulders. The sight of her all sleep-tousled made his heart race.

She seemed to become aware in an instant, blinking, and scrambling to her knees. "You're awake."

Since he was looking right at her, he didn't see the need to confirm her statement. Though moving awoke new pain under the bandages, he lifted their locked fingers.

Her sleep-flush deepened to a rosy glow. "Miles—" She broke off, confusion flashing in her eyes.

"Later, Addie. We'll sort all of that out later. Tell me what happened after I passed out."

The cell door clanged. "I'll tell you what happened." Deputy Pearson edged inside. "Your lady-love here pitched a pan full of lye water into Hap Greeley's face." Pearson carried a cloth-covered tray. "Doc said for you to wake up and eat something. Said you needed to get your strength back." He used his boot to drag a chair close. "Addie, how's about you sit there and spoon some of this stuff into him."

A moan ripped through the air, and Miles turned his head. Cuffed to the bars in the adjacent cell, a man he assumed must be Hap Greeley lay on a cot, his face swathed in wet bandages.

Jonas sat beside him. He soaked another cloth and placed it over Hap's eyes.

"Here, let me help you sit up." Addie leaned over him. He inhaled her perfume as he struggled upright—difficult considering Doc had used enough bandages on his upper arm for a hospital.

"How does that feel? Doc said if you got dizzy to stay lying down."

The room did wobble for a minute, and his arm throbbed, but he refused to give in to it. "I feel like a rag doll with half the stuffing drained out, but I'll be fine. I have a powerful thirst though."

Addie helped him drink and insisted on feeding him, though he felt like a fool. Addie wouldn't quite meet his eyes and kept herself busy with trays and napkins.

He wanted to grab the spoon and hurl it away so he could kiss her senseless and somehow convince her they were meant to be together, that their pasts didn't matter, only their future. He wanted her promise that she'd meant forever.

Miles forced himself to be patient. By the time he'd finished the soup, strength began to return to his limbs, and the grogginess in his head lifted.

Bat came into the jail and entered Hap's cell. "Greeley, it's time to answer some questions."

Miles started to swing his legs to the floor, but Addie stopped him by putting her hands on his chest and pressing him into the pillows. "You're supposed to rest."

He captured her fingers with his right hand. "I feel fine." It wasn't strictly true, but he wasn't going to let a little pain stop him. "I won't go far. I need to hear what Hap has to say."

Miles edged down the cot until only the bars separated him from Hap. Bat took Jonas's place near Hap's head, and

Jonas leaned against the wall in Hap's cell and opened up his notebook.

"What happened to your head?" Miles noticed the swollen and bruised cut on Jonas's forehead for the first time.

"Had a little run-in with Vin Rutter." Jonas shrugged. "Don't worry. He won't be bothering anyone ever again. I'll tell you about it later."

Addie scooted her chair closer to Miles, and he reached over to hold her hand.

Bat leaned over the prisoner. "Hap, Doc says you can talk just fine, so go ahead. What happened?" He unlocked the cuff from Hap's wrist, freeing him from the bars.

A moan filled the air, and Hap dragged the wet bandages off his face. Red welts and blisters covered his skin.

Addie's breath hitched in her throat, and Miles squeezed her fingers.

"I killed him. I killed Wally." Hap's red, weeping eyes blinked, but his voice was strong and controlled, not like the demanding, demented voice from the studio. "He was going to dissolve the partnership."

"Why?"

"My gambling. He said he couldn't trust me anymore, not after I took some money out of the till to gamble."

"Take us through everything that happened on the Fourth."

With a sigh, Hap began. "I was over at the fort for a party at the quartermaster's. Gambling, drinking. There was a lawyer there, too. He said Wally had come to see him the day before about breaking up the business. I was so mad I hopped right on my horse and headed back to town to confront Wally and talk him out of it." He shuddered, and Bat handed him another wet cloth, which he pressed to his cheek. "When I hit town, there was some kind of ruckus going on at the livery, so I went around back of the store and tied my horse up. I let myself in, and Wally was there, counting money, just like I figured he would be."

Jonas's pencil scratched as he recorded every word. Miles pictured Wally alive as he'd last seen him, counting out stacks of bills. Then his mind drifted to those smoke-filled moments in the livery when he nearly got himself trampled to death.

Hap's voice brought him back. "We argued—I know we fought all the time, but this time was different. Wally wouldn't budge. Said he'd had enough of working like a dog to keep me in gambling chips, and that the next day, he was going to file the papers. I was so upset I hardly knew what I was doing. I don't know exactly what happened, but all of a sudden, I was standing over Wally with a can in my hand, and he was on the floor dead. I panicked. I never meant to kill him." He moaned again, pressing the cloth into his face. "It was an accident. I just wanted to make him listen to me."

Bat's eyes glittered in the lantern light. "Then what did you do?"

Hap sucked in a big breath. "I tried to make it look like a robbery. I unlocked the front door, and I took the money off the counter. Wally had most of it bagged up to take to the bank. I ducked out the back and hid just outside of town until it got dark. I figured I'd stroll into town and pretend to be shocked when I heard the news."

"Which you did."

"That's right. I went to the store, and there were deputies there, and it wasn't hard to act like I was upset. I *was* upset. Like I said, I didn't mean to kill him. Just being in the store made me want to throw up." Tears tracked down his ravaged face. Though he was upset, he seemed to be in his right mind. Did madness come and go? Miles tucked that question away to ask the doctor sometime.

"What about the picture? Why attack Miss Reid and Deputy Carr?"

"I thought I'd gotten away with it until I saw that picture she took. I knew I had to destroy the photograph and the plate, or eventually, someone might put me there at the time of the murder. I pretended to get upset when Carr showed me the picture, and I tipped a bunch of papers off the desk. In the mess, I shoved the picture into my pocket."

Miles grimaced. So that's where the first photograph had gone.

"I figured Miss Reid would have the plate at her studio."

Addie's hand tightened on Miles's shoulder. "How did you get inside? The lock wasn't broken."

He shrugged. "Skeleton key. Wally changed locks on me once, trying to keep me out of the store when he wasn't there, so I ordered a skeleton key a few months ago. I used it to get into your place."

"And you ransacked my studio."

"I couldn't find the right plate. There were hundreds of

glass slides and photographs."

Addie's hand shook. "So you ruined everything you could find?"

Hap's shoulders hunched. "I was mad. And scared. It was like I couldn't stop myself once I started breaking things."

"What about my room at the boardinghouse?"

He scowled and winced. "I was afraid that I'd missed the plate somehow at your place. What if you kept it in your room? When the old woman left, I went in and searched, but I couldn't find it. And the anger took over. I don't remember what all I did to your room. It was like I was out of my head."

Out of his head was right.

The door opened and Fran slipped inside the jail. Miles's jaw dropped when she made a beeline for Jonas in the cell doorway. Jonas grinned at Miles and put his arm around Fran, who didn't seem to mind in the least. Something drastic had happened there, and Jonas jerked his chin, a promise to divulge all later.

Fran tugged something from her pocket. "Here they are. I found them hanging in the darkroom and brought them both." She turned the papers to reveal two copies of the photograph of Wally sprawled on the mercantile floor. "And I noticed right away why Hap would want the picture destroyed. I wish you'd shown me the photograph sooner. It would've saved us a lot of trouble."

Hap groaned and sank back onto the bunk.

"What is it?" Bat reached for one of the pictures.

"Look beside the register, just at the edge of the photograph."

Fran ducked out of Jonas's arm and pointed over Bat's shoulder. "Right there."

"A pair of glasses?"

She nodded. "Hap's glasses. He never went anywhere without them, but he was always taking them off and rubbing them or shoving them up on his forehead. He often took them off when he fought with Wally. Like a habit, you know?"

Bat tugged at his moustache, studying the picture.

"Was that it, Hap? The glasses?"

"Yes."

Jonas shook his head. "But when Addie and I met you at the mercantile, you were wearing your glasses. I remember because you kept taking them off to wipe your eyes."

Miles nodded. "That's right. You had them when you came to the jail."

"The minute I got out of town to hide, I realized I'd left the glasses behind. I knew I'd have to get them back or someone would be bound to notice. When I snuck back into town, I went right to the mercantile. There were two deputies in there, so I had to act shocked. The place was a mess, and someone had knocked the glasses onto the floor behind the counter. The deputies didn't even notice when I picked them up and pretended to take them out of my pocket before I put them on. I was caterwauling and carrying on, and they were only too glad when I left."

Bat scowled. Miles wouldn't want to be either of those two deputies when the boss caught up with them.

Fran shook her head and returned to Jonas's side.

"I thought everything was fine," Hap continued. "When no new picture showed up, I figured I must've destroyed the right plate after all when I hit the studio. Then *she*"—he pointed at Addie—"chimes in about how she had the plate with her the whole time."

Addie shuddered and stood up, as if she couldn't bear to be near him anymore. Miles levered himself up and put his good arm around her waist.

Bat shook his head. "So you went to the studio to kill them and get the plate once and for all?"

Hap nodded.

"How were you going to cover up killing them?"

"I don't know!" His hands fisted on his thighs. "I wasn't thinking. I just had to get that plate!"

Bat stood. "That's enough for now. Hap, you're under arrest for the murder of Wally Price, the attempted murders of Miles Carr and Addie Reid, the destruction of property, and about half a dozen other things."

Miles guided Addie out of the cell toward Bat's desk, and Jonas and Fran followed. He leaned against the desk, careful to keep hold of Addie's hand and not to tip over any stacks of paper still cluttering Bat's workspace.

Jonas ripped out the notebook pages and placed them into a labeled file folder, along with the two copies of the photograph. "Not going to lose anything related to this case." He tucked the folder into a cabinet and took Fran's hand.

"You two look like you have a lot to tell us." Miles raised an eyebrow in Jonas's direction.

Jonas grinned, and Fran blushed. "Let's just say things worked out all right in the end." He raised Fran's hand and brushed a kiss across her knuckles. "We're going to be getting married in a couple of weeks and moving out to my new ranch." Without another word, they walked outside together.

Addie sighed. "It sure took them long enough."

Bat locked the cell door and tossed the keys onto his desk. "Carr, why don't you get some air? Take Addie home. With Hap in jail, no reason why she won't be safe over at Mrs. Blanchard's place. At least for the time being until you two sort some other arrangement out." His eyes twinkled as he took in their clasped hands.

Glad for the excuse to get her alone, Miles didn't hesitate.

Addie breathed in the cool night air, still unable to fathom all that had happened. It would take a long time to sort through all Hap had said and put all the pieces together. Some things they might never know. "Jonas killed Vin. Did you know that?"

Miles stilled. "Did he?"

"Jonas followed Vin to his hotel, and Vin bashed Jonas on the head and left him for dead. Then Vin tried to attack Fran. Jonas got there in time, but he had to shoot Vin. Over at the mercantile."

"I always figured he'd wind up getting killed by some lawman somewhere."

"I guess coming that close to losing Jonas for good made Fran see things clearer." Standing on the jail porch, she soaked in the touch of Miles's hand in hers. "Are you sure you shouldn't be resting? You lost a lot of blood. Does your arm hurt?"

He led her down the steps and up the street. "I'm fine. Not up to running any races, but I can see my girl home."

Addie stopped.

His girl.

They walked in silence the two blocks to her boardinghouse, and Miles drew her into the deeper shadows of the cottonwood tree beside the house.

"Miles, about what I said to you in the studio. . ."

He turned to her and put his fingers to her lips. "Shh. I don't want to hear an apology. We both said things we shouldn't have because we were hurt and scared and churned up."

She blinked, caught sideways by the warmth and forgiveness in his voice. His hand dropped away, and she felt the loss of his touch on her lips. "Everything happened so fast, I was angry and confused. I thought you were only after the stolen money, that everything between us had been a lie. I'd already been told so many lies. And then you were shot, and I thought you might die. I was afraid I'd never get the chance to tell you how sorry I was."

He shook his head. "No, I told you, no apologies. This is one time when I think we should just let the past go. Both of us have let things in the past determine who we are and what we do. We can't change the past, but there's no sense in chaining ourselves to it and letting it drag us around." His arm slipped around her waist, and he pulled her close. "I love you, Addie Reid, and I've been waiting a long time for you to say you love me, too."

Careful of his wound, she eased her arms around his neck. Happiness sang in her veins, and she tunneled her fingers into his hair, drawing him close. In a whisper, just loud enough to be heard over the tinkling sigh of the night breeze in the leaves overhead, she gave him the words she needed to say. "I love you, too, Miles. Forever."

Chapter 21

How do you like living on a ranch?" Addie dug through excelsior to find another bottle. She lifted the jar, studied it in the sunshine, and placed it on the darkroom shelf.

Fran, her hair tied back with a kerchief, put her hands on her hips. "It's wonderful. But you know what? I'd live in a rabbit hole as long as Jonas was there."

"You talking about me?" Jonas stuck his head into the darkroom. "Wife, what are you doing standing around while we labor away moving all these boxes?"

"Standing around? I'll have you know. . ." Fran started after her husband of two weeks, swatting him with the cloth in her hand, sending clouds of dust into the air.

Jonas beat a hasty, laughing retreat.

Addie shook her head and went back to arranging supplies. She smiled when Miles came into the darkroom and slipped his arms around her waist. She leaned back, reveling in his strength. "Did you get everything from the depot?"

He nuzzled her neck. "Mmmhmm."

"Are those two still squabbling out there?"

"Nope."

"What are they doing?"

He pressed a kiss under her earlobe. "Pretty much the same thing we're doing."

Addie laughed. "Deputy Carr, don't you have work to do? We have to get everything unloaded and set up before the grand opening tomorrow. I've got customers lined up."

His arms dropped away. "You're a tough taskmistress, Mrs. Carr. I thought new brides were supposed to like billing and cooing with their husbands." He tilted his head, giving her a reproachful, forlorn look. "Married for a week, and she's already tired of me."

She grinned, leaned into him for a quick, dusty kiss, and gave him a playful push. "Someone around here has to keep us on task. I can't count on those two." She waved to the studio where Fran's laugh reached them. "And you're just as bad, trying to distract me when I have so much work to do."

Taking her hand, he tugged her out of the room. "Come see what we all brought."

A half hour later, a shining new Chevalier stood on glossy tripod legs in the center of the studio. Miles and Jonas dragged packing material and crating out to the alley, and Fran pirouetted with a new parasol from the replenished prop box.

Tears pricked Addie's eyes. God had been so good to her. To all of them, but especially to her. The court had ordered Hap to make restitution for all the damages, as well as compensating Addie for her distress and all the business she had lost as a result of his actions. She'd immediately paid off the mortgage—much to Archie Poulter's and Heber Donaldson's chagrin—and set about ordering new equipment with the money.

Fran studied her reflection, dragged the kerchief off her hair, and shrugged at her disheveled appearance. "You never told me what Poulter said when you went in to pay off the mortgage."

Addie grinned. "He looked like he'd swallowed a hedgehog and it got stuck halfway down." The satisfaction of counting the bills and coins out on his desk down to the last copper penny had stayed with her for days.

"You know," Fran said, "my first thought when I saw the studio that night was that Donaldson must've done it. He was so mad at you for getting the Arden contract, and then everyone on opening night was buzzing about your fabulous photographs." Fran snapped the parasol shut. "I thought he destroyed this place out of revenge."

"I thought about him, too, but it didn't make sense. Why destroy the equipment you had already put a bid in to buy? He was sure I wouldn't get the note paid off, and when I didn't, he would get everything for a fraction of the cost. He and Poulter had it all worked out. He wouldn't have gained anything by smashing up the studio."

"I suppose. He won't be any happier now that you're going to be up and running again. Still, there isn't much he can do about it, not with all the publicity you've had over Hap's agreeing to plead guilty to avoid a hanging. You've got them lining up in the street to get their pictures taken here now."

Addie went to the desk and patted her appointment ledger. She had so many sittings scheduled she would be hard-pressed to keep up with everything.

Miles came back with Jonas. "That's the last of it. Except for this stupid thing." Miles planted his hands on his hips and nudged the broken plaster pillar with his boot. "Since Jonas is here, he can help me haul it outside. It's awkward to carry very far by yourself."

"You don't have to tell me." Addie nudged the pillar with her toe. "I just scoot it around when I need it."

Miles and Jonas each got on an end and hoisted it horizontally between them. A chunk of plaster broke off and crashed to the floor, followed by a metallic *clink*. The men stopped. A bright gold coin rolled across the floor, traveled in a lazy circle, and wobbled to a stop.

Addie blinked.

"Is that—?"

"Did you drop—?"

"Addie?"

Miles motioned for Jonas to put his end down. When the pillar stood upright again, he poked his finger into one of the bullet holes he'd made when shooting it out with Hap. Fran bent to pick up the coin, and Jonas took it from her, studying it in the bright August sunshine pouring through the skylight.

"Gimme a hammer." Miles held out his hand, trying to peer into the hole. Addie handed him the hammer they'd used to open crates and gasped when he smashed it into the plaster. Wrenching it out, he hit the column again. Dust exploded and bits of wire and plaster shot across the floor. With one more blow, he caved in the whole side.

A fistful of gold coins trickled out. When the flow stopped, Miles reached into the hole and withdrew a paperbound bundle of banknotes, then another, and another. He grinned. "I'd say that was about thirty thousand dollars worth, wouldn't you?"

Addie gaped. "Vin was right. I did have the money." A cloud of fear encroached on her happiness. "I didn't know it was there, I swear."

Miles kicked coins in all directions getting to her. He grabbed her by the arms and shook her. "Adeline Reid Carr, don't think for a minute anyone here suspects you. This is Cliff's doing, not yours."

She searched his face, seeing only trust and assurance there . . .and love. Lots of love. Nodding, she moistened her lips. "The pillar. Of course. Cliff made it for me. I should've known." She shook her head at her blindness. "Where is my camera case? The Scovill?"

Fran found it hanging by its strap in the darkroom. "Here it is."

Addie unlatched the compartment in the bottom and withdrew the photo album. Swallowing hard, she gripped the book. "I meant to throw this away, but with the trial and the wedding and everything, I forgot. I want you to know, this means nothing to me, and I am going to destroy it. I kept it for a reason, but that reason no longer exists."

Miles took the book, scowling when he saw the first portrait. He flipped through the pages. "These are all of Cliff."

"I kept them to remind me how foolish I had been. But I don't need them anymore. Everything Cliff was means nothing to me now because when true love comes, lies fall away." She held Miles's gaze.

He nodded and smiled.

She took the book and flipped to the last few portraits. "This is what I wanted you to see though. In all the later pictures, Cliff is leaning on that pedestal. After he made it, he insisted that it be in every portrait I took of him. How he must've laughed, posing with his stolen money, and all the while I had no idea."

Miles snapped the album closed. "He was a fool."

"His greed and arrogance cost him his life."

"That, too, but his biggest folly was in having you and letting you get away." He threw the photo album into the trash bin and reached for Addie. "I'd never let you get away from me."

Epilogue

The front bell chimed, and Addie wiped her hands on her apron and headed to the front of the studio.

Miles entered the reception area, shaking raindrops from his hat. He grinned and tossed her the newspaper. "Take a look at this."

She read the headline aloud. "Mystery solved. Missing money recovered." The article, two columns wide, outlined the returning of the railroad's property and hailed her as a heroine.

"How do you like that?" He read over her shoulder. "They even spelled your name right. And guess what? There's a reward."

"What?"

"The railroad is sending you a 10 percent reward for recovering their stolen loot. Just got the wire today." He patted his pocket. "Can't tell you how many people shook my hand and stopped to congratulate me on the way over here."

She shook her head. The entire town now knew the story, and to her surprise, no one held it against her that she'd been linked with Cliff Walker. The returning of the stolen property convinced everyone that she had nothing to do with the robberies. The fear that had held her hostage for such a long time seemed so puny and silly now, she wondered why she'd ever given it so much power.

Miles shrugged out of his coat and hung it and his hat on the rack. "Say, that turned out great." He moved to stand in front of the new photograph hanging on the wall.

Their wedding portrait. Addie hadn't wanted the typical stiff pose of the man seated and the wife standing behind with her hand on his shoulder. Instead, with a little help from Fran, they'd managed a portrait where Addie stood before Miles with his arms around her. She leaned back against his chest, and both of them appeared to be looking into the distance toward their future.

Free of the past, with their entire lives together before them.

Picture perfect.

Even though Erica Vetsch has set aside her career teaching history to high school students in order to homeschool her own children, her love of history hasn't faded. Erica's favorite books are historical novels and history books, and one of her greatest thrills is stumbling across some obscure historical factoid that makes her imagination leap. She's continually amazed at how God has allowed her to use her passion for history, romance, and daydreaming to craft historical romances that entertain readers and glorify Him. Whenever she's not following flights of fancy in her fictional world, Erica is the company bookkeeper for her family's lumber business, a mother of two terrific teens, wife to a man who is her total opposite and yet her soul mate, and an avid museum patron.